Praise for *The Stone Maidens*

Ioulia Kolovou has written a novel full of grace, humour and loss. In *The Stone Maidens* the political is personal, the personal is historic, and the storytelling moves with ease, in ways plain and extraordinary, through characters and times. Kolovou has a historian's eye and a novelist's skill with words, and the book gives us a small focus, almost a domestic one, intimate and rooted in Argentina's Disappeared, which brings to us Milagros and her family's place in history. *The Stone Maidens* is a beautiful book that illuminates both atrocity and protection.

Elizabeth Reeder, author of *Ramshackle* and *Penned in the Margins*

Fabulous writing, intriguing story.

Emma Fraser, author of *When the Dawn Breaks* and *Greyfriars House*

Starting quietly as a coming of age tale in rural Patagonia, over six decades *The Stone Maidens* builds towards shocking events in Argentina's Dirty War. As usual, women bear the brunt of the inhumanity, sexual violence and murder wreaked by a brutish military. Innocent children become pawns. A mastery of spare – yet sweeping – storytelling that will remain with you.

Anne Pettigrew, author of *Not the Life Imagined* and *Not the Deaths Imagined*

A Blackwater Press book

First published in Great Britain and United States of America by
Blackwater Press, LLC

Copyright © Ioulia Kolovou, 2022

Printed and bound in Great Britain by Clays Ltd, Elcograf S.p.A

Library of Congress Control Number: 2022940893

ISBN: 978-1-7357747-6-3 (paperback)

Cover design by Eilidh Muldoon

Interior illustrations by Giuseppe Monterisi

This book is a work of fiction. Names, characters, organisations, locations
and events portrayed are either the product of the author's imagination
or are used fictitiously.

Blackwater Press
120 Capitol Street
Charleston, WV 25301
United States

www.blackwaterpress.com

The Stone Maidens

a novel

IOULIA KOLOVOU

For Richard (1966-2019)

At the end of the day, history is no more than an infinite succession of personal histories.

Laura Giussani

PART ONE

1948-1952

1

Milagros Riquelme

Towards the end of summer, the wind came strong from the north. It blew for weeks at a time, sweeping over flat grasslands and marshes, ruffling reeds and ancient *ombú* trees and green scummy waters, swinging sparse dark clumps of cypress and Spanish moss. It conquered the stone towers and balustrades of the Big House in Alta Gracia; it hammered on the corrugated iron roofs and adobe walls of the houses and ranches in the village. It sneaked through cracks in the roofs and windows and beneath doorsills, coating everything with layers of fine red dust. For days afterwards the women swept and scrubbed and washed: from the multi-colored tiles on the verandas of the Big House to the gold brocade mantle of the Virgin in the chapel; from the whitewashed walls of the tiny schoolroom to the earth floors of peasant ranches, everything had acquired a smell of soil and a reddish hue it took weeks to get rid of.

Milagros and the other children loved it. They ran against the wind and screamed with delight. They howled and shrieked with laughter as the red dust choked them. They spat and hissed and fought against the wind, hair and arms going wild, looking like demented windmills. Countless small insects came riding with the wind, too, dry and buzzing and biting. They drove the cattle mad. The gauchos chased the insects away with their long whips of many tails. The children ran after the riding men, teasing, taunting, but always taking care to stay well out of reach of the lead balls at the end of the leather strips.

When they were breathless with running, they abandoned the chase and turned to catching as many insects as they could. They put them in matchboxes if they could find any, or just collected them in heaps. Then they buried them. The insect funerals were long and elaborate. At the head of the procession one child chanted gibberish through the nose, holding a makeshift cross. Then followed the coffin-bearers, holding the tiny boxes or the naked dead insects solemnly in front of their skinny little chests; the mourners came behind them, boys looking down on the earth or rolling their eyes to the heavens and swearing revenge, girls wailing and moaning and tearing their hair, the solemnity often interrupted by pushes, tumbles, and giggles.

The insects were buried in shallow graves just outside the wooden fence of the real graveyard. The children had been told it was as great a sin to bury animals in consecrated ground as it was to bury Christians outwith its boundaries.

The dry windy season brought human funerals, too. The whole village turned up at them. It was a show of respect and one of the few entertainments locally available. Children were not normally allowed to attend, but followed at a safe distance nevertheless, their avid faces drinking in the signs of the grownups' distress, picking up every little detail of moist eye and downturned mouth and bent head.

Milagros herself was as familiar with death as any of them. The fourth of six siblings, she was the only one to survive infancy. When she was born, her mother and grandmother consulted together and decided to force a miracle out of the Virgin Mother. They named her Milagros, and it had worked. She had no memory of her siblings at all, besides a very vague recollection of the funeral for the youngest, Jorge Luís. Her father had held the small coffin himself. She had followed behind, holding Abuela's hand tightly. Her mother had walked next to her holding her other hand, head held high and eyes burning with a fiery grief. Doña Alejandra from the Big House made an appearance in the black and silver Rolls Royce driven by Old Man Suárez, instead of driving herself to the church in her Morris Mini. People agreed that this showed compassion for the poor Riquelmes, having to bury their fifth child. When the family returned home, the little Moses basket where the baby had been sleeping was waiting for them in the corner. Her father silently took it away.

During that night, Milagros had woken up several times, straining her ears to hear the sick baby's whimpering, but all she could hear was the wind sweeping dust and thorny balls of dried weeds in the deserted village road, all the way to the cemetery.

Milagros often thought of the dead at night, as she lay in bed curled up next to Abuela. She pictured the quiet cemetery in her head, the little graves neat and clean, her brothers and sisters resting in the well-swept flower-covered earth. Sometimes she worried about them when it was a moonlit night; her chest hurt as she thought of all that weight of dirt falling on their little chests, of how deeply they lay. How could they breathe under the earth? But when it was raining or when the wind was howling, she thought they would be rather warm and snug and out of harm's way, cocooned in their little boxes, tucked in safely in their beds of earth.

She would then listen for the sounds of the night. She would hold her breath in the darkness, trying to block the sound of Abuela's raspy breathing, and the irregular snores and sighs through the partition separating their room from her parents' bedroom, and the scuttling of mice inside the adobe and straw walls. There were voices in the howling wind, she was certain, urgent whispers in the persistent beating of the rain on the tin roof. She would pull herself close to Abuela, who always slept with her rosary entwined in her hands, in case death came during the night, her fingers twitching as if counting beads even in her sleep. The old woman slept lightly.

"What is it, Mili, why aren't you sleeping?" Abuela would whisper, the sound of "s" coming funny through her toothless mouth.

"Abuelita, do you hear?"

"Hear what, daughter?"

"I don't know, it's like...words."

"Don't worry, my dove, it's only the wind."

"But there are voices in there."

"Of course there are voices."

The snoring in the next room stopped.

"What are they?" Milagros' voice was barely a whisper now.

"It's the dead. They're trying to speak to their loved ones."

"What are they saying?"

"Unfortunately, we do not know their language."

"They don't speak our language?"

"No, you see, they are in another country now. They speak different there."

"Shut up," a choking voice would come through the cardboard-thin wall.

They would stop talking immediately, and as Abuelita counted her rosary beads to lull herself back to sleep, Milagros stayed awake for just a little longer, eyes wide open in the darkness, ears straining to hear. Could it be that her brothers and sisters wanted to tell her something? Everybody knew the dead slept in peace, but of course they ought to wake up sometimes. Maybe this was when the living went to bed.

Milagros would shut her eyes tightly and picture the small cemetery under the moonlight. Tall thin wooden crosses shaking slowly in the night air, tattered flower crowns hanging from them, wooden railings around them to keep the wild animals away. They certainly woke up, but did they rise? Did they walk? Did they run

4

against the wind? Yes, probably, and that's why she could hear them, from all that distance away. Always she wonder what they were trying to say. But as she lay there listening, wondering, her head would fall heavy over her chest and her eyelids would relax, and in the short moment when sleep was hanging above her like a thick drop of honey from the spoon's end, she could hear the voices more clearly, the urgent whispers, persistent, susurrant, rising and falling with the wind.

2

An Education

After the wind came the rain, days and days of dull, relentless water dripping from heaven. The dirt streets in the village turned into quagmires. This is how flies must feel when caught on the fly-paper, Milagros thought as she struggled on her way from home to her father's workshop on the village square, carrying his lunch which she had helped Abuela prepare. It was oddly pleasant, the sinking of feet in the soft, sticky substance, and the squelching and sucking sound it produced. Squelch, suck, squelch, suck. Her slender feet disappeared briefly and then emerged all covered in brown mud, her toenails gleaming through like white pebbles at the bottom of the river. It looked a little like melted chocolate. "I'm a fly fallen in the chocolate," she sang softly to herself. She stopped to wipe the mud off her feet on the iron boot-scrapers in front of her father's shop before she walked inside, shuddering at the feel of rough unpolished boards on the soles of her feet after the silkiness of the soft, slick earth.

Papá was sitting at the corner next to the window to catch as much of the gray daylight as possible. She usually found him work-ing, but today he was reading one of the few, well-thumbed books

6

he had brought with him from the capital a long time ago. He read and reread them: there was no place to buy books anywhere near the village, and no money to buy them with. Sometimes her mother would come back from work at the Big House and mention that boxes of books had arrived for Don Aníbal's library, and Papá would sigh. Sometimes, if he was in a good mood, he would read parts of his favorite book to her. It was called *Los Miserables*: a story that happened in the old times, her father said, far away from there. But it could have happened here, he added. Some stories in it made her cry, especially the one about the poor little girl and how she was horribly treated when she was a servant at some cruel people's house. Other parts she didn't much care for, because she could not well understand what was going on; there was one about students and how they had made a barricade, whatever that was (it involved a mattress hanging from a window) and then they were all shot and they died. This was one of her father's favorites parts. Every time he read that one, Milagros would let her eyes wander over the low buildings in the village square and the endless skies rolling above and beyond, trying to see if she could catch a glimpse of the Big House, glimmering white among the trees.

She liked her father's workshop, with its view of the square from the door, where one could sit and watch for hours and know what was going on in the village and who was going where, and she liked the smell of leather and glue and boot polish and dry wood and tobacco. This was Papá's smell, and she inhaled it deeply as soon as she walked into the dark, cluttered little place. He mumbled a greeting without lifting his eyes from his book, and she placed the enamel bowl covered with a clean tea towel on the cluttered table, clearing things away with her other hand.

With the mildly annoyed look of an owl caught in the daylight, her father closed his book and went to wash his hands at the pump at the back of the shop, stepping gingerly over the mud.

"What have you got there?" he called over the sound of splashing water.

"Stew with sausage and corn bread."

He shuffled back in, wiped his hands with a towel which he then placed on his knees, and began to eat. Milagros hovered over him, unsure what to do. If it wasn't for the rain, the other children would be playing in the square, and Milagros would join them. They would all run towards the groves and the watering ponds to the west of the village, or to the cemetery to the east, and sometimes even as far as the high fences of the Big House to the north. Milagros's mother worked there; she had recently been promoted to under-housekeeper. Sometimes the children would run up the hill to look at the train coming into the station; that was as near the station as they were allowed. And when it was hot, they would play near the streams which fed the watering ponds for the cattle and the horses, splashing about in the shallow leaping water of the streams, and the more daring ones, Pablito Suárez the indisputable leader, would dive into the scummy ponds, trawling out all kinds of horrible creatures, leeches and bloated frogs and water snakes to shake at the girls and scare them. But Milagros was never scared, and Pablito had learned not to try.

Today there were no children around. Black clouds lined up on the low sky, like the ramparts of an unconquerable city. More rain was coming.

"Do you have any chores for me to do?" Milagros asked.

"No, nothing."

He rarely did; his few customers brought and picked up their mended shoes and boots themselves, because there wasn't much else to do. Going to the cobbler's was always a good opportunity to hang out and share a *mate cocido* and gossip. But today the rain had kept customers and hangers-on away.

A noise like thunder rose in the distance. Milagros stood on the porch and wondered whether she would have time to run back home and check on Abuela before the thunderstorm broke. Another rumble shook the earth. Milagros looked at the gray sky. The clouds were dissolving. No silver seams of lightning that she could see, but still, the rumble was coming nearer. Her father rose from the table and came out, wiping his mouth.

"What's going on?"

A large military truck, growling and splashing mud, manoeuvred into the square and halted in front of the new building with the corrugated roof on the other side across from the cobbler's. This had been very recently erected by a taciturn crew from San Justo, who deflected the curiosity of the villagers with shrugs and monosyllabic replies. They had finished the job within a week; it was a humble, low, two-roomed shack, whitewashed inside and out, not different to the other buildings in the square. Nobody knew to whom it belonged or what it was for.

And now, five or six soldiers jumped out from the back of the truck and began to unload wooden crates and pieces of furniture, small desks and chairs and a larger, cedar desk, from the truck into the newbuild. It was not easy to do this in the muddy weather. Their loud voices – and occasional curses – and the thudding and scraping and banging of furniture filled the square. The commotion awoke the sleepy, huddled village; faces appeared at windows and doorways, and soon a small crowd was drawn. Four men negotiated a large blackboard through the front door, and another two carried large, framed pictures, one each, like a church procession. Milagros's papa narrowed his eyes and craned his neck to see better.

"It's the President of the Republic, Juán Domingo Perón, and his wife Eva," he told Milagros, pointing at the portraits.

The whole village watched and made loud, helpful suggestions, as the soldiers hoisted a large blue and white sign over the door. Milagros, who had been taught reading and writing by her father, read slowly:

REPUBLIC OF ARGENTINA. PROVINCE OF LAS PAMPAS.
ALTA GRACIA. PRIMARY SCHOOL "EVA DUARTE DE PERÓN"

One of the soldiers nailed another, hand-written sign on the wall. Milagros ran across the square and approached the building as much as she dared. The sign read:

PROPERTY OF THE STATE
DAMAGE WILL BE PUNISHED BY LAW

The soldiers stood with backs turned away from the crowd, admiring their handiwork. The gray clouds were dispersing, and a pale sun broke through, showing a face like a convalescing invalid. Milagros saw Pablito Suárez darting towards the truck, then backing away several times. Clearly, he was trying to find purchase to jump onto the back of the truck without being noticed. She knew well what that boy was like. She stole a sideway glance at her father. He was not paying attention to Pablito; he was gazing at the soldiers and at the sign, and his face was bright and uplifted. He looked like a younger, unburdened man.

"A school!" he kept saying. "A school! This is an important day for Alta Gracia."

At that moment Old Man Suárez's much smaller truck made its appearance at the end of the main street. It grinded to a muddy halt in front of the school, making some of the soldiers hastily move out of its way. Old Man Suárez, Pablito's father, a small, wiry man who looked like a grownup version of his mischievous son, jumped down and ran to open the passenger door. Out came a young woman with dark shiny hair partly hidden beneath a printed silk kerchief tied under her chin. She looked assertive and smart in a yellow tailored jacket and pleated skirt, and incongruous but practical black rubber boots that were slightly too large for her. Everyone stared, speechless, as she stepped down the step that Suárez had pulled out for her, looking at them and waving like a queen. She then marched up to the soldiers and exchanged some words with their sergeant, who handed her a key. She smiled graciously, and turning to the gathered crowd, she waved again and announced in a clear voice, obviously trained to carry, to the crowd of gawping bystanders:

"I am Señorita Delia Lugghi. I will be teaching your children in the Alta Gracia Primary. School starts tomorrow at eight o'clock sharp."

She then walked into the school, and the soldiers shuffled in after her. Milagros could hear her ringing voice giving orders above the din of chatter that broke outside. Some of her father's workshop frequenters had now ambled over to the porch, eager for talk.

"Don Gaudencio," they said, "you are an educated man yourself. What do you make of all this?"

But now Milagros' attention drifted back to Pablito, who was on top of the truck, dancing and making all sorts of silly gestures to a group of admiring acolytes, cheering him on from below. One or two of them emulated their chief and began to climb aboard too. Not content to rest on his laurels, Pablito slipped round the tarpaulin, up the panel and, like the little monkey that he was, he attempted to climb inside the cabin through the open window. His ultimate goal was the steering wheel, she knew. He's crazy, she thought, he'll fall and get hurt. Or worse, he'll set the truck moving and kill others – and himself! In front of his father too! But Old Man Suárez was busy bustling in and out of the school room, looking important, not paying any heed to his wayward son.

She turned back to her own papa. She had never seen him looking so delighted.

"The question is why we never had a school before," he was saying. "Yes, I know she promised she would start one, but did you ever see it? I did not."

She was Doña Alejandra, and everyone knew of that vague promise made to the village for years now, without anything ever coming into fruition.

"Well, how do you know this is not her doing then?" someone said.

"Her doing? Ha! Didn't you see those portraits? We all know how much they hate Perón and Evita. No, this is a state school."

"I wonder what they'll say at the Big House about this."

"What do you think they will do about it?"

"There is nothing they can do," Don Gaudencio said. "It's out of their hands now. They cannot fight the state."

He turned towards his daughter and pressed her shoulder softly and said, "This girl will get an education now. She will make something better of her life than serving the Goyenas."

As if to underline the triumph in his voice, the deep, resonant horn of the truck sounded repeatedly, making them all jump out of their skins.

"It's that little devil, the Suárez boy!"

Pablito was sitting at the driver's seat, beeping the horn with great gusto. But at the sight of the soldiers rushing out of the school room to find out what was going on, he swiftly clambered back up the window, on to the truck roof, dancing and gesturing like a little fiend, then just as swiftly clambered back down and burst into a run, followed by a cheering posse of kids, and vanished down the road. The soldiers uttered oaths and one of two made to follow them. But now Señorita Delia was thanking the sergeant and shaking his hand, and he gave the orders for them to climb back on their truck. Old Man Suárez jumped into his to move it out of their way. Señorita Delia stood at the door of her school, serenely inspecting the scene.

"For such a young person, she has lots of guts," Don Gaudencio said, smiling.

3

Delia's Diary – Fragments

March 10, 1948

Since I arrived at Alta Gracia – a misleading name, for I have never seen a place with so little grace in my whole life – I have been trying hard to get the school going, with little success so far. What children, what parents, what a backwater this is! The school is a ramshackle construction that I could hardly call a building. It's either roasting hot or freezing cold, stands on a little square at the end of the 'high street,' which is usually either dusty or muddy. No middle ground. A few wretched workshops – a cobbler's, a saddler's, a blacksmith's, a general store where you can buy very little – complete this picture of desolation.

I am everything in this school: teacher and headmistress, janitor and cleaner. There are very few pupils so far. The village does not exactly match one's expectations, when these are based on images of villages in story books and very little actual experience of the real thing. This is a loose cluster of homesteads, shacks really, dispersed all over the place, some in the pampas, some on the outskirts of the large oak forest, some belonging to the large estate of the same name, Alta Gracia. I'm not sure whether the village got its name from the estate or vice versa. Everybody calls it the Big House – so feudal! It is the estate of the Goyena family. Yes, that Goyena family. Who has not heard of them? One of the ancient criollo families on the land, immensely rich and very prominent in political life. There has not been a government or senate or national assembly since independence without a Goyena in office. I have actually visited their mausoleum in Recoleta Cemetery, in a guided tour. It is an immense stone building resembling a Grecian temple. A flight of stairs leads up to the massive bronze door. There are three life-sized marble statues in front of the entrance, commonly known as the Stone Maidens. One of them is a veiled woman, seated, holding the body of a young girl on her knees; another woman, winged, stands over her, one hand on her shoulder. Both women gaze sorrowfully at the beautiful, serene face of the dead girl. "Look at the flowing hair, the drapery, the detail of expression," the guide said, "this was made in Rodin's workshop and they say the Master himself added his touch here, and here." But as he pointed at the parts which Rodin may or may have not sculpted, and then went on about the immense sums of money the whole thing had cost, all I could think of was how obscene it was to spend such sums on a tomb, a place for dead, rotting bodies, for heaven's sake! How many poor families could have been fed and clothed with the money spent on a monument for the dead who had no use for it anyway? Apparently I had been thinking out loud, and some people looked at me with annoyance, but others nodded in agreement. I was gratified to see that the majority agreed with me.

When I found out about my appointment, I went to see the Goyena town house in Buenos Aires too. It is an elegant mansion on a leafy street off Avenida Alvear. I vaguely remember having read Doña Alejandra's articles about women's emancipation in one of the literary magazines from back in the 1940s; like everyone else, I've heard the story about how Don Anibal Goyena survived an assassination attempt a long time ago. And so here I am, living in a small village attached to the Goyena country estate, which *looks like something out of a nineteenth century novel. Who would have thought that such an insignificant, godforsaken place would boast such illustrious residents, senator Aníbal Goyena, and the son and heir, a lauded youth who is the namesake of the Faustino Goyena, father of the nation, but apparently nothing like him. This one is always in the pages of the gossip rags one finds lying about at a hairdresser's salon or a dentist's waiting room — not that I would ever read them.*

March 13, 1948

For such a small place, it is hard to believe that Alta Gracia has its own railway station. The colonial white stucco building, complete with large clock and colonnade, is rather an anomaly — why would such a tiny hamlet have a railway station at all? But it is obviously the clout of the Goyenas. This small family of three outweighs a village of a few hundred people, or indeed a province of a few thousand more. At least the railway is for everyone, and the journey to the provincial centre of San Justo, which is really just another village, albeit much larger and with a few real shops, takes just over two hours. If it all gets too oppressive here, that will be my escape, I hope, even though there is only one train per day, and this would mean staying in San Justo overnight.

Living here is really like taking a long dip into the past of our country. It is like finding oneself in the pages of Martín Fierro. Not much has changed here since that great epic of our literature was written, I'm afraid. Unless you count the railway. And the wireless. At least this is something to keep one company in the long dark winter evenings, so pleasurably spent by city people in cinemas, bookshops and cafés. In fact, the wireless is my tenuous link with the life I've left behind, a life that seems more distant, more fabulous day by day. I often wonder if I am the same person: Delia Lugghi, twenty-four, spinster, born and bred in Buenos Aires, lover of cafés and theatres and concert-halls, of books and interesting discussions with friends, or if somebody has taken that young woman's place and inhabits her body, a somebody who walks on dusty roads and lives with an old deaf woman who talks loudly and non-stop, a somebody who has sacrificed so much, for so little in return.

I still question my decision to leave everything behind and bury myself out here. How could I not, after everyone tried to dissuade me, and my parents nearly threatened to disinherit me? But the answer is clear: it is my duty to my country and its people. Unless we all make little or greater sacrifices, our beloved country will never fulfil its great destiny. Juán Domingo and Eva Perón set the example for me with their tireless dedication and courage. If the President and Eva ask each one of us to offer what we can, to fight from whatever post life has placed us in, who am I to refuse? I do my duty, as the rest of the country does, or at least should.

March 17, 1948

My best pupil in the school is a girl — it is always a girl, isn't it? She was the very first one to walk through the door. She is the daughter of the cobbler, a dark-haired, sort of brooding man with a limp, whose workshop is situated right across from the school. Milagros Riquelme is a lovely, serious, pretty girl, half-indigenous of course, like the majority of the villagers, with the straight black hair and long, narrow eyes of those people. Most people here are indigenous; you see comparatively few European faces. This takes a little getting used to, to be honest. But she is very bright and alert. She is very clever. She could already read and write, but her handwriting was the squiggly, illegible sort that passes for calligraphy among certain classes. I taught her to print plain and sensible letters, so that I can read what she writes. She picks everything up immediately and she has a good hand for drawing, too. She has never been farther than San Justo. I keep forgetting how isolated people are here, how little they know about the wide world we live in. But she shows a great willingness to learn and make something out of her life. I understand she is an only child; all her siblings are dead. Her mother works at the Goyenas' house, and the grandmother, who is a Guaraní woman, is something of a healer, and apparently in communication with people "from the other side." They mention the ghost of an old Jesuit priest that counsels her. People are rather superstitious here, which is unsurprising for uneducated populations. They are not particularly religious. It seems the Goyenas are some sort of free-thinking liberals who don't care much for the Church, regardless of the beautiful Jesuit chapel on their estate, and are not really interested in the spiritual welfare of the village, or the physical one, for that matter.

April 10, 1948

The school is now set up, with the help of that nice sergeant from San Justo (he's married though, so I've been very careful not to give any grounds for gossip). However, it appears that my problems have only just begun. Our local petty tyrants, and I refer to the Goyenas, the Family (I cannot begin to describe how it exasperates me to hear the capital F in their tone of voice, to see it in the expressions on their faces) are clearly not very happy about the school. They sent two heavies. Or they may have fancied themselves as heavies; in truth there were two wrinkled old indios, rather pathetic.

Here is what happened. One morning last week, Tuesday or Wednesday, I cannot exactly recall, at a quarter to eight, the men appeared at the school. I was wearing my flowered dress with full skirt and my Ferretti court shoes (so it must have been Tuesday after all). Whoever said that a well-dressed woman can conquer the world was absolutely right. As Eva Perón has shown us. Anyway, I had just put on my white duster coat over my clothes and was about to start ringing the first bell, when I heard the thunderous sound of galloping horses. I went out to see what was going on and saw two horsemen dismounting in front of the school. They had a sour look on them, as if they were burdened with a duty they didn't like and wanted over with soon. They came up to the front door and stood in the threshold as if unwilling to proceed. I gestured for them to come in and I sat at my desk, leaving them to stand in front of me. I don't think they have ever been to school, but the teacher's desk is a wondrous, powerful object; it can sap any man's will to dominate. I let them stand in front of me as I sat staring them in the face, not uttering a word. It always works. By the time they had summoned courage enough to say their piece, only a mumble came out. In the meantime, the school children had gathered at the door, and adults behind them, drawn by the news that spread like wildfire (I had noticed the cobbler and his daughter standing at the porch of the workshop as I walked in).

When I had enough of an audience, I asked the men what they wanted. They muttered something about Doña Alejandra wanting to see me. No doubt their script, or the delivery, would have been different with someone more diffident than I was. But even though my heart was beating more quickly – some drama, at last! – I was cool and collected and never stopped staring them in the face. "Am I summoned?" I said, just about managing to make my voice appropriately low and threatening. "Is she bidding me?" I stood up and showed them the way out. I stood at the door as they sullenly mounted their horses, and said loudly for my now quite sizeable audience around the square to hear:

"This is a democratic country, and a great democracy is built on education. A school in every village! These are the orders of President Perón himself! Anyone who has a problem with that, let him lodge a complaint. Here's the address: President Perón, Casa Rosada, Plaza de Mayo, Capital Federal, Republic of Argentina!"

The next day nothing happened, and the next, and the next. My blood boiled every time I thought of the nerve of the woman, Alejandra Goyena, to send her servants to summon me to her presence. A nice little invitation on paper would have done the trick, as she should very well know. She could have treated me with the dignity that my position deserves, instead of sending the gauchos, as if I were some outlaw they wanted to chase out of town.

So then this morning she came to see me herself, and the meeting was not at all what I had expected. She is an interesting type, I must admit. She must have been some kind of suffragette in her youth. She was urbane and sweet-spoken, if a little condescending, but I suppose those people cannot help it. She said she would support my every effort and assured me that nothing that could promote the welfare of the local people, and especially the local women, could be disagreeable to her.

"There are women here who've had incredibly hard lives, Señorita Lugghi," she said. "Wait till they begin to open up to you and tell you their stories. Mind you, most of it is the fault of their fathers and their husbands, such lazy, rough scoundrels as you'll ever find."

"Well, this is where I will disagree with you, Señora Goyena," I said. "If those men had been given the education and opportunities denied them for so long, things may have turned out differently for them. What can they have known so far, but oppression and injustice, which of course they take out on the weaker ones? But trust me, educate the masses and you will see a very different attitude, you will see civilized and fair men everywhere."

"If being just and liberal were only a matter of education..." She paused and shook her head. "Don't count on education too much, Señorita Lugghi," she went on. "When you reach my age, you'll realize it cannot really change man's nature very much."

Which is of course the kind of thing a person of her class would say.

"Don't be offended," she hastened to add. "I have a great respect for what you do, and I think it's very brave of you to leave the luxuries of the capital behind and come out here to help these poor people."

It is irritating that she, of all people, seems to appreciate the immensity of my sacrifice. Everybody else just takes me for granted. She did not say a word about the portraits, though I caught her looking at them with what I thought was distaste. I know the President and Evita are anathema to those people; it is one thing to be high and mighty and benevolent, every inch the enlightened despot, and another to actually see the objects of your benevolence and philanthropy having rights independent of your patronage and condescension. I would have liked to ask Old Lady Goyena, "Why don't you like Evita, since she is a strong woman who is not afraid to defy men and demand whatever is due to women? Isn't this what you claim you want for women, too? Aren't you supposed to be on the same side?"

Of course I didn't ask her that. I know better than to make overt enemies out here. I must depend on their good will, up to a point. And who knows? She might be converted with time.

I could ask Old Man Suárez to get me my mail and shopping from San Justo when he goes into town on Goyena business. True, if I want my complete independence, I should buy my own car. But it is unlikely I could afford it anytime soon, and asking my parents to help is out of the question. Mother was clear about it: anything I wanted was mine as long as I stayed in Buenos Aires, but away from it, they would have nothing to do with me. So I'll have to be diplomatic instead.

April 15, 1948

My accommodation is tolerable. The Widow Pérez may be deaf and rather slow, but she keeps an immaculate house and is not a bad cook either. I heard a story about her which I do not know if I should credit or not: apparently, she was of somewhat questionable morals in her youth, and for a time lived in this house with two men, her husband and a young man about whom the village could not decide whether he was her lover or his. That he must have been one or the other was in no doubt, according to the narrator of this story — none other than Old Man Suárez himself, who has a gift for tall tales — or else why did the two men end up murdering one another? Was it a duel, I asked him, did they fight over Mrs. Pérez? No one knows, he replied, they were just found dead in the room, in a deep pool of blood, the walls and furniture and floor all crimson. The Widow found them herself. According to Old Man Suárez, it was whispered at the time that she murdered them both, which is patently ridiculous, for how could such a small woman (she weighs no more than a small goat now and could not have been much bigger in youth) knife two adult men? Suárez said in a positively ghoulish tone that he believes my room is the scene of the double or mutual murder, but he shut up when I gave him a look. I must admit that since he told me this horrid little story, I look around my room with trepidation at the hour of sunset when everything turns red. My room looks out west. I would have preferred a view to the southeast, towards my beloved, distant Buenos Aires.

September 16, 1948

One of my main problems living here is having somebody to talk to. I'm sure the length of my entries is an indication! How I miss civilized, interesting conversation! For a moment I had believed — against myself and my better judgement — that the people from the Big House might offer the possibility of a social life, but I am too low for them, apparently. Never mind. It just goes to show that a leopard can't change its spots. They may claim they are interested in education and the mind, but in truth all they care about is keeping the distance between themselves and the rest of the world. For them, 'the people' is a derogatory term, an insult, something too low to be despised. For us, it is a badge of honor, it is an ideal, it is the one thing that matters in our list of priorities for our nation.

On days when there is no school, I can spend the entire time without uttering a word aloud. The old lady is a kindly soul, but there is not a chance for anybody to say a word when she opens her mouth. Poor woman, she must have been lonely for a very long time.

I try to take every day as it comes and not think about the future because if I do, it seems like a long, endless landscape of emptiness and repetition, just like this place. I must not forget I have work to do, and very important work it is.

October 13, 1948

Don Gaudencio is the father of my best student, Milagros Riquelme. He was born in Galicia, Spain, and came out here as a young man. He is, surprisingly, very good company. A quiet, tactful man. He seems a little aloof at first, but once you get to know him you realize it's because he simply conducts most of his conversations in his own head. His wife works for the Family, a sort of cook or housekeeper, I'm not sure exactly. I have seen her; she is a good-looking woman, tall for a native, rather fierce. She is one of those people, I believe, who support and perpetuate their own oppression through their outlook on life. She doesn't seem to care about her daughter's education very much. She obviously believes that the best thing that could happen to young Milagros would be to secure a position on the estate. I don't think Don Gaudencio is happy with her. Of course we are not on such a footing as to discuss personal matters. I have to be extra careful, too, because all people do here is talk about what others are doing, and I must be a beacon of morality and beyond suspicion. Caesar's wife etc. But it is good to have someone to talk to, even if the interaction consists only in an exchange of innocent remarks about the weather. I have a hunch he is a progressive, and potentially a Perónist.

Don Gaudencio came to Argentina in the twenties. That makes him quite old, though he doesn't even remotely look his age. Who would have thought he's approaching fifty? That's double my age! He lived in Buenos Aires for a few years before ending up in this backwater. Why he chose to come out here is a mystery. I hope to discover it someday. If only we could sit in a café over a cup of coffee and talk. From what I've gleaned from the few words he's spoken on the subject, he left for the usual reasons: poverty, unstable political situation, a perpetual fear of war. However, it seems he was disillusioned, as he found more of the same here. I cannot begin to imagine what it would be like to leave a place only to go and find the same situation, and worse, at the other end of the world, but I am sure that permanently unhappy look he has owes a lot to this. And of course, he has buried five children. Poor man! I wish I could convince him that things are changing now, politically. A new dawn is rising over our country. Just give it some time, I tell him.

Nothing good ever lasts for long around here, he always replies. I wish we could get rid of that fatalism, or cynicism, or just plain old despair, in this country, for once.

November 3, 1948

Sometimes I stay late in the school to write my reports and prepare my lessons in peace – there is no such thing to be had at the Widow Pérez's house with the radio on all day long, and those endless insipid radionovelas the women aorund here are crazy about. I like to be alone in the school after hours; I like the smell of paper and sharpened pencil. I like to look at the children's drawings lining the wall. We are having an Eva Perón drawing contest. The best drawing will be sent to the capital to compete with drawings from all over the country. I hope to persuade Milagros Riquelme to take part. She is a talented girl in many ways, and it really breaks my heart to think that all her life she will be here, in this empty, abandoned, dusty old village of three houses and one shop. I look outside the window and see the empty square and the dilapidated buildings and the forlorn trees and it breaks my heart. Nothing to do here, nobody to see, no pleasure or interest to pursue. Yet people live here, and they have lived here for a long time. I find it baffling. But I will try to persuade the best of them – not that there are many – to leave this place as soon as possible and get to the capital. There is opportunity for clever, industrious people, though perhaps Don Gaudencio would not agree. Why did he leave the capital, a man of his education and mental ability, and decide to come to this place of exile?

May 27, 1949

When night falls in the winter and the bitter wind blows with a threatening howl and I walk home from work, wrapped up as best I can but still shaking with the cold, walking the deserted dirt streets where only a few lights are switched on, I look around me and think that maybe I'm already dead and don't know it yet. News travels very slowly out here.

Don Gaudencio came and had mate *with me today. I invited him, and to hell with conventions and small-town talk. Let them talk. Why should I care? I have nothing to reproach myself with. He is the father of one of my students, of my best student, in fact, and I am a teacher, a member of the Justice Party and an educated, enlightened, modern woman. Plenty to talk about.*

He is a kind man. He is a lonely man. I am lonely too. Is it such a crime to admit it and to try to do something about it? I mean no harm to anyone. I only want someone to talk to.

June 15, 1949

I had no idea how difficult it would be to organize a school in this area. In my second year now, and still not very much progress has been made, at least not to the standard I had hoped. There are few children who come to the school regularly, only those that live nearby. Pablo Suárez's attendance record is much better than I had expected, given his penchant for mischief. But his father can drive him, whereas others don't have that choice. I must speak with Mr. Tévez in San Justo, maybe we could arrange a bus or truck to pick them up in the morning.

December 9, 1949

I am quite satisfied as to attendance now. Thirty-five children come to school every day. The truck brings them in the morning and takes them back in the afternoon. I understand there may be some children in more inaccessible areas or with more backward parents, but I am confident: when they begin to see that school is nothing terrible, when they begin to see the results of education, they will be motivated, too.

Now my worries are of a different sort. I see that many of these children are...how to put this politely? Underfed. Undernourished. Starving. It is a pitiful sight to see. Many of them just sit there and stare at me stupidly, as if they don't understand a word I'm saying. Too passive, too weak to do anything. Something has to be done about this. How can I teach these children anything if their stomachs are permanently empty? Physical nourishment first. I wonder where are all those good and charitable intentions of the great lady Goyena. I heard they had another batch of guests from the capital, with dinners and parties and shooting and heaven knows what. Expense and dissipation. And the local children, starving, as though they weren't their responsibility. Well, now they are mine, and I'm glad I'm here to help. The Big House all ablaze with lights every night. You can hear the music out here in the still of the night. Oh, my country! I hope the sword of justice falls on their heads quickly. I must write to the Foundation. She who cares for all the destitute and hungry will surely spare something for us up here too. I heard some worrying rumors about her health when I was in Buenos Aires over the winter holiday. I hope they are just that, idle rumors. I ardently hope, and am not alone in this, that she may live long to accomplish her plans, and may she succeed in leaving those rich parasites destitute in the end. It will serve them right to feel what it means to be the underdog for once in their lives. I don't expect this to happen in my lifetime, though. Perhaps the next generation, these children we are now educating in the lights of truth and justice.

September 20, 1950

School dinners have begun! Long live the President! Long live Evita! I told the children that they should thank the good Lord for their food and ask Him to grant long life and health to our beloved President and Evita, because it is to them they owe it the most. Plain but nourishing food: milk, cornbread, soup, polenta, quince jelly. The occasional morsel of beef. For many of my students this is their only meal. I let them take time over it, because I think that they should become aware of how education can really make a difference in your life materially too. The life of the spirit is all very good, but try to tell this to someone with an empty belly.

I am glad to say that the stupid, empty look is vanishing and that sparks of intelligence begin to light up in my poor students' eyes.

Doña Celedonia, Gaudencio's wife, is helping in the kitchen. She sneaks up at night to cook, after coming back home from work. She's asked me not to tell anybody. They may be affronted at the Big House. I was indignant when she first said this. Is it our fault they have been negligent of their Fduty to the poor people in the area? Apparently Mrs. Goyena is against charity, because she thinks giving money to the poor only results in them drinking more. Why it never occurred to her that philanthropy is not just giving money, that she might actually feed the people directly, I don't know. Celedonia said that even if you give them in kind, they

26

sell it and buy drink anyway. Well, I don't know about that. Except for Old Guacho, the village idiot who loiters in the plaza and is generally harmless, poor soul, I've never seen another drunk in the area. But then again, I don't frequent their dances and have never been to the pulpería *beyond the train tracks, or to the* boliches *of San Justo. Too vulgar for me, I'm afraid.*

The greatest surprise in all this is that Celedonia offered to help. I think I may have misjudged her. She looks daunting, a handsome woman, her face chiselled like stone, but her heart is in the right place. I thought she might suspect me of bad intentions because I had befriended her husband and was trying to take her daughter away from her, in a way. But I could not have been more wrong. She actually wants her daughter to leave Alta Gracia. She told me so herself, to my astonishment.

"She must make something better of herself," she said one evening, as she was spooning filling onto dough, then folding up the empanadas *in neat, elegant half-moon shapes. "What life would she have here? A servant in the Big House? It's a fate I wouldn't wish on my worst enemy."*

The fierce way in which she spat those words, in a loud whisper as if she was afraid someone might overhear, made me turn and look at her, taken aback.

"I agree," I said. "Your daughter deserves much better, and we'll make sure she gets her chance."

March 4, 1952

Tomorrow I will have been here exactly three years. How things have changed since I first arrived in Alta Gracia, an innocent who'd never been outside of the capital before, who had no idea how the rest of my country and my compatriots lived. There were so many difficulties, so much to do, so much to fight against, so much to organize. Thankfully, much has been accomplished. I look back at my younger self — I was nearer twenty then and I'm nearer thirty now, going on to middle age fast — and think of that wide-eyed young woman fondly, as if she were a younger sister or friend who's gone forever.

I am a very different person now. More hardened? I couldn't say. It still brings tears to my eyes when I see some of my students, or should I say, most of my students, and their parents: how they live, how poor they are, how every chance has been stolen from them even before they were born. But also tears of hope and pride, for they are not alone. Perón is there for them. Eva is there for them. So many things have changed in my country in recent years. All for the better.

Many changes in the area, too. Many people have left. They are going to the capital, and I don't blame them. There is work there for them; there is hope. Don Gaudencio was saying the other day that he too would go if he were younger, but he feels it's too late for him. Too old to begin again. But we all hope that Milagros will leave when the time comes. She has been my assistant for the last two years. She helps with the younger children; she is so good at teaching them songs and showing them how to draw. She is so patient and sweet-natured. After that conversation I had with her mother way back, I always thought there would be a way to help the girl. Things I have heard since about what has happened to some young, pretty girls that went into service have made me more determined to assist her in making something better of her life. And now that I have taught her for a few years, I firmly believe that this girl will be wasted if she does not go on with her studies.

She could become an excellent teacher; I've told both Don Gaudencio and his wife. Especially for younger children. She will have her salary; she will have a permanent job. They both agree. But there is always the problem of money. They can't afford to send her away to study, and they have no family or friends that could help by putting her up, for example. They have very little money. I tell them there are scholarships and surely something can be arranged. I am looking into it anyway. It would be such a credit *to the school to have a teacher come out of its ranks! Living proof of the President's and Evita's aspirations for the people, and their firm belief in the power of education to better people's lives! Yes, young Milagros must not be another slave to the backward feudal powers that rule this place. She must escape, and I have a plan, which I believe is going to work. I have written letters, and have received responses, and any day now I am waiting for the confirmation, so I can tell the Riquelme family about the extraordinary luck that is coming their way soon. Well, not just luck. Plenty of hard work involved, some by me, but most by the girl herself.*

4

Don Faustino

Except for that first brief visit by Doña Alejandra Goyena, Delia did not have any further contact with the family in the Big House until almost a year later. She had rather expected a follow-up to their initial meeting sooner, and had almost given up hope of it, until an invitation for "tea and a friendly chat," written in an elegant script on thick, pearl-gray paper with a silver monogramme was delivered to her by the Widow Pérez, who clucked and fussed like the old hen that she was.

"The chauffeur delivered it. In *full* livery!" she announced, emphasising the "full" in her awed tone, her eyes round and rheumy.

"It's only Old Man Suárez in his uniform, Señora Pérez," Delia said, laughing. How those people loved pomp and circumstance! It was true that Old Man Suárez was friendly enough when going about in the village in his ordinary clothes, but quite a different man, formal and distant, in his cap and uniform.

The following day, Delia wore her white dress with the red and blue cabbage roses, with a matching three-quarter sleeve coat, and her most expensive hat, an elegant little toque perching on top of her head. She was dying with curiosity to see the inside of the Big House. She expected palatial interiors and old-world charm mixed with European sophistication. She had never been anywhere that grand before, at least not a private residence.

As she walked up the expansive avenue leading to the house, under a canopy of gigantic jacarandas, she felt she was inside the central nave of a cathedral. The house rose in front of her, an off-white, sturdy, beautiful structure, built for the centuries, built for ease and pleasure. She wondered how such majestic beauty could comfortably exist sitting only a few hundred yards away from the shabby, forgotten village. They just don't see it, she thought. They come and go in their fast, shiny cars; they are picked up at the train station by Old Man Suárez doffing his cap; they have their own private road to their palace. The village might as well be on another planet.

It was a warm day and she was feeling hot; her shoes felt too small for her feet as she climbed up the wide stone stairs. The front door was open; obviously she was expected, but there was nobody there to receive her. How strange! She had expected liveried footmen, as one saw in films. She walked inside the cool hall with its black and white chessboard marble tiles and its enormous bell-shaped Tiffany lamp hanging from the faraway ceiling. She felt a little nervous, a little apprehensive. What good could come of this meeting? She was sure Señora Goyena didn't much care for a state school teacher, a civil servant, polite though she may have wanted to appear, and Delia herself didn't want anything from the Goyenas. She did not believe in patronage; she was suspicious of it and resented it, rather. She believed in a powerful, all-providing, socially minded state administration instead.

Doña Alejandra came hastily down the stairs towards her, extending her arms. Delia's experienced eye took in the beautifully cut silk tea dress, definitely made in Paris; the cropped, silver hair on a small, neat, bird-like head; the pink sheen of pearl earrings and necklace on tanned skin; the thin lips painted in coral by

Coty. In spite of all those effects of youth and softness, the woman looked old and hard and dried-up.

"Señorita Lugghi, I am so glad to see you again, do come in," she said, extending a bony hand with ringless fingers. Her grip was firm, slightly cold and waxy. "I hope you haven't waited long? That useless girl was supposed to wait for you at the door."

A maid in uniform appeared from the depths of a corridor off the hall, a young girl who reminded her a bit of Milagros, except that this one, though slender and glossy haired, had a plain face and large, almost obscenely pouty lips. The girl plainly heard her mistress's comment, because she pouted even more. She took Delia's coat without looking at her.

"Bring us tea to my sitting room, Hortensia," Doña Alejandra said in a firm voice, and turning to Delia said more softly, "Come along, you'll need your refreshment, I'm sure. I know I do. Such a hot day today!"

Delia took off her gloves and furtively patted her perspiring upper lip with them as she followed the woman. There were large paintings on the wall by the stairs, many of them abstract, modern ones, she was surprised to see. The stained glass on the enormous window between the landings refracted the afternoon light into shafts and pools of mellow colors. An eerie silence enveloped the place, elegant and stacked with beautiful objects in every nook and cranny as it was.

"We are rather quiet at the moment," Doña Alejandra said as if she were reading Delia's mind. "My husband is in the capital. The Senate is in session, you know. Politics is a very demanding business, I'm afraid. And my son – oh well, you know young people these days."

Delia mumbled something polite about the country needing all hands on deck in such crucial times, but in the privacy of her own head she resented being put in the same category as her host. I'm not much older than your idiot son, she thought.

They entered a room facing southwest. From the French windows Delia could see the azure swimming pool glinting in the sun, the art deco pool house and the lounge chairs on the mowed grass. It was cool and calming. Doña Alejandra's sitting room was painted a rich, creamy yellow. It smelled of beeswax polish and autumn roses, arranged in crystal bowls and vases. All this luxury was beginning to give Delia a headache; it was getting on her nerves. She couldn't explain how or why, but it occurred to her that she was somehow being patronised.

"I'm aware this is not much of a welcome, but I thought it would be more...cosy if we met here, just the two of us," Doña Alejandra said. "Our first meeting was rather brief."

You were afraid I might not be presentable to polite society, thought Delia viciously. She only smiled and inclined her head in thanks. They sat on two opposing Queen Anne settees, Delia perched on the very edge of hers, as if ready to take flight.

"I'm not one to stand on ceremony," Doña Alejandra said. "We seem to complicate our lives all the time, so many unnecessary rituals, *n'est-ce pas*?"

"Well, I think–" Delia began to speak, but Doña Alejandra leaned forward and cut her off:

"Well, what do you make of our little backwater then? Isn't it so charmingly quaint?"

"Yes, it is rather forsaken," Delia said. She hadn't meant to sound acerbic, but she didn't regret that she did.

"You've settled well in your lodgings, I hope?" Doña Alejandra asked, pretending she hadn't noticed. "You live in that house by the railroad, isn't that so? A Mrs. López, isn't it?"

"Pérez."

"Of course. You must forgive me. It's the prerogative of age: one is allowed, even expected, to be forgetful," she said with a little laugh.

Delia smiled politely; it was getting more difficult by the minute. She had to resign herself to the fact that she wouldn't be allowed to contribute to this talk, or probably even finish a sentence. Just let the lady do the talking if she loves it so much, she told herself.

The maid who had taken her coat clattered in with a trolley full of tea things. Fine bone china, silver teapot and milk jug, sugar cubes in a silver saucer, cakes and scones on a platter, crisp embroidered linen napkins. The maid's expression was still sullen. Her movements are strangely awkward for such a slender person, Delia thought, she moves like a fat woman. There was a damp patch from spilt milk on the exquisite doily lining the trolley. Doña Alejandra pursed her lips, casting a look of disdain at the girl, who – Delia would swear – shrugged and, without offering any excuse or uttering any word at all, turned her back to leave. The maid's uniform was too tight on her pert bottom.

"Those country girls," Doña Alejandra said. "They are immune to learning, as I'm sure you will have already discovered in that little school of yours."

She poured the tea.

"It depends," Delia said. "Certainly, it is difficult for many of them, with so few resources and mostly uneducated parents, but it's not as bad as one might expect."

"Oh, I don't mean they are not naturally apt, I just believe they are not really interested in broadening their mind. Give them tangos and movies and silly magazines, that's all the knowledge they want. Such a pity, really."

"I believe this is the case everywhere, in the cities, too, not just the village, and in all social classes," Delia said.

"You are right there, I'm afraid," Doña Alejandra said with a slight grimace. "The majority of the people have always been like that and probably always will be. Nothing can beat bread and circuses!"

"Not necessarily," Delia said drily. She was getting hot again. She put her teacup and saucer on the small table next to the sofa and pulled at her imitation pearl necklace. She could not help comparing it to the string of pearls round the Goyena woman's neck. A soft breeze came through the open French doors, bringing a subtle fragrance of roses. The fine linen curtains stirred. Delia stretched her neck towards the current of air, trying to place her face on its way. The ceiling fan was whirring hypnotically above her head. She had a sudden vision of it coming loose, falling from its ornate nest, beheading her and Doña Alejandra with its sharp blades, scarlet drops of blood splashing all over the curtains and the plush settees and the velvet rug.

"Are you feeling all right?" Doña Alejandra said. "Perhaps you would like some iced water?"

"No, thank you, I'm fine."

"You'll get used to our climate eventually. Sometimes the shock of finding oneself in a new place, having to adapt all one's habits to the new conditions...it's not the easiest thing in the world. Here, try some of these scones. Would you like some cream with them?"

"They are very good."

"Yes, we are very lucky in our cook. Celedonia Fernández is a rare jewel."

"Her daughter is my best pupil."

"Really? How old is she now? I thought she was too young to be in school."

It was Delia's turn to laugh. "No, she's old enough to be half-way through, had she started in time."

"You don't say," Doña Alejandra drawled and Delia wondered if it would be unforgivably rude to get up and leave within the next five minutes. Aloud she said:

"Yes, and what's more, she seems destined for better things than...what I mean is that she absorbs knowledge so quickly, so thoroughly. I have recently made her my official assistant. She could make something of her life, perhaps get into teacher training college eventually."

"Oh?" Doña Alejandra looked genuinely interested. "Do you think so? A teacher! She would have to live away from home, isn't

35

that so? I don't know how her poor parents would like that. They have been through so much, you know. She is all they have left. So much death in that family, so much pain...Surely the daughter's duty is to stay with them."

"Milagros's duty is primarily to herself," Delia said. "I'm sure you would be the first to recognize it. In that article of yours in *Austral* about women's emancipation, you wrote that–"

"Emancipation is all good and fine," Alejandra interrupted, "but the big city is a dangerous place, especially for young unprotected women from the provinces."

"She won't be unprotected inside the college. She will learn much and she will earn her living. She will be her own person. She will serve her country and will make it a better place for others, as it was made for her." She said this with her eyes fixed at the silk-wallpapered wall, her own voice sounding harsh and tinny to her ears.

Doña Alejandra did not reply. She sipped her tea looking at the swimming pool. The only noise in the room was the whir of the ceiling fans. Then she said:

"This President Perón of yours – I understand you support his government, *n'est-ce pas*? – he seems intent upon destroying the fabric of this country, uprooting the people from their own land. He promises the earth to them. They all rush to the capital expecting to find streets paved with gold. At the end of the day, all he will have, if he stays in power much longer, which I doubt, all he'll end up having is displaced and dissatisfied masses in the city right under his nose. There is nothing more pathetic and sinister than the urban poor, Señorita. Believe me, it's not doing them any service, taking them away from home on false promises of ease and wealth."

"Perhaps they don't feel that the country as it is is really much home to them, Señora Goyena," Delia replied. "And there is certainly something far more pathetic – I don't know about sinister

– than the urban poor, and that's the rural poor, as you're well aware."

"We do all we can to help, I'm sure," said Doña Alejandra, lowering her eyes modestly over her fine bone china cup.

Delia felt a surge of hot blood going up to her head. I can't believe this, she thought, I'm accusing her to her face and she takes it as a compliment. What sort of people are these?

"I really must be going," she said after a while, "so much to do at the school." She felt spent and light-headed as she got up.

"Of course, of course, I understand," said Doña Alejandra, getting up in turn. "Just don't wear yourself out too much. You are so young, it's a pity to waste your youth in this manner. Young people are meant to enjoy life."

Ah, so I'm young now, Delia thought. "Doing one's duty is more important," she said. In another, fairer world she would have smashed the teacup over the smug woman's head.

Doña Alejandra walked her downstairs to the front door, beaming patronage, promising books and writing utensils and even fitted cupboards to store them in. Delia knew these were about as likely to materialise as Alejandra Goyena converting to Perónism. The fake smile she'd been wearing during her stay made her face ache. As they reached the hall, the sulky maid appeared from the shadows bearing Delia's coat. As she was putting her arms through the sleeves, wishing that she didn't have to wear the coat, it occurred to Delia that Don Gaudencio's wife was a few metres away in the kitchen, and she felt somehow worse for it. She offered her thanks and goodbyes and left as quickly as politeness allowed. Halfway down the avenue, she took off her coat, then her high heeled shoes, and sank her naked feet into the soft dust with a sigh of relief. The thought came to her that she might be watched from the Big House, by mistress and servants alike. What would they think, seeing her walk away with her coat over her arm and her shoes in her hand, as if she had escaped a burning house?

"Well, fuck the lot of them," she said out loud, shocked at her own profanity, but also rather pleased she had uttered it.

A bird took off, wings fluttering in the late afternoon peace. It was getting cooler as the sun went down.

Delia ignored any further invitations from the Big House; she didn't care what they'd think of her, and then the invitations stopped coming. Every time she happened to see Doña Alejandra's sports car from afar, she felt red hot rage rushing to her head. This reaction baffled and displeased her. She could not explain it to herself, but she felt as if she had been insulted somehow, or worse, that she had been tried and found wanting. Delia was not used to failing any tests. In Buenos Aires, social differences did not matter to her, at least not in any concrete sense. She had no connections in the higher circles of society and she never wanted or missed them. Apart from a general suspiciousness towards them, fuelled by her political allegiances as a thinking woman and an intellectual, and apart from an occasional stir of curiosity as she leafed through pages of women's magazines at the hairdresser's, it would never occur to her to give any thought to those men and women sitting in the plush parlors of the palaces and mansions of Avenida Libertador and the Barrio Norte. But now she had come into very close orbit with them and felt that this brief and transient contact had somehow poisoned her life and mission in Alta Gracia.

One early winter evening, after her private class with Milagros had ended – for now she was coaching the girl for her exams twice a week in the afternoons – the Widow Pérez burst into Delia's room without waiting for permission. She was all aflutter.

"Don Faustino Goyena is coming this way in the car. He intends to pay you a visit, I'm sure."

Delia cast a quick look in the mirror. She was just preparing for bed, and looked pale and frumpy in her housecoat and curlers.

Quickly she began to remove the curlers from her hair and throw them in a drawer. She gave her hair a quick brush and applied lipstick, blotting it with her finger and passing it quickly over her cheeks to give them a blush. She stood in front of the wardrobe, her eyes like dark glistening pools looking back at her through the slightly rusty mirror. She sidled to the window and peeked through the curtains; she could see the glint of the sun as it hit the fenders of a large, sleek car in the distance, hear the engine's deep throaty roar. Why was she behaving like a stupid girl of fifteen? Somewhat annoyed with herself, for her heart was now beating very quickly, she retreated back to the wardrobe and lit a cigarette. She was still in her housecoat. She should change into a dress. The red floral one that accentuated her dark colors, or the navy blue that made her look aristocratic, as she had once been told, a very long time ago?

She smoked her cigarette trying to calm herself down, despising herself for needing to. Faustino Goyena, whose picture was everywhere in the social columns, had that golden shimmer around him that film stars had, a sheen of unreality, like a character from a book come to life. In the polo field, at the exclusive clubs, at the horse races, at galas and parties, surrounded by other young men like himself, and beautiful girls in dreamy dresses, he looked at ease, as majestic as a young king in his court. And now he was coming to visit her in the faded old parlor of an old house in an old, godforsaken village. How strange was life! Imagine if it became even stranger. She too had read novels and seen films in which a simple but extraordinary young woman captivated the young, handsome, rich man and lived a charmed life to the end of her days, or at least attained the promise of such a life.

She snorted, even more annoyed with herself now. What idle thoughts! Still in her housecoat, she shrugged and approached the window again. The sun had now sunk below the horizon and the edges of the sky were painted in sombre purple tones. The face of the earth was quiet, peaceful, like someone who has given up the fight. A few lights flickered in the distance: the railway station, a few sparse homesteads. There was no one on the road, just the hum of an engine getting fainter with distance. Then silence, broken only by the mournful hooting of an owl and the faint murmur of the radio in the parlor, a few strains of a tango tune.

No one was coming. Mrs. Pérez must have got it wrong. He was not heading this way. Delia shrugged and took some blotting paper to her lips for the lipstick, glad she had not changed into a dress and heels to wait for a visitor who was probably completely unaware of her existence.

Don Faustino watched the girl in the white dress walking along the dusty road. She was slight and slender, and her glossy black hair hung gracefully over her straight back. Her feet were light on the ground, barely touching it, like a ballet dancer. Was she real, or was she one of those spirits that you read about in European folklore tales, a fairy that would lead you deep into a forest where you would perish and be glad of it?

"Who's that?"

"This is the cobbler's girl, Milagros Riquelme," Suárez said from the driver's seat. "A good family, hard-working. Unlucky though, their sons all dead. Her mother is in your service, Celedonia Fernández. Her grandmother is a witch, they say."

"Oh," Don Faustino said. "Of course."

He turned to look at the girl as they overtook her on the road. She lifted her hand in greeting, and her face was shining soft and silver in the gathering dark, like a perfectly minted coin, lost in the wilderness, unclaimed.

Very pretty, he thought, and smiled at her.

As she walked back home from her lesson, Milagros heard the car behind her and turned back to look. Her heart began to beat wildly, because she saw that it was the young Señor inside. As the car passed her by, the young man turned to look at her, and he smiled. He was so beautiful, his smile so dazzling; he was like the sun. She blushed to the roots of her hair and jumped out of the way of the car. She nearly tripped and fell, and blushed even harder. What an idiot he'll think me, she thought.

5

The Train Station

1952

Milagros ran against the wind, hair streaming like a banner, arms cutting circles through the air, feet barely touching the ground. She could swim in the air. She could fly. She opened her mouth wide, swallowing the cold, delicious air, bursting with joy. She skipped and she leapt, she twirled her skirt, she laughed out loud, her laughter carried by the wind and scattered over the flat land with no edges, no beginning and no end.

She was running up towards the hill overlooking the train station. It was the only high ground for miles and miles, an island rising softly in the sea of tall grass. Many years ago, long before she was born, hundreds of cattle were slaughtered, their carcasses burned and buried in a large pit under the hill to stop disease from spreading. Men piled up rocks on top of the hecatomb, then time and the wind brought dust and piled it up on top of the rocks, forming a grassy knoll. A network of streams at the foot of the hill irrigated the ponds where cattle used to drink before Don Anibal modernised his estate. Now the water on the surface of the ponds was green with scum and buzzing with large insects of metallic colors and sounds.

This was a land of vast emptiness and huge domed skies. Birds plummeted down from the heights spreading their wings, they cawed, they soared again. This was a land of sibilance, bursting with buzzing and swishing, rustling and hissing; a land of long straight roads that led to places where Milagros had never been, and railway lines that extended into the horizon and dissolved in the distance, taking people and cattle to the capital and to the port, and then to the unimaginable seas beyond. It was an ugly-beautiful place and Milagros loved it, and never more so than on that day.

A few weeks earlier, Señorita Delia had invited Milagros into her office, really just a niche in the corner of the classroom, stuffed with an old wooden office desk and cabinet overflowing with books and papers. Milagros thought she was needed to help with tidying up and cleaning and looked around for the duster.

"Sit down, Milagros," Señorita Delia said. She was holding an opened letter in her hand. "Do you know what this is?"

Milagros didn't know what to say.

"It is your ticket to the future," Señorita Delia said, beaming at her. "You have won a scholarship to the teacher training academy in Buenos Aires, paid by the Eva Perón Foundation."

Milagros looked at her, hardly daring to comprehend.

"Do you realize what this means?" Señorita Delia went on, almost breathless with joy. "Eva Perón is giving you the opportunity to make something of your life, and to contribute to the greatness of your country."

She began to describe life in Buenos Aires. The parks, the exquisite buildings, the cars, the shops. Milagros's mind was filled with bright lights and shiny shop-windows and music and elegant men and women going out on the town. "You'll be one of them," her teacher was saying, "you'll be a young lady with a career, a future, money of your own, friends, a social circle. You'll be Señorita Milagros to your students. They'll look up to you. You'll be Señorita Riquelme to the world. You'll be somebody. But remember, you have to give back to your country and to your people, like we all do, in the example of our dear Evita Perón."

Milagros tried to say something but no words would come out of her throat. She was feeling dizzy and slightly nauseous, as if Señorita Delia had grabbed her hands into hers and together they were spinning round and round and round till the whole world had become a blur. She felt her eyes prickling with tears. She took Señorita Delia's manicured hand and kissed it.

"Thank you, Señorita," she said.

Now gazing at the train station, Milagros dreamed. Soon it would be her turn to board that train. First graduation, and then wearing her Sunday best, suitcase in hand, Milagros would board the train that would take her to San Justo, and from there to mythical, golden Buenos Aires, and to teacher training college. Far, far away from Alta Gracia. All expenses paid by her scholarship from the Eva Perón Foundation, and even a little bit of pocket money. Señorita Delia had helped, but Milagros had put in all the hard work, studying by lamplight until the cockerels crowed three times and the shadows vanished from the wall, swatting mosquitoes away, closing her ears to all the siren voices calling her to bed or to head outside and abandon her studies. Her girlfriends were now beginning to wear lipstick as soon as they were out of their parents' sight, and listen to the radionovelas, and smile at the boys. But not Milagros. Even though young Pablo Suárez, now suddenly grown taller, but still cheeky and mischievous as ever, was always within her sight, now teasing, now full of tender gestures.

She watched as the station awakened from its usual lethargic state. Men were bustling about with trolleys and wheelbarrows and carts ready to be laden, jostling for space on the platform. Two cars appeared on the dusty road from the direction of Alta Garcia, racing against each other, raising clouds of dust, then stopped outside the station. It was the formal cream and crimson limousine from the Big House, and Doña Alejandra's gleaming red two-seater. She jumped out of her car, small and straight in pristine white, and made a sign to Old Suárez, in his uniform with the gleaming buttons, military-looking cap held respectfully in hand. They had come to meet the train.

"What are you looking at?"

The voice in her ear made Milagros jump up.

"Oh, it's you again," she sighed. "You can't keep away for five minutes, can you?"

Pablito Suárez laughed; he blew into her ear and received a smack for his pains.

"Just leave me alone, will you?" she hissed. "For heaven's sake!"

"There's my old man!" Pablito cried. "Oh, look at that beauty of a sports car! One of these days I'll be driving that car myself."

"No, you won't!" Milagros scoffed. "This boy has such a big mouth. Someone must put him in his place."

"My old man drives every single vehicle on that estate."

"Not that one," she said, pointing at the sleek sports car. "Doña Alejandra will never let anyone drive it, not even young Señor, as you very well know."

"I'm driving my old man's cars all the time!"

"They aren't his cars. They belong to Don Anibal."

"He's the one who drives them, which is as good as," said Pablito. "Sure, they belong to Don Anibal and Doña Alejandra and young Señor – they've got more cars between them than all the population in San Justo. But it's my old man that holds the wheel, and I've been in each and every one of them, too."

"What a big mouth!"

"When I grow up I will be the driver and I'll get all the cars to drive as much as I want. And then..." He leaned over her and whispered into her ear, "I'll take you any place you want."

She swatted at him like at an irritating mosquito.

He didn't know that she was leaving soon. No one did, except her own family. Her father was constantly beaming with a joy he could barely contain, bursting to tell his friends at the shop, but keeping his solemn promise not to divulge a word until Milagros was safely installed at the academy. Her mother was her usual silent self, but also wary and non-committal, as if she could not believe the good luck that had befallen her daughter. Good things rarely happened in Celedonia's life and she did not believe in that possibility, but now she had to. It was all arranged. Yet Señorita Delia advised them to keep quiet about it and Milagros agreed. Why tempt fate? Why attract envy and sorrow? She knew she would die of jealousy if she had to listen to another girl announce that she was going, while she, Milagros, had to remain behind.

She had a vision of herself in that station, not leaving but returning, many years later, tall and sleek in a brand-new dress and coat and a silk scarf around her neck, her black hair in an elegant bun, in brand new leather shoes and handbag. Señorita Milagros, teacher. What would life be like then for her? Anything would be possible. Doña Alejandra would invite her to the Big House. And Don Faustino would be there to see her...

Her eyes were bright with hope and desire.

"I bet you are dreaming of the day when you'll be sitting in that car next to me," Pablito Suárez says.

She pretended she didn't hear.

A long whistle in the distance: the train was coming. They could see it, a long black centipede crawling slowly until it stopped at the station. The platform was teeming with people. Doña Alejandra cut briskly through the crowd, the stationmaster following closely behind. Old Man Suárez sauntered back to the limousine, gave a last polish to the door handles with his sleeve, then stood to attention next to the back passenger door. Some men came round the station hauling a large box, the sort used to carry horses in, shouting directions at each other.

Soon Doña Alejandra walked out of the station with a small group of people. Don Faustino, dressed all in white just like his mother, towering over her like a young birch, walked just behind her next to another man. The sun had just come out and was shining on his fair wavy hair. He was holding his hat in his hand and was talking to his companion: a dark, burly sort of fellow, dressed in black riding clothes with silver trim that caught the sunlight. Milagros narrowed her eyes, squinting in her effort to see better, to discern the features of this newcomer. And this was the first time she laid eyes on Ramona Irribaren – not a fellow at all! – although Milagros did not yet know her name or anything else about her, except the reason she was here.

"This is a lady?" Milagros cried, hardly believing her eyes. "A lady in man's clothes?"

"She must be the new fiancée," Pablito Suárez said, snorting.

It had been the talk of the village for weeks now. Don Faustino was getting married. Milagros squinted trying to see what the bride looked like, but all she could make out was that she walked just like a man, legs astride, shoulders square, chin held high. Not at all what she had been expecting.

Could this be the woman who had captured Don Faustino's heart? But of course it was not a question of the heart. As Milagros' father had said, airing his opinions to his clientele, it was always buy and sell for those people, nothing more.

"He's marrying her for money," Pablito said. "Her father owns half of Buenos Aires. He doesn't even know how much money he's got."

"Well, apparently *you* do," Milagros said.

They watched the odd company: elegant Doña Alejandra stiff and small and upright; then the couple; then another man following the unlikely bride-to-be, close to her, at one with her shadow. He walked in the stiff, open-legged way that was common to men who had spent their whole lives on horseback. The new fiancée turned to him every so often, but Milagros could not see if she was speaking to him or just making sure he was following. Could he possibly be her immensely wealthy father? From afar, he looked like an old gaucho.

As the group reached the cars, Old Man Suárez bowed and opened the door for the fiancée to enter the limousine. But she abruptly turned her back to them all and strode away towards the big horsebox, the old gaucho trotting at her elbow like a bodyguard. She gave an order to the men, and they opened the door and out came a magnificent black horse, its mane and tail long and sleek like a beautiful woman's hair. In a flash the fiancée snatched the reins from the handler's grasp and placed her other hand on the horse's muzzle. The old gaucho shouted out an order and an attendant ran towards them with a saddle; another led a chestnut roan along, and the old gaucho grabbed its reins. Then the new bride and the old man mounted their horses in a flash and galloped away without so much as a backwards glance towards the assembled crowd. Doña Alejandra, Don Faustino, the station master, Old Man Suárez, and all the bystanders stood there like pillars of salt, Milagros thought.

Doña Alejandra got inside her car, slamming the door, and drove off with the engine roaring. Don Faustino got inside the limousine on the passenger side. Old Man Suárez closed the door softly after him, got behind the wheel and started the car. The fiancée and her gaucho attendant were now small black specks on the horizon.

"Well, look at that! Don Faustino is marrying the Lone Ranger!" Pablito Suárez whooped. "Complete with Tonto, too!"

Milagros did not even look at him. There was nothing to laugh about, nothing at all. She felt sorry for Don Faustino with his lovely golden hair and his white suit and elegant boots, insulted like that in front of his own mother, in front of all those people, his employees too! She must be a cruel, heartless woman – if indeed she was a woman.

"I must go home," she said. "It's getting late. Abuela will be up from her siesta and will be needing me."

She turned back and began to walk fast down the slope of the knoll towards the village.

"Hey, Mili, where are you going?" Pablito called out from the top of the hill.

"None of your business," she called back, walking even faster.

"Milagros Riquelme, I swear to God, I'll marry you one day!" he yelled. "And I won't catch you playing such tricks on me like the Lone Ranger out there!"

"Go to hell!" she shouted back, suddenly angry, even though she did not know why.

She burst into a sprint, and the earth was shaking beneath her feet.

6

The Ticket to the Future

The late afternoon sky was frowning. Dark purple clouds, the color of three-day old bruises, gathered at the edge of the horizon, as Milagros walked towards the house of the Widow Pérez. It was quite a long walk, and for the millionth time Milagros wished she too could afford to buy a bicycle like Señorita Delia's. One day, not too distant now, when she was a teacher herself – Señorita Milagros! – she would have her own bicycle with a bell and a basket at the back where she would carry her books and knitting and shopping.

The house was on the way to the railway station, and it was the largest in Alta Gracia – the Big House excepted. It was constructed for the men who came to that place long ago to build and run the railway that would carry produce and cattle to and from the estate. At that time, except for its ancient chapel, the village consisted of only a few shacks around the plaza. Don Anibal's father, the Half-Gringo, as those who remembered him still called him, had actually been one of the major shareholders in the railways.

According to Milagros's father, the Goyenas lost a heap of money when the President repossessed all the railways in the country and made them property of the state. He used the world "nationalization" and Milagros had to ask Señorita Delia what it meant. Señorita said that everything that was for the use and benefit of the public should be the property of the state, and it was quite right that the railways should belong to the people and not to some foreigners and their local pawns. "Now the railways belong to me and you, to all of us," Señorita Delia said. "When this happened," Papá said, "you could hear Don Anibal shouting miles away; he'd stormed and ranted and sworn that that army thug of a President and his harlot of a wife, the ex-actress, were set to ruin the country and someone should stop them before it was too late." Mama's brow turned dark as the coming storm and she told Papá off for using such language in front of their daughter, though this wasn't fair, it was Don Anibal and not Papá who had used it really.

Milagros didn't dare ask Señorita Delia what "harlot" meant; she had an idea this wasn't a thing Señorita would care to explain.

Milagros, slightly out of breath, reached Señorita Delia's house and mounted the stairs, which were flanked by two large, rather dusty and elderly-looking palm trees. Storks built their nests just above the roof cornice in the spring; you could see them from miles away, standing on one reed-like, gangly leg.

As she knocked on the flimsy door and entered without invitation as she always did, Milagros wondered if Señorita Delia had heard the strange and sordid tale of this house, the one that ended with the Widow Pérez, not yet known by this name, of course, running down the road in her nightgown, supposedly splattered head to toe with blood. Apparently the place was like a slaughterhouse when the police arrived, with both of the men who had been living in the house lying dead. Milagros decided that she wouldn't broach the subject with Señorita Delia, whether she already knew or not.

In the enormous front room, the Widow Pérez was fast asleep in her red velvet moth-eaten armchair; the lace antimacassar had fallen on her head and its end was rising and falling steadily with every sonorous snore. Milagros passed her by without making a noise, and treading softly on the threadbare carpet in her *alpargatas*, went up the staircase without extracting a single creak from it, congratulating herself for the feat. She knocked on Señorita Delia's door and waited until she heard a muffled, "Come in!"

"Good afternoon, Señorita Delia," Milagros said, taking in the familiar smell of polished furniture and floral perfume and cigarette smoke.

The teacher nodded at her. She was sitting at her large worktable by the window with a few pins in her mouth. The afternoon sun fell on her gleaming chestnut hair, gathered in a bun at the nape of her neck. The radio, a big boxy thing with bulbous buttons, was playing softly what sounded like a melancholy bolero. There were swathes of material on the table, crinkly paper patterns, a stack of fashion books, an overflowing ashtray, a cup of coffee, and a saucer with a few cigarette stubs. Señorita Delia was wearing black today, and her string of pearls. There were purple circles under her eyes, and she looked pale. It was that black dress, Milagros thought, that made her look haggard; she should be wearing something bright all the time, green or royal blue or even red.

"Good to see you, Mili," Señorita Delia said, tucking the last pins from her mouth into the yet shapeless fabric on the table. "Come sit by me, I've got something to show you."

She picked up a pile of fashion books from a chair. Some of the books slipped on to the floor with a thud that made them both jump. Milagros bent down quickly and picked them up. Señorita Delia placed them neatly on the table, emptied the cigarette stubs and ashes into an empty flowerpot. She then picked up one of the fashion books and began to leaf through it, putting small pieces of paper here and there among the pages.

"I think I've found the perfect dress for your big day," she said. "Now, that's one of life's most underestimated pleasures, a beautiful new dress."

Milagros sat on the chair next to her and breathed in the perfume and the cigarette smoke and also something else: a hint of rain, of eucalyptus and of high quality material wrapped up in mothballs. It was quite a pleasant smell, and she inhaled again, deeply, flaring her nostrils to capture the scent to the full. They looked at the fashion magazine together.

"This looks lovely," said Milagros pointing at a crinoline dress with ribbons and bows on the sleeves, hem and neckline.

"Oh no, not at all!" Señorita Delia said, horrified. "No, this is a dress for ugly girls. They need elaborate clothes to take people's eyes away from their plain faces. Besides, it's not a wedding but a graduation. We want something with simple lines for you. Just like this. Look! Isn't this perfect?"

Milagros looked at the picture her teacher was showing her. Oh no, she thought, what's this plain thing! It's like a nightgown. Why would she want to wear a nightgown at her graduation? Out loud, she said politely, "Yes, this is quite it."

"We'll buy the material at San Justo," said Señorita Delia, lighting a cigarette and puffing with gusto. "Or maybe I should order it at the capital. I know just the place, a lovely shop at Plaza Once. Cotton and lace...*broderie anglaise*...or perhaps rayon? Yes, rayon, it looks like silk but cheaper. And satin ribbon for the trimming."

She tore a page off the fashion book and pinned it on the table, making a few notes on a piece of paper. She took out her tape measure. "Stand up, Mili!" She took measurements and noted them down. It felt strange having one's own teacher fussing over one's person. It was ticklish, too, and Milagros stifled a giggle or two.

"You'll look divine in this dress," Señorita Delia said. "Such a big day for you, and for your family, too. The first one to graduate from school! You'll never forget it as long as you live."

"Will I need to wear a veil, too? I've got a nice one from first communion, with pearls and flowers and–"

"A veil! Heavens, child, no, of course not. It's not your wedding or your first communion, is it? It is much better, infinitely better than that. It's your entry to a new life, and you'll be the boss of that life and nobody else but you."

"But don't you think marriage is good at all, Señorita Delia?"

Señorita Delia picked up some stray pins from the table and began to stab a red satin pincushion. Milagros blushed, feeling exactly the way she did when – albeit it was a rare occasion – she got an answer wrong at school. She went to the sewing machine and turned the big wheel slowly. Her mother had one just like it in the house, only hers was old and battered, another cast-off from the Big House.

"No, I don't think marriage is a bad thing, not at all. It's just that I'm not interested in marriage at the moment," Señorita Delia said. She smiled at Milagros, a weary smile. "I know it's unusual to say such things. People don't believe a woman when she says she is not thinking of marriage. Not that I have anything against marriage per se. Look at our First Couple, the perfect union of grace and power. If you could be soulmates with someone special, like the President and Eva, yes. Otherwise, what's the point?"

Milagros let out a sigh and took her books out of her carpet bag.

"Yes, it's time for our lesson," Señorita Delia said, getting up from the table and switching off the radio. "But it has to be a shorter one today. I want us to listen to the news soon."

After the lesson, Señorita Delia switched the radio back on and sat in the worn velvet brocade armchair, lighting another cigarette. Milagros collected the books and notes and put them away, then she went to the window and looked outside. Darkness was falling over the empty stretches of land. In the distance she could see tiny lights from the village houses, and farther ahead, the Big House, all lights blazing through the large trees.

"It will be night soon," she said. "Señora Pérez will have to lend me the lantern."

She looked at the room wistfully; there was a pool of light over Señorita Delia's chair, and the red oval rug looked mellow and cosy in the soft light. They sat and listened to the melancholy tunes on the radio, hardly saying a word. Milagros thought it a strange thing that all music was sad today, no tangos or milongas tonight at all. Then the music on the radio abruptly stopped and the speaker was saying something about an announcement to the nation. Señorita Delia rose briskly and turned up the volume.

"Quiet!" she said, even though Milagros wasn't speaking. "They are saying something about Eva Perón."

A solemn voice over the radio waves spoke slowly, a warm, passionate, teary voice:

"Thousands of people are gathered outside the presidential residence, disregarding the cold and the rain. Tonight our hearts are being ripped out of our breasts and our souls are being torn apart. Our beloved Evita, the angel of kindness, protector of the poor and the downtrodden, our great nation's spiritual leader, is slowly passing away to eternity. Our hearts are with the President, who has hardly left her side these last days and hours. What will become of us without Evita? God have mercy upon us all..."

Milagros looked at Señorita Delia. Her eyes were closed, the circles under her eyes a deeper mauve.

"She can't die, she is only thirty-three years old," Delia whispered. "And if...and if she goes, what will happen to her work? What will happen to all the poor she's helping? What will happen to your scholarship?"

Milagros could hardly understand what she was hearing; her heart was wrung with dread. Hadn't they just been discussing what dress she was going to wear? She looked on, stunned, uncomprehending, as Señorita Delia covered her face with her hands and began to weep softly, bitterly, inconsolably.

PART TWO

1953-1957

7

The Big House

In the soft early morning light, Milagros and her mother walked on the road to the Big House. Doña Celedonia was speaking to her in a steady drone, instructing her on her future duties and comportment. Birds were chattering in the trees, insects darting through the grass; the world was vibrating softly, awakening.

"You must wash your hands after your morning chores because you are not allowed to touch anything with dirty hands and soil it. When you tidy up Don Faustino's study, be careful how you handle every single thing, and as soon as you're done dusting, put it back in its exact place. He doesn't want his things to be disturbed. Make sure you do your work when he is away. You must not be seen by any of them, ever. Your work starts once they leave a room."

"And if they don't?"

"They always do. When they are having breakfast, you are tidying up their rooms. When they leave the house, you tidy up his office and her dressing room. She's always away riding anyway, even now in her state."

"Her state?"

"Never you mind," said her mother. "I didn't say her state, you misheard. Just make sure you are invisible and out of everyone's way. Only use the back stairs, from the kitchen to the upper floors, I'll show you when we get there. They never use it, but if you happen to meet any of them, just curtsy and go, but say nothing. Flies do not enter a shut mouth."

"And if they speak to me first?"

"Do as I told you, just smile and listen to what they say, or pretend to listen at least, and nod and go away immediately. You must be especially careful with Doña Alejandra. Keep your eyes on the ground and look sharp when she is giving you any orders. She doesn't like people to be slow, especially those who serve her. Make sure she never catches you anywhere near the rooms after 10 o'clock in the morning. Never hang around any of them, especially Don Faustino's rooms."

"Why?"

"Because I, your mother, tell you so, that's why. No more questions, girl, here we are." She stopped to catch her breath. "This is not what I had hoped for you, no, not at all. But there's no arguing with God." She squeezed her daughter's hand and walked quickly ahead.

Milagros nodded. There was nothing more to say or do. She was all cried out now. She had shed the last of her tears a few days ago, when she had waved at Señorita Delia as she boarded the train to Buenos Aires. The news of her departure had struck Alta Gracia like a thunderbolt, though really it was only to be expected in the tempestuous times following Evita's death. The scholarship was gone, as the Eva Perón Foundation floundered. Señorita Delia had confirmed the terrible news to Milagros with tears in her eyes, but had also tried to console her, to build up some hope. "You will continue to help me here at the school," she had promised, "we'll find a way for you to hold on to what you've learned, and who knows, something else may turn up, another opportunity for you." But then within a matter of weeks, the little village school too was gone: no more funding. Students that could manage it transferred to San Justo, while their beloved teacher was transferred back to the capital. For one last time, Señorita Delia and Milagros had wept together, clinging on to one another at the doors of the train, and then she was gone.

Mother and daughter walked up the avenue lined with jacaranda trees leading to the main entrance. The path was thickly carpeted with star-like lilac flowers; when you stepped on them, they were crunchy and gave a sweet smell. Milagros could not help but feel as if she had been transported to a magical place, a fairy land, where she was a princess, a fairy herself. Oh, it was beautiful. So, so beautiful. Nobody, not even her father, could deny it. The house rose, its marble walls white and elegant and majestic, adorned with many windows, some open, some not. The whole structure felt secure in its permanence and beauty. And this was where she would be spending most of her days from now on. That was it then. Not teacher training college, not Buenos Aires. But, she thought as the house loomed larger, had she really expected all of that to become reality? Now that the possibility of it was vanished, the whole thing seemed to her like a dream she had just woken from; she could hardly bring what might have been to mind at all. And this really was such a splendid place. Not to mention that the thought she would be seeing Don Faustino every day, handsome Don Faustino with the sandy Hollywood hair and the warm smile, made her a little tingly and light-headed, only a tiny little bit.

"Move along and don't gape," Celedonia called out as she turned off the main avenue, into a path leading towards the back of the house.

They walked into the kitchen, a room so cavernous that it was still gloomy in spite of the growing light outside and the huge fire already roaring in an enormous fireplace. In the middle of the room there was a massive cedar table with benches on either side. A middle-aged woman in a black dress with a starched white lace collar was sitting at one end, pouring hot water into a teapot then into a silver and leather *mate* gourd. At the other end, as far from her as possible, sat an old man wrapped in a worn black alpaca blanket. He wore tall riding boots, old and scuffed but of quality leather. He rose briefly as Celedonia and Milagros came into the room and said good morning, and the lady at the table smiled at Milagros. She was a broad, sturdy woman, with silver strands in her black hair. She was older than Milagros' mother.

"So this is your girl," she said, by way of a greeting. She looked at Milagros with grave, piercing eyes.

Milagros blushed. "How do you do," she said politely.

The woman smiled, and Milagros beamed back with a feeling of relief, as if she has just passed an exam. "Come in, come in," said the woman. "We'll all have a cup of tea before we get started. Doña Celedonia, your daughter is a lovely girl."

"Thank you kindly, Doña Herminia." Milagros noticed how her mother sounded more mellow, less curt, but still very dignified. The two of them sat at the table as Doña Herminia put a cup and saucer in front of each. Celedonia poured them tea. There was a bowl with little pinkish cubes of sugar. Milagros observed how her mother picked up one daintily with a pair of tongs and dropped it in her teacup. She imitated her movements as best she could. She was about to pick up a second cube but her mother's slight frown stopped her. She drank her almost bitter tea, the flavor strong and full. It was good.

"Here's your *mate*, Don Rafael," Doña Herminia said, and put the filled gourd in front of the old man.

The old man, who had his eyes fixed on Milagros, took the gourd with a nod of thanks and turned back towards the fire.

"Well, it's good to meet you, Milagros," Doña Herminia said, her voice lowered. "Though I wish we didn't have to meet in this place. Your mother has told me about your hopes and I am very sorry it did not work out for you. However, that's that, and I hope you will find working here a good thing. It depends on you, of course. I am sure your mother has told you what is expected of you."

"Yes, ma'am."

Doña Herminia looked at Celedonia, who promptly said, "She is a well-behaved girl."

"It's not *her* behaviour I'm worried about," said Doña Herminia shortly.

Whose then? Milagros wondered.

"I see her dress is a bit too large for her."

"We did not have time to alter it," Celedonia said, "but I can just put a few tucks in–"

"No, on second thought, it's better this way," Herminia said. "The less attractive, the better. Having very pretty girls around, especially maids, is not a good idea in this house, when the mistress is so..."

She whispered something to Celedonia which Milagros didn't catch. She noticed that the old man, Don Rafael, was staring at her again from his corner of the fireplace.

"But she will find out for herself soon enough; that's why I urge utmost caution. I just wish we kept her down here, but Doña Alejandra insisted. She thought that a girl with some education should be doing better work than being a kitchen skivvy."

"Yes, that's so kind of her," Celedonia said.

"She is kind in her own way, but as for wise, I'm not so sure," Herminia said. "As for the other one, I don't think she notices or cares about anything with two legs. Four legs now, that's another story. Horses, that's where her interests end. She loves them more than her own family."

"Maybe they are her own family," Celedonia said. The two older women looked at each other and sniggered.

Milagros knew then who the man was. She had seen him from far away on the day the young Señora had arrived at Alta

Gracia. The old gaucho who was her shadow. Everyone in the village talked about the woman's love for horses. A story was going around that on the day of her arrival she rode into the Big House on horseback, and her horse left his manure all over the expensive rugs. But Milagros did not believe it.

Herminia turned towards the old man. "Eh, Don Rafael, what a pity your mistress only cares for her horses and not for people." Then she turned towards Milagros, and winked.

"Don't worry, he's as deaf as an old piece of wood. Aren't you, Don Rafael?"

The old man didn't move but kept staring at Milagros. She was sure he had heard every word. She didn't know what to make of that, but felt very sorry for him, old and decrepit as he was. Then, suddenly, he said, "Too pretty for her own good, that one. Yes, go on, keep her hidden, much good will that do." His voice was loud and raspy with a strange intonation, like chanting.

Herminia looked at Milagros. "Don't mind him, he's a crazy old man." She tapped her temple with a finger. It was impossible that the old man hadn't seen the gesture. He turned away and looked glumly into the fire, sipping his *mate* slowly.

Doña Celedonia took Milagros through a door leading into a small room. Most of the space was taken up by a large stone basin and a wood stove with an enormous kettle on it, black with age and use. It was bubbling softly. There was a drying rack hanging over the basin with pulleys and ropes. White aprons and gray poplin dresses were hanging from it. There was another door, leading to a further room.

"This is where you report first thing in the morning and last thing at night before we go home," her mother said. "You put on your work dress, and you take it off and wash it every night, then iron and put it back on in the morning. You will also iron my and Doña Herminia's aprons and dresses. Not her lace collars, she does those herself. The ironing room is through here. Look, there are many irons. These very small ones are for cuffs and collars only. Mind that you iron them the way I taught you, smooth them out flat and start with the sleeves."

She showed her a storage cupboard behind the sink.

"This is where we keep the soap. Green soap for *our* clothes, white for the family. You will be doing some of their washing and ironing. Only the young Señor and Señora's, the white linen, shirts, the delicates. You'll be collecting them after you've done their bedrooms.

"And here are the coals for the fire. And these are the aromatic herbs for the water. You put your hand in the bowl and then sprinkle. Our clothes, too. Doña Alejandra cannot stand bad smells in the servants' clothes."

So much for my education, thought Milagros. That's all it was good for apparently, washing their dirty clothes.

Still, she could not help but be impressed by the place. Look at that, she said to herself. One room for washing, one room for ironing. Only for the servants, too! Imagine what the rooms of the masters are like! And the thick frosted glass on the small high window! And the immensity of the kitchen! She was sure their whole house could easily fit in that room alone.

"Are we the only servants?" She wondered out loud. "I thought there would be more."

Celedonia said, "There is that useless girl, China, she's somewhere around, you'll meet her soon enough. But she won't be staying long. Don Anibal is in the capital and Doña Alejandra will be leaving for Mar del Plata soon. Don Faustino will take her there."

"Isn't the young Señora going too?"

Celedonia shrugged. "Not our business. Come, put your uniform on, lots to be done and no time to lose."

She turned and left the room, leaving Milagros alone and wondering.

Milagros slipped out of her own gingham dress, folded it carefully and stored it in the cupboard. She was in just her slip, passing the new dress over her head, when she heard the door open suddenly. She panicked – could the old man have followed her in there without anyone noticing? She struggled inside the darkness of the unfamiliar garment, fearing she would suffocate. But she heard giggles, and when her head was finally through the neck opening, she saw a girl, about her own age standing at the door, staring and laughing. She was wearing a gray poplin coverall over a square, thickset body. Her permed hair was shiny with oil, her eyes small and bright like a bird's: one of them smaller than the other, with a drooping eyelid that created the impression that she was permanently winking. She had just left a pail of dirty water and a couple of big brushes on the floor in front of her and was wiping sweat off her brow with her sleeve. She had now stopped laughing and was peering at Milagros curiously.

"So you are the new girl," she said. "You *are* pretty. Have you got a boyfriend?"

Milagros stared. What kind of question was that?

"Don't look at me like a suffocated fish," said the girl. Milagros realized she was agape and shut her mouth tight. "They call me China, or Chancha, and a lot of other names too. And you, pretty girl? What do they call you?"

"I'm Milagros."

"Ah, I know. Doña Celedonia's girl. You were going to be a teacher and then Evita died and a teacher you never were."

She snickered and began to wash her hands in the sink, singing in a surprisingly sweet voice, "My poor dear old mother, languished all alone…"

"Your mother is a very serious woman," China said, after a verse. "A good cook too, but too serious. Too serious for her own good. This is not a serious house."

Milagros didn't know what to say, so she said nothing.

"You are serious too," China said. "But you are really pretty, so I don't know for how long you'll stay serious." She wiped her hands on her coverall and went to the door, looked outside and then came back in, too near Milagros for comfort. A strong odor of sweat and carbolic acid came off her.

"Let me tell you a secret, for free, Señorita Teacher," China said. "I know a lot of secrets about this place. Here's one: do you know where Hortensia is?"

"No. Who is Hortensia?"

"The other girl, before you. You know why she's not here?"

"How should I know?"

"She went to the capital." China quickly peeped through the door again. "It's only that old idiot Rafael out there," she said. "The young Señora's pet. She's got her horses and dogs and she's got old Rafael, too. No one is serious in this house. So, I'll tell you about Hortensia, but promise you won't say it was me who told you." She lowered her voice to a whisper. "Hortensia went to the capital to have an abortion."

Milagros stared at her. What was she supposed to say now? She didn't even know what the strange girl meant. Surely something very naughty, judging by the secrecy and the leering and the whispering. She just shrugged and made to go.

"You don't know what an abortion is, do you?" whooped the girl.

Milagros went all red. She hated to be caught in ignorance. And now that Señorita Delia was gone, she couldn't ask her about it. Not that this sounded like the kind of thing she would have dared ask her about anyway. "Listen, I've got work to do, and my mother might come in here any moment now," she said, and tried to leave.

But the girl grabbed her by the dress. "Don't worry, innocent lamb, your Ma is doing the accounts with Doña Herminia – there's another one who pretends to be a serious person but isn't. But for your own good I'll tell you what an abortion is, and then you must be careful the same doesn't happen to you. But it can only happen if you have a boyfriend. If you don't, no problem. But perhaps a baby like you doesn't even know what a boyfriend is."

Milagros made a gesture of protest, eager to go away. She knew that she shouldn't be listening to such idle talk but her curiosity was aroused.

"So, that Hortensia, who wasn't a serious person like you or your Ma, was running up and down the stairs all day to do the young Señora's work for her, and she did more than her due, and before you know it she was doing it with Don F–"

"Mili, where are you?" Doña Celedonia called out. "Aren't you ready yet?" She burst into the laundry room. Milagros instantly took a couple of steps to distance herself, feeling guilty but also wishing her mother hadn't interrupted what sounded like a very interesting secret.

Celedonia bristled as she saw them both standing there.

"What are you doing here, lazy girl?" she asked China sharply. "Get out of here, double quick. You still haven't done the passage to the back door, it's all muddy. Dirty creature! Not for nothing they call you a pig! Move on! And you, daughter, what are you doing there staring like a wooden idol? Your first day, too! Come on, get on with your work. It's not going to do itself."

China gathered her pail and mop while muttering away, "It's not my fault if those stupid old boys from the stables are always coming and going in here. We've turned the house into a stable now. Horses will be eating at the dining room table soon. This isn't a serious house and no one in here is a serious person. Present company excepted."

"Cut it out!' Celedonia said. "Come, Mili, start ironing these."

As China stomped out, water sloshing out of her pail, she winked at Milagros and mouthed "abortion."

Milagros set to work, silently wondering what that unsettling girl would have revealed to her if her mother hadn't interrupted the conversation. All sorts of dreadful – but so intriguing – possibilities churned about in her mind. Was that China going to say something terrible about Don Faustino? Was this house really not a good one? But then why would Milagros' mother bring her to work here? No, that girl was just weird, maybe crazy.

At least she was grateful that her mother had reverted to her usual brisk tone; that other sweet-spoken and subdued Doña Celedonia she had witnessed earlier was somebody she didn't know. She wondered if she was a different creature herself now from the one that walked through the back door of the Big House at dawn. Perhaps this place changed everyone who went inside into someone else, just like the enchanted castles in fairy tales.

8

Ramona Iribarren

When Señorita Ramona Iribarren saw Faustino Goyena for the first time, she thought, "So this is the man they want me to marry. He is pretty like a girl." It was the way he stood at the threshold of the ballroom in her father's house, in an almost effeminate posture, shoulders squared but neck thrust forward and head slightly bent towards his chest, gleaming blond hair glazed over with brilliantine catching the glint of the parquet floor and the sparkle of the chandeliers. He had extended a pale, long, elegant hand to her, but his eyes were casting sideways glances at the group of girls assembled at one end of the large room, like birds of paradise with their many splendid colors and their cruel eyes and their strident chatter and giggles.

Ramona tossed her head back and looked haughtily around the room. It looked unfamiliar now, with all the people and the lights and the flowers, although she had paced the shiny floorboards time after time, creeping into the ballroom when there was nobody there, only the chairs stacked against the wall, shutters drawn over the French windows, sunlight peeping in through the horizontal slats. She had played hopscotch on the temporary grid formed by the light, a lonely child who was not allowed to bring home any friends from school, and had no friends to bring anyway, even if she *were* allowed. She had skipped and jumped on miles and miles of these parquet floors, stopping to sniff the air, a faint fragrance of orange blossom and perfume wafting, teasing, its source elusive.

She had stood beneath the shrouded chandeliers and the mirrors that reflected their faintly stirring shadows and she held her breath, trying to imagine how she would make her entrance into a room full of people she had never encountered. In this living fancy, her mother and father and all the aunts and uncles and neighbors would disappear; and other, unknown, attractive, interesting people would take their place, dressed in perfect clothes and speaking in low and refined voices, smiling and laughing and drinking colorful drinks out of tall glasses. She could even see the colors, mint-green and turquoise-blue and amber; and then Someone would turn up, the Someone she had been taught to expect, dangerous but irresistibly so, even as she was warned against their wickedness and shallow and fearless ways.

She knew she should not be wasting time daydreaming in the ballroom. Mama didn't like her to be idle. Ramona was supposed to be working at her embroidery or following the housekeeper as she counted teaspoons, or making sure to point out undusted cornices and unpolished spots to the maids. "The first duty of the mistress of the house is to make sure the servants know how to do their jobs well." Mama kept hammering at them day and night. She practiced what she preached: a fat and perspiring woman panting behind lethargic, somnambulant girls, just come from their Patagonian villages to be trained into service.

Mama had been the youngest of a family of girls, and the only one to be married. Her two sisters lived in the house. "They came with the dowry," Papá said when he was in a good mood. He was less kind with the phrasing when he wasn't. They were all three of them fat and ugly now, and Ramona wondered what had made her father pick her mother over her sisters. She had been pretty as a young girl, people said. Ramona could not tell. Everyone in those old sepia photos looked the same to her: all the women plump and uncomfortable with their huge heads of hair and their strange frilly clothes that seemed a burden to carry; all the men moustachioed and pinched and prematurely old. Sometimes she would look at herself in the mirror with apprehension, lest she would see Mama or Tía Bonifacia or Tía Leonor staring maliciously back at her from behind her own eyes.

The one thing she had liked about the convent where they had sent her – against her will – for her education was that mirrors were not allowed there. Her dislike of mirrors and of having her photograph taken had gained her the reputation of not being vain, which made her mother and aunts temporarily fearful that she might shun marriage and become a nun instead. But Don Ignacio had other plans for his only child.

And this ball formed part of them. Ramona knew it, and this is why that evening she stood among the loud girls and tossed her head loftily, thinking: I'm not going to giggle and scream like them. She was certain her aunts and Mama were like that as young girls, undignified and loud and overdoing it. This is why they stayed unmarried – all except Mama, and then she had only married her own father's foreman, the ambitious Iñaki Iribarren, who had come on the boat from Navarra with all his earthly possessions in a carpet bag, barely able to read or write. He changed his name to Ignacio later, believing it was more dignified. His naturally taciturn demeanor served him well; the less he spoke, the fewer mistakes he made.

Ramona was ashamed of her father's origin but proud of his erect, upright posture and neat appearance and stately silences. He was a talented social climber. He intended for his daughter to have the best; he wanted her to marry a member of the aristocracy so *he* could become one by marriage, albeit not his own. He had his own catechism: what is the point of a good education? Good social connections. What was the aim of good connections? An excellent match, the best money could buy.

So his only child was now standing at one end of the ballroom, heart beating fast, fingers itching to grasp and twist the skirt of her new dress, only arrived this morning in a large satin-lined box. She did not like wearing dresses. She did not wear them well. She was too large for them, and they made her feel like a trussed-up turkey. She didn't care what she looked like to others. Early on in her life she had decided that she would not live under the tyranny of the mirror. A tall, ponderous child, she could have never grown up to be attractive in the sprightly, pretty, frisky way that everyone considered charming. Once she had overheard herself described as "statuesque" – she could have kissed the old lady who said it. She had been trying to live up to the attribute for some time now. When she thought of statues, it was not any Venus of Milo or art-nouveau angels that came to her mind; it was the great equestrian statues that she admired. She spent most of her time outdoors riding horses. Mama did not dare to complain, because Papá approved and encouraged it.

He considered himself very lucky in his daughter. She seemed to be driven by the very same need as himself. He trusted her blindly and indulged her every whim; he knew she would never be frivolous and would never betray their ideals. By the instinct that informs akin spirits, he knew that love and romance were unimportant to her. Thank God, she had inherited nothing of the silliness of her mother and aunts. When his wife talked about how important it was for young girls to be good housewives for example, he almost lost his patience, seasoned though he was in restraining his temper.

Don Ignacio never talked about what he had left behind in the old country; if it still lingered in some hidden recess of his memory, nobody knew. He neither supported or undermined others who came from the same arid yellow lands he knew he would never see again. He belonged to no immigrant group, club, or lobby; he became a naturalized citizen as soon as it was possible. The only country he recognized himself a citizen of was the one for which money was the passport. His bank accounts, his deeds of property, the neat stacks of gold coins in the secure safe in his bedroom – these were his credentials and identity cards. His homeland, if anywhere, lay in his own vast acres of land. He grew rice, bananas, and coffee; he owned farms and orchards; shops, depots, storage-houses; endless rows of tenements and masses of tin-roofed bungalows in the slums; and of course the mansion and the town-house, to which he secretly added the luxurious pad across the water in Montevideo, of which his family knew nothing, not because he felt particularly guilty of what went on there, but because he wanted his daughter's respect and was afraid of her, her lip curled in unspoken scorn.

Like many men of his past and of his disposition, he was tight-fisted and generous at the same time, but never to the same people. There were two completely different worlds he inhabited in this respect, and the one knew nothing about the other. That was his way of adhering to the biblical advice of the one hand not knowing what the other was doing. He entertained his business associates lavishly, as long as they belonged to what in his mind was the aristocracy: old families, wealthy men whose grandparents had been born in this country, who lived in large white palaces within walking distance from the large garden parks of the capital, and met each other daily at the Jockey Club. His one ardent desire, second only to a good marriage for Ramona, was to become a member of that club, which he imagined as some kind of Olympian mansion untouched by pain and fear. He believed that if he succeeded in the one goal, success in the other could easily follow: a suitable son-in-law could be his introduction to the Jockey Club.

Until recently he had been collecting the rents from his properties all over the country himself. "You can't trust anyone in these troubled times," was his excuse to himself. He made sure Ramona knew nothing about it. This hard-faced old Basque with eyes that would remain unmoved watching employees overworked to death, half-starved women and children thrown out on the street because they could not pay the rent, or pale men who walked out of his office straight into financial and social ruin, even suicide in a case or two – this man could not bear a reproachful look from a girl of seventeen, his own flesh and blood.

The night of the ball, the Iribarren mansion was filled with people, la crème de la crème. Don Ignacio would have invited fewer young unmarried women if he could; he did not have any illusions about his only daughter's ability to charm. But she had the irresistible allure of a huge fortune, and her father was pleased to see that every eligible young man he had invited was now in his house, filling the large ballroom – one of the largest in any private residence in the country. He had personally examined and vetoed each and every one of the suitors. His wife would have been useless at that: she would have laughed with that silly giggle of hers and fawned over the young and good-looking rascals who kissed her hand and cast languishing looks. No, his wife only had eyes for the cheap, lustre-haired, thin-moustachioed lovers who bowed and danced and had more debts than assets. The featherweights. But he trusted Ramona to do the right thing. The girl knew the value not only of money but of old family names and large estates in the country, as well as mausoleums in the necropolis of Recoleta. That last one especially was of great importance. Don Ignacio knew that when it came to decisions, certain things weighed with his daughter as much as they did with him. Together they could not go wrong.

When young Faustino Goyena walked into the room, Don Ignacio turned to look at his daughter and his heart almost skipped a beat when he saw her standing tall and dignified, even graceful, in her long draped dress. He knew she had starved herself for the last few weeks in order to look like this and he admired her self-discipline. And now, standing in front of the Goyena heir, she looked like a queen. She knew that he had settled on this young man as the most desirable of all of them. Family name, fortune, fame. Everything Don Ignacio's heart could ever desire. His time had come at last. His invitation to the Jockey Club would be arriving any day now. His son-in-law and especially the son-in-law's father would make sure of that. He would have smiled with approval and encouragement to his daughter, if he wasn't sure that she would find it vulgar.

Meanwhile, Ramona wished with all her heart that she was somewhere else: in her father's estate in the north, where the wind rustled among the thin blades of the rice plants and the surface of the water rippled and the creepers and Spanish moss, cascading from weeping willows, swayed gently in the drizzle. She missed her horse, El Moro, and her attendant, Don Rafael, a weather-beaten gaucho who had once saved her from the path of a raging bull when she was a small child. She did not remember the event, but now neither could she remember life without Rafael and the horses. He had taught her everything she knew about them, and she knew everything there was to know. That was the one thing in her life that wasn't vulgar or common, she felt: riding on her horse in the night, her hot face soothed by the fine rain, with the loyal Rafael by her side, Rafael who did not care if she was pretty or clever and wanted nothing from her, and did not see her as part of any plans.

She loved being in the country and hated the capital. It had been the scene of her first humiliation, at the boarding school of the Sacred Heart, an exclusive establishment run by nuns, in which only the daughters of the very finest families were accepted. Her father had made them a very substantial gift, but what clinched the deal was that to the nuns, Ramona looked like someone who would not cause them any trouble; they were weary of spoiled, wayward young beauties and took to the big, plain, shy girl immediately.

But she had been unhappy there. She felt graceless and even slightly ridiculous among the slim, elegant, cruel girls who lifted their eyebrows and smirked as she shuffled among them, ungainly and miserable. "The bear," they called her behind her back. She hated them. She hated not riding every day. She had no particular issue with the nuns, even though she felt their kindness to be patronising and rather uncomplimentary. She could see that they were nice to the ugly girls and harsh with the beautiful ones, like Eugenia Quintana and Alicia de Grant, the indisputable leaders of that beautiful and vicious pack.

Ramona had spent her first weeks at the school shuffling around with her rather flat-footed, heavy tread. She was not used to walking; it got her all tired and sweaty. She was in a relentless sulk during the day, and plotted escape and revenge during the night. She was constantly fantasizing during the lessons; she would write to Rafael. He would come in the stealth of night on Canela, his mare, bringing El Moro for her. She would jump over the wall behind the greenhouses and join him, knocking a few nuns out of the way, if necessary. She was bigger and stronger than most of them. Then she and Rafael would set fire to the school and ride away, watching it burn from a distance; the thought threw her into ecstasies of almost physical delight. They would all burn: the nuns, the simpering music and dance teachers who laughed at her ineptitude, the girls who whispered unkind words to her. Bear. Gorilla. Fatty.

She hated lessons. She was a slow and uninterested learner. Once she walked out of a classroom in the middle of a long-winded lecture. She didn't even know what the subject was, but as the teacher happened to be talking about Federalism, everyone thought Ramona must be the most pronounced Radical. This temporarily earned her some friends and many more enemies, although she had no idea about politics and did not wish to learn.

Eventually she was more tolerated than accepted per se, and afterwards became invisible.

The girls' school was, rather unfortunately as far as the nuns were concerned, situated next to the boys' school, only separated from it by a park and a series of vegetable and flower gardens. The gardeners who tended them day and night did not allow any of the girls to come near, but the foolhardier students always found a way to sneak through and climb up on the wall to peer over the other side. Ramona was never among them. She did not care about boys and she had given up on the girls.

But one day, out of the blue, she was invited to join them on their expedition to the wall, by no less an authority than Alicia de Grant. Ramona could not decide whether the invitation was a sudden impulse of kindness or a ruse to get her into trouble, but whatever the motive, she found herself following the girls. They climbed up the wall, Ramona with some difficulty, wincing as the rough stone surface scraped her palms and wrists. She would have given up had she not sensed the presence of horses on the other side; she could hear riders' cries and thundering hooves. When her eyes were just above the parapet, she saw that over the wall was a polo field. There was a game in full progress: horsemen and mallets and loud voices everywhere. She and the rest of the girls watched for a few minutes, transfixed by the way the horses weaved between one another in the afternoon sun, by how the men timed their swings at just the right moment.

Suddenly one of the riders lost control, and with a cry he fell from his horse, which began running toward the wall. Ramona did not even pause to think. Ignoring the girls who hissed at her to stay down and not be seen, she scaled the wall and before she knew it she was on horseback. A wanderer in the desert, left without water for many days, wouldn't have been that fast or that desperate. She heard nothing but the wind rushing over her hair and ears, she felt nothing but pure relief and light-hearted joy.

Later that week, Don Ignacio made another huge Donation to convince the nuns not to expel Ramona. He even made arrangements for her to take riding lessons, which she didn't really need, being a better rider than her teachers. But it was an opportunity for her to be around horses again, to have a few hours away from the school and from the girls, who were even more hostile to her since her "shenanigans" had alerted the nuns to what was going on in that remote part of the grounds. As a result, the walls of the perimeter were no longer accessible to any of the students.

One day Ramona was wandering alone in the grounds, resigned to the fact that she was now untouchable, resented fiercely by her classmates, and though she pretended she didn't care, she felt truly desolate. This was made all the worse when she saw Alicia de Grant approaching. It was Alicia who had conceived the unfortunate idea to invite her to that fatal foray, and she would surely feel her kindness had been met with a very poor return. Ramona's heart beat wildly and she braced herself for a confrontation.

Alicia greeted her with an unsmiling but not angry expression. She was so flawlessly beautiful – all alabaster skin and ash blond hair swept in a neat bun, her tall, elegant figure making the austere navy-blue uniform look like an haute couture design from Paris – that Ramona felt breathless, smitten. But she disliked the effect the other girl had on her, and responded with an ungracious shrug at her greeting.

Unperturbed, Alicia said, "I want you to know that I don't blame you for doing what you did. It must be hard for you to live in such confinement after being used to open spaces and horses. You obviously have a way with them."

Ramona did not speak and barely breathed, trying to ensure her heartbeats, deafening to her, remained inaudible to Alicia. She would have liked to be able to say something nice, appropriate, natural. To start chatting away, to become friends with Alicia, to belong. But it was too late. She couldn't help feeling that Alicia had only come to tease her, to make fun of her. Perhaps there were girls hidden all over the place right now, watching, waiting for her to do something, anything, so that they would howl with laughter. They would never consider her as one of them. Her father was stupid to expect that, no matter how much money he threw into this stupid place. The more Alicia spoke in her simple, friendly, dignified manner, so mature for someone her age, the more Ramona became angry and bitter and thought how much she hated them all and especially Alicia de Grant, the nosy do-gooder, with her airs and graces and superior tone. Why could they not leave her be? Why did she have to be here?

As Alicia de Grant, slightly baffled at Ramona's hostility, but not particularly bothered, said goodbye with a light shrug and turned to go, part of Ramona wanted to call her back; part of her begged that Alicia would turn and say something to her, anything, to give her another chance. But she did not, and even though she was always distantly polite, she never attempted to approach Ramona again. And Ramona hated her for not persevering with her friendliness, and she hated herself even more for not accepting that single offer of it.

And now, many years later, Ramona stood in the middle of the ballroom, the queen of the ball, if not the belle – but who cared? She was soon going to receive a marriage proposal far better than most of the other girls in attendance ever would, some of them her own classmates of old, who once had snubbed her but now came to her own party as guests. They seemed stunned by the splendor and honored to be there, and would soon be witnesses to her triumph, when the engagement was announced. But she knew what they were thinking and what they were saying behind gloved hands and silk fans; she could see their laughing, mocking eyes, and she felt the old resentment coming back. She wanted to turn her back on the lot of them, including her poncy fiancé-to-be, and never set eyes on any of them again.

9

The Duties

The things you learned about people when you washed their clothes, Milagros thought. Silk and linen, cashmere and vicuña, cotton lace and chiffon velvet, calico and poplin and twill, and all these new fabrics that cleaned so well but retained all sorts of smells and crackled with static. How they bore the smells of the people who wore them, and those smells, repulsive when put into the hot soapy water, came out all fresh and subtle in the ironing, and it almost felt as if the real person who wore them was there.

Stains and marks, streaks and smears; traces of the food they ate and the drinks they drank; where they'd been, what they'd touched, even who they'd been with. It was all there, a testimony of their lives. Faint traces of perfume and cigar smoke on Don Faustino's shirts, whiffs of expensive surroundings, of soft leather chairs and polished furniture. The rough smell of horses and saddle, of leather and hay and stale sweat on the young Señora's riding clothes; jasmine and stale sweat on her dresses. Milagros knew all about their secret lives too. When you washed their bed-linen and their underwear, things you knew people did but which you were not supposed to talk about became plain, though of course that girl China whom they also called Chancha, Pig, for being so dirty and coarse, did talk about them. Milagros was sure she was the first, however, and maybe the only one so far, to know that the young Señora's shape was soon about to change, along with her life, and probably everybody's life too, especially Don Faustino's. The young Señora was not the easiest of women to like, but Milagros was glad for her. She had been married for a year now, and people were getting anxious, and Doña Alejandra had been bitter about it all, even from her remote Punta del Este residence.

As she tiptoed down the corridor past the young Señora's bedroom, Milagros tried to imagine what it would feel like to own all these beautiful things, to feel as comfortable and entitled to it as she was to her little bed in her parents' house. The crystal chandeliers that had fascinated her ever since she first saw them – hers. The plush soft-leather sofas and chairs with the buttons that were such a hassle to clean but so pretty to look at – hers. The porcelain ornaments, little elegant ladies and gentlemen in white wigs and baby-pink coats and dresses – all hers. She passed the soft downy duster over them like a caressing hand.

Well, perhaps they *were* hers in a sense. She enjoyed them as much as their rightful owners, maybe even more. She didn't think the young Señora enjoyed them very much at all. She hardly wanted to stay indoors among them. She would even break some of them because she was clumsy and indifferent. Maybe that's what owning things did to you: you forgot about how beautiful they were and you treated them badly. Imagine if she, Milagros, broke something – what fuss! She had never broken a single thing, of course, although there was that one time when the window had been left open – not by her – and a sudden gust of wind knocked down the green lamp in Don Faustino's study. Doña Celedonia was furious but Don Faustino had said, "Bah, it was a hideous old thing anyway." Very kind of him. A few days later a new one arrived from the capital, similar to the one that had been broken. It made Milagros wonder how amazing it would be to just be able to get anything you wanted and replace everything that was broken, just like that, without a second thought.

A new batch of guests arrived, most in white or cream sports cars, gleaming under the sun like new-born colts. Milagros watched them get out, smoothing their coats and dresses, patting the dust of the road off themselves, calling out to each other with joyous, unfettered voices. They obviously relished the comfortable drive, the fine day, the smell of the jacaranda flowers strewn in their path. As they approached the house, they cast cheerful, frolicking shadows on the freshly mown lawn.

"Don't stare, Mili. Come back in here and help me prepare the drinks."

Milagros let herself in through the screen door and began to wipe china cups and crystal glasses, but kept casting looks outside trying to catch more glimpses of the guests. By now everybody had moved to the front veranda. Their voices wafted over the lawn, carefree, full of fun and laughter. There were some young ladies in the company. They wore short white dresses and sporty shoes and elaborate hairstyles, looking exactly like Tita Merello. The young men who escorted them wore white linen jackets and candy-colored shirts and their hair was glossy and their teeth white. What problems, what fears could ever touch these people? Milagros imagined them in their palatial houses or apartments in the capital. She imagined the women's wardrobes, entire rooms filled with all that was desirable, white fox furs and slinky silk and damask dresses, sparkling jewelery scattered in front of crystal mirrors. The young Señora had all those things too.

And yet she doesn't look at all happy, Milagros mused.

"Who doesn't look happy?" Doña Celedonia asked, her mouth stiff like the opening of a miser's purse.

"Nobody. I was only thinking out loud."

"Hm, thinking too much, I think. Just finish up here and go upstairs to do the music room. They are sure to be using it later what with all those guests he's brought in again."

She sounded ill-tempered and tired and it was unlike her to be criticizing Don Faustino, even indirectly. She had often been like this during the last few months, ever since her old mother had died, Milagros's beloved Abuela. That was the one good thing about her not going away to the teacher's academy: Milagros was there with Abuela, holding her hand and wiping perspiration off her waxy brow as she slipped softly into that other world. But the gloom that had fallen over their little house since her scholarship plans had sunk with the shipwreck of Eva Perón's Foundation was becoming ever deeper. Her father especially had taken it to heart. He had retreated into himself again, all the shine in his eyes and pride in his bearing gone; he was like an empty house, the fire at the hearth and the lamps all extinguished.

"Guests and drinks and living the life, while folk are starving," Celedonia muttered under her breath. "And horse riding and all kinds of carry-on. And not a baby in sight yet, over a year of marriage now."

Milagros thought about the blood-free white linen of the last three months, but kept her own counsel.

She thought of Don Faustino – Tino to his family and friends. The first time she heard them use that name, she found it adorable. Not that there was much family around: old Don Anibal had never stayed much in Alta Gracia anyway, preferring the pleasure of the capital and his club, but Doña Alejandra was around even less frequently now that her son's wife was there. She disliked her heartily – it was no secret. The feeling was reciprocated. Everybody knew that the only creature with two legs the young Señora cared about was Rafael. She was rude to her in-laws, dismissive to her husband, and indifferent to everyone else. They were not a happy family; it was not a happy marriage. It was common knowledge that the expensive Goyena preoccupations – politics for Don

Anibal, cars for Doña Alejandra, and Don Faustino's general extravagant lifestyle – required a river of money to finance them, and as the Goyena assets had been receiving blow after blow in the volatile political climate of the times, Doña Ramona's vast fortune could supplement this. She knew it and she let it be known that she knew, which did not help her relationship with Doña Alejandra. The older lady now spent most of her time in Buenos Aires or Mar del Plata and Punta del Este, with her own set of old friends, who despised the nouveau riche and made unkind jokes about them all the time.

The new lady of the house liked Alta Gracia a lot, and hated the capital with a passion people could not understand. It was clear that she would never become the kind of wife that a family like the Goyenas needed, and it was still unclear to many people why Don Faustino, so young and handsome and apparently rich, would marry that ungainly bulk of a woman when there were plenty of pretty rich girls in his own circle. Milagros had once overheard a group of old ladies, Doña Alejandra's friends on a rare visit to Alta Gracia, gossip amongst themselves, wondering why Tino had not married Alicia de Grant, for example. Can you imagine the two of them, tall and shimmering and perfectly mannered, king and queen of the crème de la crème? But Alicia de Grant wouldn't have him, another lady said, not with his *propensities*. Yes, men were lecherous pigs, but Alicia de Grant or someone like her, who could have any man she wanted, would never put up with this. Whereas a nobody, albeit an extremely wealthy nobody, like that Iribarren girl, would be grateful and put up with anything.

That's what was said, and even Milagros had got the gist of it, although she knew that whatever his alleged *propensities* were, they were surely being exaggerated. A servant, walking in and out of rooms and parlors and drifting by doors left ajar, can hear and learn a lot, but must also learn who says what for what reason. It was an education, a very different one from poor Señorita Delia's for sure, but an education all the same. And someone as clever as Milagros could easily note that Ramona Iribarren could put up with a lot, but feigning gratitude for her circumstances was beyond her. Milagros could see that her mistress was mostly uninterested, but also resentful.

At any rate, she did not deserve him.

But Milagros kept her thoughts to herself. She never had any secrets to keep in her life, but now every day there were more things that she kept quiet about. The back stairs, for example. She had unexpectedly come across Don Faustino a few weeks earlier, as she was climbing up in a hurry and did not see him descending, and she almost crashed into him. He had put out his hand to steady her, and it was like a thousand bees began to buzz on her skin. She could only manage to lift her eyes to his face for a brief moment and when she did she saw…what did she see? His eyes, gazing straight into hers.

Face burning with shame, she whispered, "I am so, so sorry, sir," and made to run, but he held her and peered into her face. His eyes dazzled her. He said, "No, I am sorry, I should not be here. Are you okay? You were not hurt?" "Oh no," she said, "I am fine, thank you, sir." And she made to go again and the second time it was harder, like wrenching herself away, and her forearm was burning hot where he had placed his hand, and it was icy cold at the same time. And she thought of him and the young Señora, the big sulky woman who lived for horses only, alone in their bedroom, and averted her blushing face from him and gently but firmly she pulled her arm away and ran up the stairs and kept running up and up until she reached the dark attic, where she sat for a while, waiting for her heart to stop kicking wildly about and for her blood to flow slow and steady again.

She had long begun to suspect that in many ways her mother knew less than Milagros did herself. Of course, her duty as a daughter was to show due respect and say nothing. "But I must remember this when I am a mother myself," she thought. "My children will know much more than I do, and this is how it should be, too."

Later that day, a sudden noise drew her attention away from her polishing: a man standing outside the kitchen door. Milagros could see his outline behind the screen. Rather small, black hair, holding a beret. One of the *estancia* hands, the younger ones. Doña Herminia had noted, with a twinkle in her eye, that since Milagros had come to work there, the visits from them had increased. "Lord, it's as busy as the *pulpería* around here lately," she said. "I'm sure they are not coming here for me." Doña Celedonia had many sharp words for them. "Much good will it do," old Rafael would say if he was around at such times. "You can't keep bees away from flowers nor flies away from shit." This would elicit stern reprimands from both ladies, and Milagros would blush and feel sorry that Rafael did not seem to like her at all, but of course it was common knowledge that he hated all women – and all men, for that matter – except his own mistress and protégée.

With a weary sigh, Milagros went to the door. "Do you want anything?" The young man looked nice enough, and smelled of water and soap.

He smiled at her. "You." Milagros felt red hot around the ears, but he quickly added, with a mischievous smile, "Doña Ramona sent me to fetch her riding jacket. She said you know where it is."

Milagros wondered what the young Señora's exact words had been. "Ask my maid," or "Ask the girl in the kitchen." Maybe even: "Ask Milagros," if she was in a good mood.

"She said you were the only one who always knows where everything is. That you're the best."

Milagros cast him a look. Surely the Señora would never say so many things to a farm hand. "She didn't!"

The young man burst out laughing. "No, she didn't," he admitted, "but you are a clever one, aren't you? People were right to warn me about you."

Milagros smiled in spite of herself. "People have been talking about me to you?" she said.

"Who's been talking about you?"

Milagros and the young man both started and turned towards the voice: it belonged to Pablito Suárez, who had suddenly appeared out of nowhere, grinning like a mischievous cat. Milagros felt her cheeks burning. He had been doing that a lot lately, bursting in on her, especially when there were any other young men around. Everyone knew that he wanted to marry her. He would tell everyone who would listen. He treated her parents with deference as if they were already his in-laws, and every week he asked Milagros for her hand. His father and Milagros's father had agreed that it was too early, that it was not a good idea to start a family on the meagre salary Pablito was making as a man of all jobs around the *estancia* and the village. His father was still the driver in the estate, but since Doña Alejandra had more or less moved out, there was not very much for him to do involving cars. The young Señora would ride everywhere. Old Man Suárez had to supplement his income by taking odd transport jobs in San Justo. But Pablito had other plans. He sometimes talked about them, when Milagros stayed around long enough to listen. "Buenos Aires," and "factory job," he repeated over and over, ignoring her skeptical looks or ironic comments. "You will be living like a queen," he'd tell her, but she shrugged. She did not discourage him though. It might be a way to see the capital after all, the place where she would have been residing now, if fate had not decided otherwise. Imagine if Pablo was the one to make it happen! Señorita Delia would call that an irony.

But these days Milagros wasn't thinking of the capital that much. Often she simply didn't have the time, her hours being filled with task after tedious task. But also, she found that whenever she did have a spare moment, her head was usually in the clouds, the way she'd never understood when she used to see it in other girls. She found herself mulling over those times when Don Faustino caught her eye as he descended the stairs – he was using the back stairs more often recently, it seemed – or when he turned around to peek at her from the library as she walked swiftly down the corridor. Sometimes she heard Señorita Delia's voice in her head at these moments, scolding her for these idle fantasies. Yet as the days turned to weeks, and the weeks to months, it seemed that Delia's voice was coming from somewhere further and further away.

10

Stay with Me, My Darling

"Where is that girl now?"

Doña Ramona was losing her patience. If it wasn't for all this, she could have been riding now. For the last few days, she had been doing little else. She had come to depend on her maid very much. Life had become much easier now that she had her to herself most of the time. The girl's mother, who was, Ramona believed, the cook, wasn't very happy about the promotion. She was jealous, Ramona supposed. It was nothing new to her, parental competitiveness and envy. Hadn't she caught her own mother's looks, the way she narrowed her eyes at Ramona's dresses and Ramona's furniture and Ramona's husband, the faces she made at the mention of his name, his money, his position and his family? The woman Celedonia had tried to tacitly take the girl back into the kitchens, the scullery or the washroom, and Ramona had to ask for this to stop in no uncertain terms.

"She will soon find out what's what, and it won't be my fault," said Doña Herminia grimly to her friend María Asunción, who came in once a week to help with the heavier loads of laundry. "The young Señora is trying to gouge out her eyes with her own hands. But it won't be me who'll put her right."

"Can it be possible she has no idea what he's up to?" her friend wondered, sipping *mate* thoughtfully. "You'd think someone would have dropped a hint."

"It's amazing how blind people are when they want to be. Besides, she doesn't seem to have much experience in life, poor soul. But if I may say so, who would go out of his way to give her experience, the way she looks?"

Doña Herminia, still a handsome woman in her fifties, snorted merrily.

"Poor Celedonia!" said María Asunción. "And her poor girl. It was bad enough what happened with that teacher from Buenos Aires who only came here to cause mischief. She raised their hopes and then upped and left."

"It wasn't her fault. Nobody's fault. Bad luck. Plenty of that in poor Celedonia's family. The question now is how to protect the girl."

"She is a good girl. She wouldn't do anything like that."

"It's not *her* behaviour I'm worried about," Doña Herminia said, sighing deeply.

STAY WITH ME, MY DARLING (episode 123)

Man's voice:

In the luxurious mansion of the Posadas family, Romilda goes into the dining room to clean the silver. She thinks she is quite alone, and for this reason she does not hold back her tears. Thick pearly teardrops fall on the elaborate silver like the rain. Tonight the engagement of Rodolfo will be announced, with whom she has been secretly in love ever since she came to his house as a servant. But suddenly...

Romilda:
Oh!

Rodolfo:
Don't be afraid, dear girl, it's only me.

Romilda:
Oh, Don Rodolfo!

Rodolfo:
Don Rodolfo! I thought we were friends. Haven't I asked you to simply call me by my name?

Romilda:
Yes, but…it's not appropriate. Your mother wouldn't approve.

Rodolfo:
She is not here now, is she? Besides, what has my mother got to do with it? I'm telling you, so you listen to me.

Romilda:
Yes…Rodolfo.

Rodolfo:
That's better. But why are you so downcast today? It hurts me to see such a pretty face look so sad.

Romilda:
Oh, it's…it's nothing.

Rodolfo:
Come, come, you and I are friends, aren't we? You must tell your friend now. What is it?

Romilda:
It's nothing, I tell you. Please don't ask me, Rodolfo.

Rodolfo:
But you're crying. Oh, my dear, what's the matter? Please tell me.

Romilda:
No, you are not supposed to do this. What would people say if they walked in here right now and saw you holding me?

Rodolfo:

I don't care what they will say. It's my house and I'll do as I please. And if I feel like taking you in my arms, I'll do it. There. And if I feel like—

Romilda:

Rodolfo, please, don't!

Rodolfo:

But I love you, Romilda. I love you. I have loved you since the first moment I saw you. You walked into the room dressed in your maid's uniform and I thought I had never seen a more beautiful girl in my life.

Romilda:

Oh, Rodolfo.

Rodolfo:

Can it be true? You love me, too?

Romilda:

(whispering) Yes...

Rodolfo:

Say it out loud, mi amor. *Do not be embarrassed.*

Romilda:

(a little more loudly) Yes. I love you too. It is the first and last time in my life I'm in love. I could die for you.

Rodolfo:

Oh, my girl, my love, my soul! I adore you.

(Sounds of kissing)

Romilda:

But we must not do this.

Rodolfo:

Romilda, don't turn your back on me, please. I adore you.

Romilda:

We must forget this ever happened. It breaks my heart, but it is so. What would your mother say? What future is there for us? You are rich, you are an aristocrat and I am only a poor servant girl in your house.

Rodolfo:

I am a free man and I will do as I please. It's none of my mother's business. What is social position for a heart that is in love? I adore you, and you'll be my wife.

Romilda:

Dear Rodolfo, I adore you, too. But...your wife? This is not possible!

Rodolfo:

Why not, silly girl?

Romilda:

You can't...you can't marry someone like me.

Rodolfo:

Yes, I can. I will marry the only woman I have ever loved and ever will love.

Romilda:

Oh, Rodolfo!

Rodolfo:

My beautiful Romilda!

(more kissing sounds)

Romilda:

No, please, Rodolfo, I'm scared.

Rodolfo:

Of what, my sweet love?

Romilda:

Of...society. Of your mother. They said you were getting engaged to the daughter of the Fernández family tonight. Is this true?

Rodolfo:

Of course not! My mother thinks she's arranged it all, but it's not going to happen. I have a plan. You'll see, we'll be happy together. Now let me kiss you once more. And once more. Oh, my love, you drive me crazy, I feel like a drunken man...

Romilda:

Yes, Rodolfo...

Man's voice:

(over music) And now let's leave the young couple to enjoy their love for a short time, because the future is not as bright as they want to believe. Will Doña Fernanda Posadas catch them out? Will Rodolfo be as true as he promises? We'll be back with you tomorrow with more exciting events from the estancia Las Jacarandas. And don't forget, ladies: Limpiex is the only detergent that transforms your household into a fairy palace of cleanliness. Limpiex, for all household tasks! Limpiex, simply the best!

Doña Herminia switched off the radio with a sigh. "That horrible mother of his won't let this pass, oh no," she said.

"I don't know," said Doña María Asunción. "When two young people are in love, they can do anything they set their minds on."

"I'm not sure it's good for the girls to listen to that sort of thing, a new episode every day," said Doña Celedonia anxiously, looking at the face of her daughter: pensive, remote, perfectly beautiful. She hoped that she was not paying attention to the radionovelas, educated girl that she was.

"Oh, how I wish a man like Don Rodolfo would fall in love with me," China sighed. "Then I wouldn't have to work in a kitchen and I would be a Señora myself."

"Nonsense! See, that's what I mean," said Celedonia. "This sort of thing can introduce ideas into girls' heads. Listen, stupid girl, this is only for fun, all right? This kind of thing never happens in real life, do you hear?"

"Yes it does," said China, watching Milagros's face as she spoke, like a cat watching a bird, not missing a movement, not even the tiniest flutter of an eyelid.

"*Yes it does*," Doña Herminia mocked, imitating the girl's whiny voice. "Get out of here, lazy pig girl, it's never going to happen to you at any rate."

"I didn't say it was gonna happen to me, but I know it is happening very near here," said China. "Too bad the gentleman is already married! What fun when it all comes out in the open!" She made as if she was shaking with mirth, wiping pretend tears off her face.

"Shut up and get out of my sight!" Doña Celedonia hissed. She began to tidy up the pots and pans in the shelf above the enormous stone sink, with furious clattering and banging about.

Milagros did not raise her head to look at any of them. She concentrated hard on her ironing, the expression on her face exactly the same as when she did her homework, back when she was still in school, her mother thought.

"None of you are serious people!" China yelled suddenly and left the room, banging the door behind her.

"Enough of this," said Doña Herminia, putting down her *mate* gourd. "If that's what happens when we listen to the radionovela, I'll take the radio back to my room and no one will be welcome to listen anymore."

Milagros was passing the iron carefully over the creases of a peach silk slip, thinking about the radionovela. Were such things really possible? Could love beat every obstacle and transform a poor girl into a great lady in a powerful family? Perhaps. She remembered the story of Eva Perón, so often told by Señorita Delia: how she had risen from the slums of a provincial town to become the leader of a nation in all but name. And all that because President Perón had made her his wife. But could this happen to her too?

Don Faustino came into her mind, unbidden: images she tried to not see, thoughts she tried to shut out. When he walked into a room she was happening to clean, now undoubtedly a more frequent occurence than before, she trembled and couldn't *not* lift her eyes to him. Her vision became a tunnel, everything darkening around the object she tried to focus on. If she lifted her eyes to him, she would be blinded. She would be burned as if staring directly at the sun. Like the sun, she felt the heat of his gaze on her skin, the soft fuzz on it bristling like the hair of a cat, then singed. Looking was dangerous, but touching was fatal.

"With your permission, sir," she would say, and move quickly to the door.

He would usually say nothing, do nothing, just stand there, filling the space with radiating heat. But yesterday...She brought back every single detail of the moment, how the sun shone through the windows, how the white stucco mouldings on the ceiling and the chandeliers like fountains of crystal dazzled her with sparkling sunlight, how her heart beat as she lifted her hand to touch the door handle that looked molten under the heat pulsing on her own skin.

He had said in a soft voice, "Why such hurry? Do I scare you?"

His voice seemed so different from any other man's voice: slow, deep and vibrant. What was in his voice this time that made it all change? She lifted her eyes slowly, looked at him, and then quickly away; in the very short moment she gazed upon his face she saw his honey-coloured eyes, long eyelashes like a girl's, a kind smile. Why did everybody speak of him as if he were some kind of monster? He did not look angry or scornful, as she had expected. Her cheeks were glowing as she murmured, "Excuse me" and slipped past him out of the room. Once out of his sight, she exhaled: cool now, safe, able to breathe, but devastated. She had left something behind in that room, but what? She had no word for it. Or maybe she did, but she did not dare think of it. As she ran quickly down the back stairs, her heart was beating violently again; she could feel large wet patches spreading under her arms. Twice, she stumbled and almost tripped down the stairs, catching herself on the banister just in time. She was feeling cold and feverish at the same time. She found herself entering the kitchen. Her mother was there, sitting at the table with Doña Herminia, deep in consultation about the menu. Milagros was thankful that they ignored her. She went straight into the scullery; she could not face her mother, and she was scared that she would look at her and know exactly what it was that just happened, even if Milagros herself did not.

STAY WITH ME, MY DARLING (episode 278)

Man's voice:

In the big city, night is falling and a chilly wind is blowing. Happy couples walk arm-in-arm in the streets, going out to enjoy themselves. Bright lights, expensive perfumes, laughter of the carefree, the happy, the loved ones. But the young woman at the corner, selling flowers, is not part of the gay scene. She has a melancholy look. She is dressed in clean but threadbare clothes. She would be beautiful if she smiled, but her sad face looks careworn, lined with misery.

Romilda:

Flowers...please buy my beautiful flowers...flowers...

(Laughter, songs, mirth, unintelligible voices of people calling each other)

Romilda:

(waning voice, sad and close to tears) Flowers...please buy flowers...

Antonio:

Here, girl, give me those violets. How much?

Romilda:

Four pesos, sir.

Antonio:

Here you are. Keep the change.

Romilda:

Thank you, sir. Most kind. Flowers...please buy my beautiful flowers...

Antonio:

Romilda! Oh God, it's you, it's really you! don't you recognize your old neighbor, Antonio Sandoval?

Romilda:

Oh, Don Antonio. Yes, yes, of course it's you.

Antonio:

What are you doing out here in the cold so late at night, child? Does your mother know where you are?

Romilda:

My mother, sir...She knows, of course she knows.

Antonio:

But what is the matter child? Are those tears that I see on your pretty face? And what are all those flowers? How is it you are selling them? A flower-seller, you?

Romilda:

...

Antonio:

You're shivering. Come, let's go, you'll catch your death.

Romilda:

But, Don Antonio, I have to sell my flowers, I can't afford to...

Antonio:

Nonsense. I'm buying them all. There now. Let's go to that café. I must find out what this strange business is all about.

China snorted, and Doña Herminia shushed her. There was a shuffling of feet, as the gaucho Rafael stood at the kitchen door; he glared at the women and took his place by the fireplace. Milagros stopped rocking the baby Adolfito, who was fast asleep in her lap, and moved uneasily in her seat by the stove.

(sound of a busy café)

Romilda:

I had to run away. I couldn't destroy him, I had to think of his place in society, his mother, his happiness...

Antonio:

My poor girl, what a sacrifice.

Romilda:

No sacrifice is great enough for him. His love for me will never die, and I will take it with me to my grave.

Antonio:

Brave little woman. What a shame his mother almost died when she found out about you and him.

Romilda:

She is not the forgiving type. She said that as long as she lived, she would refuse to speak a word to him if he was with me. And his political career would be destroyed. He couldn't have a poor girl like me for his wife. He needed someone with the right connections.

Antonio:

But he is not married yet.

Romilda:

He can still marry a woman from his class, I could never offer him what she could.

Antonio:

Well, what did you do then?

Romilda:

Like I said, I ran away. I had to. There was nothing else to be done.

Antonio:

But why do you have to do this graceless job, all alone in the big city, with so many dangers around for beautiful young girls like yourself?

Romilda:

I have no choice, Don Antonio. You see, I have someone to support.

Antonio:

To support? But who?

Romilda:

My child. The light of my life, the only happiness left to me now.

Antonio:

So there is a child...and pray, does Don Rodolfo know about it?

Romilda:

No, I would never do that to him. I could never allow his heart to be torn in two like that. What would you do in my place, Don Antonio? I cannot make him choose between his mother and his child. Wouldn't it be terrible to have to make that choice? No, no, I couldn't let him know. I want him to be free and happy.

"Ha! As much of a father as a tomcat," China said.

"Won't you hush your mouth so we can hear," hissed Doña Celedonia.

Antonio:

But it is his child too, Romilda. My dear, you must not do this to a father. He has a right to know, he must take care of you both. It's his son!

Romilda:

A natural son, Don Antonio, has no rights.

Antonio:

He has the rights of blood. This is enough for me. I'll take care of this business. Leave everything to me.

Milagros lifted her eyes from the baby's serene face. China was watching her with her unsettling eye. What did she know? What did she suspect? Milagros felt a blush creep down her face and neck. To hide it, she bent over the baby and kissed his little rounded forehead. The baby smelled so sweet, looked so peaceful. He sighed in his sleep, a deep sigh which shook his whole tiny body.

Antonio:
I'll come with you. For your mother's sake I will help you. She was the only true love of my life. I will take care of you all. And tomorrow I'm going to find that man and have a word with him.

Romilda:
Oh, no, please, Don Antonio. Please, no. I don't want him to know.

Antonio:
He has to know the truth. A hidden truth is as lethal as a hidden dagger. You never know whom it might hurt.

Romilda:
Then I'll have to run away again. I'll hide somewhere he'll never be able to find us. Farewell, Don Antonio, thank you for your kind words and for the coffee.

Romilda:
No, come back, you silly girl. Come back!

(sound of a chair scraping, Romilda's receding footsteps)

Antonio:
She's gone. A strange girl, indeed. Now what should I do? Shall I go to find this young rascal Rodolfo tomorrow and tell him about his child? Maybe I should have told Romilda that his marriage to that haughty Patricia Ferrero was announced this morning. I must think...

Man's voice:

(over music) Don Antonio has a difficult choice to make. But for yourselves, ladies, the choice is simple: Limpiex, and keep it clean. Join us tomorrow and find out what fate has in store for poor Romilda. And remember. Limpiex, simply the best.

"The stupid things women listen to..." grumbled Rafael, as Doña Herminia switched off the radio. "They learn to be unhappy and unsatisfied with everything. No man's good enough for them after they listen to this crap."

"Who asked you to come in here and listen to it?" muttered Celedonia under her breath, even though she had often expressed the same view herself. She got up and said loudly enough for him to hear: "Don Rafael, I'm warming your dinner now, and once you've had it you must go to bed. You need your rest, there's a good man."

STAY WITH ME, MY DARLING (episode 280)

Man's voice:

There is a grand ball tonight at the mansion of the Posadas family. A veritable army of chambermaids, valets, cooks and butlers have been scouring, cleaning, shining, cooking, preparing the household for the big feast. The celebration of a betrothal between Don Rodolfo Posadas and the beautiful Patricia Fernández is one of the biggest events in the capital: two illustrious families will be united tonight. Don Rodolfo is in his room, getting ready. There is a knock on the door.

Rodolfo:

Enter. Ah, it's you, Ramírez.

Ramírez:

There's a gentleman to see you, sir.

Rodolfo:

A gentleman? Didn't he give his name?

Ramírez:
Antonio Sandoval. What's the matter, sir, are you ill? Do you want me to send him away?

Rodolfo:
Don Antonio...Yes, tell him I'm too busy to see him now, he can come back tomorrow.

Ramírez:
Very well, sir.

Rodolfo:
Wait, on second thought, just show him in.

(Sound of man rushing in)

Antonio:
Thank you for accepting to see me, Don Rodolfo. I know you must be very busy today of all days.

Rodolfo:
Don Antonio. To what do I owe the honor of your visit?

Antonio:
I came to offer you by best wishes, sir, on your imminent marriage.

Rodolfo:
Thank you, that's most kind of you.

Antonio:
Also to warn you that if you do marry, you will commit a sin unforgivable in heaven or earth, sir.

Rodolfo:
What!

Antonio:
Yes, sir, I stand by what I just said: an unforgivable sin, a crime really.

Rodolfo:
How...who...what gives you the right–

Antonio:

Listen, Don Rodolfo. We are not children. I am a man of the world myself. I understand how things work. But let me tell you something: what matters most in this life for a man of honor is to be true to his word.

Rodolfo:

True to his word...whatever do you mean?

Antonio:

You know very well what I mean, Don Rodolfo. You promised true love to one woman who loved you more than anything in the world. She was as pure as spring water from the mountains, as innocent as a newborn lamb. And she trusted you, she gave everything to you. She gave you herself. And this is how you repay her. You are about to get married to someone else, and she—

Rodolfo:

Romilda! Where is she? Have you seen her? Is she well?

Antonio:

How can she be well after you let her go like this? As if she were a stray cat. You turned her out in the street. Do you know where she is? Have you any idea how she lives? She sells flowers at street corners, to feed herself and her child.

Rodolfo:

(whispering) Her...child!

Antonio:

Don Rodolfo, I'm really horrified. I had a higher opinion of you, sir. How can you speak with such nonchalance about the true love of your life, your true wife, sir? And of your own son.

Rodolfo:

A son! My own son!

Antonio:

Yes sir, your own son. And this heroine, this saint, did not tell you anything because she didn't want to set you against the wishes of *your family. But I'm asking you, young man, which one is your true family? How do you expect to find true love anywhere else? True love is not found in alliances of money and power. True love is what this poor, brave little woman is feeling for you. She sacrificed her happiness, so you won't have to shed a tear.*

Rodolfo:

Listen to me, Don Antonio. I'm not the scoundrel you think I am. I know I have done wrong. But I will make amends. I will send her money right away. I will see to it that she lacks for nothing. As for my son, of course he must come to me, I cannot have him live in heaven knows what hovel, in a slum probably. No, whatever the circumstances of his birth, he is a Posadas, and he must be raised like one. Patricia will accept him. She will have to.

Antonio:

What! You mean...you mean you will add another injustice to the one already perpetrated! Not only do you intend to carry on with this travesty of marriage, you will take this woman's only joy away from her! What kind of man are you? Shame on you!

Rodolfo:

Come, come Don Antonio, what would you have me do? You are a man of the world yourself, like you said. You can't expect me to abandon everything, my prospects of success and happiness, for a mistake made because of my youth and inexperience! You can't expect me to marry an uneducated servant girl!

Antonio:

Oh, the fool, the fool, what have I done! She will never forgive me if you take her son away. She will never forgive me.

Rodolfo:

As a prudent man you can see this is the only possible solution, can't you?

Antonio:

No, sir, I cannot see any such thing. I will never tell you where she is. I will warn her right away. I will help her to escape from your clutches, far away from here, where you'll never find her.

Rodolfo:

You'll do no such thing. You will tell me immediately where she is, or else...

Antonio:

Do you dare threaten me, young man? Have you no respect for my white hair? Have you no goodness in you, that you want to break the poor girl's heart and mistreat an old man?

Rodolfo:

Tell me at once, I say!

Antonio:

No, I will not. Let go of me, you rascal!

Rodolfo:

Tell me!

Antonio:

No! No! Stop that!

(Noise of fighting, things falling over. A crashing sound and a cry.)

Antonio:

Oh, no. Oh, no. Don Rodolfo, Don Rodolfo. Oh God, I think he's dead. Oh my, so much blood. I'd better make my escape. But at least the villain cannot hurt my poor Romilda any more...

Man's voice:

(over music) As Don Antonio leaves in a hurry, unobserved by the servants, nobody knows the tragedy that has taken place in the house. Join us again tomorrow to find out the repercussions of this tragic fight. Is Don Rodolfo really dead? Even more importantly, will Romilda find out the truth? And what will the reaction of the

Posadas and the Fernández families be to this mess? As for you, ladies, you know that Limpiex is the only detergent that could clean up a mess like this. Limpiex, keep it clean!

A hush had fallen in the kitchen. Some of the women were wiping their eyes. Celedonia hit her closed hand against the palm of the other and said, "The villain! The treacherous scum!"

"She should have seen it coming," said China with a sneer. "All men are like that, isn't it so, Mili?"

Milagros lay the sleeping baby in the portable crib and busied herself folding clean laundry in the ironing basket. She didn't look up.

"Why are you saying this to her, what would *she* know about men?" said Celedonia in a belligerent tone of voice.

Milagros got up. "I don't have time for this nonsense," she said calmly. "Speak quietly or you'll wake the baby."

"No time for this nonsense," China mocked. "Señorita Milagros is too busy and important to speak to us."

"Yes, she is," said Doña Herminia, "and unless you can keep up at least a semblance of civility, you won't be allowed to listen to the radionovela again, do you hear? Come, Don Rafael, Doña Celedonia will get you your soup, you must be hungry. What's the matter now, don't tell me you were listening to the radionovela as well? It moved you to tears, didn't it? All right, don't get angry, I was only joking. It surely must be the fireplace. This chimney has been smoking ever since that sou'wester began blowing again. Enough smoke to bring tears to a man's eyes, surely."

11

What is Love?

She was standing behind the door. He could see her through the crack between the door and the frame, but she didn't know that. He was playing Chopin's Nocturne in B-flat minor. She was standing there behind the door and the music was holding her captive, invisible chains of melancholy notes binding her to him. He couldn't see the expression on her face; he could only see her forehead gleaming like the moon, the arch of her delicate brows and the thick eyelashes set on the soft curves of the cheeks. Stood there behind the door, slender and pensive like a young cypress tree, listening to the music.

She was only a village girl working for his wife, for him. He desired to go to her, to grab her arm and shatter her serenity. But he knew the only way to keep her there, spellbound, was to keep on playing; the minute he stopped she would vanish, she would run downstairs or wherever it is they went when they were out of sight. He wanted her to remain, listening, her delicious body tense but ready to give in to him, as she was surrendering to the music. The music slowed, three, four minutes in. He felt her just on the verge of ripening, ready for plucking, for tasting. She was his. He had her. He could wait. He had all the time in the world. But for the moment, he would keep on playing.

His face, his fingers, his hands. She wanted to stay here and look at him forever as he played the piano. Amazing how one could do that, pass one's hands over the keys and make this miracle. She could stay there forever and listen. But this would not get the ornaments dusted. This would not get the mirrors polished. It would not get baby Fito fed and burped and changed. She could stay there forever and still he'd never look at her.

The young Señora didn't care very much for music. She yawned and fidgeted on her seat. She looked bored to death whenever he played. Could she love him? She didn't even seem to like looking at him any longer. Could they love each other as husband and wife should, as even her own old and tired parents still loved one another? Her bed linen always looked untouched. Her clothes never smelled of man; they smelled of horse. He rarely went into her bedroom after she had Fito. He didn't care about the baby very much, but ever since Milagros had officially become the child's nanny, he hovered around them both. He peeked at the sleeping baby and brushed his hand against Milagros' arms, and when no one was looking, her breast. She shivered and blushed as his breath became faster. He whispered words to her, sweet, kind words. She wanted to be caressed by him, to let herself go and sink into his arms, to let him touch her as much as he wanted, and she feared it. She loathed herself for standing so near and wished she could tell him to stay away from her, to leave her alone. His golden eyes and luscious hair, and that low, tender voice. And his hands moving over her just as they moved over the keys of the piano. Had she been a rich girl perhaps...But no, she must not allow such thoughts to come. She should keep them firmly away. She must get moving, the baby would wake up soon, and there was so much to be done before she gave him his mashed sweet potato and cream.

Ramona looked at her husband as his besotted eyes followed the movements of the maid with the sweet face and the long, brown, graceful limbs. Milagros, her name was. He was eating the girl up with his eyes, savouring every morsel. Ramona stomped out of the room and out to the stables to ride. She could outride him – easily, she thought with a grim satisfaction.

The hooves pounded the earth, the horse's nostrils flared and let out steam. She was seething with anger. Marriage was so humiliating. To be married was to be humiliated. Always at another's mercy, at another's beck and call. Always a witness to another's intimate moments, and they to her intimate moments as well. She hated using the toilet knowing there was this man next door. And the undressing, and the putting up with another's hands upon herself, especially the parts of herself she was most ashamed of and wished she didn't have.

Why had she accepted to be married? It was for her father. He counted on her and she had not wanted to let him down. When he coaxed her into accepting Faustino Goyena, she had felt powerful and important, and the thought that this gift to her father would improve his status was all the sustenance she required. But it would seem her sacrifice – for it now felt less a gift than a sacrifice – had all been in vain. Not much had changed in his life. He had finally been accepted at the Jockey Club, but he was still unhappy; he complained that they snubbed him in subtle ways, excluded him from discussions, did not extend private invitations that were given gladly to others, much less wealthy than he was. He had implied that perhaps she could say a word to her husband. She was furious with him.

"What more do you expect me to do?" she had yelled. "I've done everything you asked me. I married this ponce. I even gave you a grandson. Did you ever care what I wanted, what was good for me?"

Only Rafael loves me for who I am, she thought. But he was getting so old that he could not ride with her any longer. She wished that he was her father, that they lived far away in the pampas, wandering from ranch to ranch, free and away from the Goyenas and that stupid world they all lived in, where she was restrained, a prisoner for life.

That night, alone in her bedroom, Ramona remembered how Tino looked at that girl Milagros as she went about her work dusting with a feather, shaking bed covers, patting cushions. His eyes had caressed her, lingering on every nook and cranny of that sun-dappled body. Ramona was fascinated, though she knew she ought not to be. It was like watching a snake eyeing a nest full of little birds, and she knew she must not do anything, she must not interfere, and besides there was nothing she could do. Nothing could be put between that look and the girl, her maidservant, who was moving about quite innocently, ignorant, exposing more of her flesh than she would if she knew she was being watched. She bent over, patted the cushions, picked things up from the floor, all with efficient and effortless movement, like water flowing softly in a peaceful stream, her long and lean legs exposed, the white edge of her knickers, a shadow of firm curves, of soft swellings. His eyes followed every move and soon his hands would too. How was it possible to look at a fruit hungrily and not extend your hand to pluck it; how could you resist sinking your teeth into it, knowing it would be firm and succulent under your teeth, knowing your tongue could plunge inside its juicy sweetness. Hands, tongue, skin...

For what felt like the entire lunch, Ramona looked on fascinated as her husband leered at her maidservant, and she couldn't help but follow where his eyes led. She too saw the olive skin and the soft neck and the small round breasts, pointy but not too pointy – in bed, Ramona felt her own breasts, large and overripe – the small waist and the narrow but rounded hips. Ramona tried to trace with her fingers the girl's exquisite shape on her own thick waist and square body, the girl's slender legs to her own broad ones – strong and muscular as a man's – and she knew her body was as ugly as the girl's was delicious. But the pleasure she felt in tracing the lines was so great, and she was so surprised and shocked that her ugly body could give her such excitement, such pleasurable shivers, that her hands continued to move all over it, and as she imagined the eyes of her husband moving shamelessly, recklessly, possessively all over the body of the maidservant, she trembled, felt a flutter, and then was blinded by pleasure.

All of a sudden, she came back to her senses with a jolt, and there she was in her darkened room, a faint moonlight seeping through the cracks in the blinds. She was embarrassed and disgusted at herself, cold and quite alone. A woman whose husband was craving someone else, only a few years into their marriage.

The ranch hands were coming and going in the kitchen. They wanted the salt, the knife, the sprinkler, a bowl to mix the meat juice with the chilli powder. They hung around for longer than necessary. Milagros was the main attraction, particularly for Pablo, who could not stop smiling and laughing out loud at any comment anyone made, even the most trivial ones. He was happy, and even Doña Celedonia's thunderous face did not manage to spoil his good mood. Herminia shooed him off but not too sharply. Her broad face was glistening with sweat and her breath came out in short gasps. The fabric of her silk dress was stretched to the limit of its tensile strength over her bosom.

"It's just too hot for me," she said as she bustled about.

"Lose some weight then," Rafael muttered from his seat in the corner by the fireplace, which was on even during a hot day like this. It was never too hot for him, or too cold. He looked like a very scrawny old cat.

"Rich of him to talk," said China, who also found an excuse to come into the kitchen as often as possible, attracted by the constant stream of young men. "He should take a look at his beloved mistress."

Rafael paid her as much attention as he would to a fly on the ceiling.

"I wish we didn't have the *asado* so near the house," said Doña Herminia, fanning herself with a small linen handkerchief after she wiped her face with it. "Especially today with the north wind, the house will be full of ashes and dust."

"It's not you who's gonna clean it up," said China.

"Are you still hanging around here, you? Get a move on, there are loads of dishes out the back. Bring them in carefully. In two or three trips. They've already broken two plates today, those clumsy idiots. I wish Don Faustino didn't take traditions so seriously. You'd have thought he'd give it a miss this year, what with the young Señora's condition and all..."

Rafael gave her a sharp look.

Milagros came in the room carrying a load of freshly ironed linen towels and tablecloths. Her face was very pale, almost pasty, tendrils of glistening black hair stuck on her temples and the back of her neck. She stumbled as she dropped the pile on the table.

Doña Celedonia lifted her face from the enormous bronze pot she had been stirring and tasting regularly for the last hour.

"Daughter, are you all right?"

Milagros gave her a faint smile and mumbled something about being fine, but her voice sounded distant, exhausted.

"How could anybody be all right in this heat?" Doña Herminia complained, resuming her fanning even more vigorously. "The poor girl has been in there ironing for hours now. In this heat!"

"I don't mind," Milagros said, barely a whisper.

"Better you than me then," said Herminia. "I know I'd have died."

"Imagine what it'll feel like in the eternal fires of hell," chimed in China, her head poking round the door.

"You again? Didn't I just tell you to get out?"

"I am out, what do you want?"

"Watch how you speak, horrid creature," Celedonia growled. "Or else."

"Here, give me that, my dear," said Doña Herminia kindly to Milagros, getting up with some effort. "I'll put it away for you. Oh!"

Suddenly Milagros sank onto the floor in a small heap like a cast-off dress. She barely made a sound as she fell. Bed linen scattered around her, luminously white on the dark flagstone floor. With a cry and a loud bang, Celedonia threw the pot cover and ladle she had been stirring the soup with into the sink and ran to her daughter. China rushed through the door with a pail of water.

"Don't you dare throw that on her," Herminia warned.

"It's clean, I've just–"

"Get out! NOW!" Celedonia, beside herself, kneeled next to her daughter and patted her cheeks and hands, touched the pulse on her neck, wiped sweat off her brow with her apron.

"She's cold, she's frozen," she said. "Cold like ice, frozen." She repeated the same words over again, patting, patting.

"It's this extreme heat," Herminia said, bringing a bowl of water, dipping one of the scattered towels in it, wiping the girl's face.

"The heat of animals," muttered Rafael. "Bitches in heat."

The women ignored him. Milagros's eyelids were sunken and purple, her breathing faint; she was perspiring.

"She's coming to, thank the Virgin," cried Celedonia. With stiff, awkward fingers she tried to unbutton Milagros's dress at the neck.

"Here, let me do it," said Herminia, her usual brisk self, forgetting the heat. "What did you think, poor woman? Of course she's coming to, she's not dead, is that what you imagined?"

"Better off dead, better off dead," Rafael said, but nobody paid him any attention except China, whose small eyes glittered.

12

Milagros and Pablo

The moon was rising over the pampas, the familiar place already starting to appear foreign to Milagros. She shivered in her new coat: stylish, but the thin rabbit fur collar not warm enough for the chilly night. Señorita Delia had brought the materials from Buenos Aires, and had helped her make it. It was supposed to have been her good coat as a trainee teacher on her days off in the capital. Milagros looked good in it: taller, more grown up. When Pablo saw her, he let out a low whistle, forgetting they were supposed to keep as quiet as possible. He then kissed her on the lips and pressed his body onto hers, which filled her with cold fury. He acts as if he owns me already, she thought. She wondered what the other one would think if he could see her in her beautiful new coat and lipstick. She chased the thought away quickly, as if swatting a bug. They got into the car. Milagros fixed her eyes on the bright path ahead formed by the headlights.

"How could you do this to us?"

She tried the phrase in different versions in her mind, imagined hearing it in different voices. Her mother, her father. Doña Ramona. She even imagined baby Fito extending his little arms to her, wishing to be picked up, the accusation written all over his sweet face, on his mouth puckering up to cry. How could she do this to them, how could she leave them and flee in the middle of the night, like a burglar?

She wanted to imagine *him* saying it to her, but she knew he wouldn't. He would not care. It was over. The fuzzy haze that enveloped her when she was in the same space with him was gone. His eyes passed her over, as if she was just another piece of furniture. He did not hang out on the back stairs or lurk by the doorway, pulling her by the waist into his dressing room, fragrant with his spicy cologne, where they had spent intoxicating moments a hundred years ago, it now seemed. The world had become a cold, gray desert, except for the fierce flicker inside her, growing, growing...

"So how's my little wife feeling?"

"I'm not your wife yet."

"No, not on paper. But in everything else, eh? Soon the magistrate will make it all right and proper, and then..."

She could see the white glimmer of his teeth, but she did not feel like smiling.

They arrived at San Justo just after midnight. The train station was empty, but they sat at the darkest part of the platform, hidden in the shadows, waiting silently. Milagros had to push away Pablito's wandering hands several times, or shushed him when he became exuberant. They were not supposed to draw any attention to themselves. People might see, hear, remember. The train for Buenos Aires arrived at 2:10 a.m. They boarded silently, bleary with sleep, unsaid words hanging over them like a mist.

As they passed by Alta Gracia again on the train, being cruelly forced to return in that direction in order to reach the capital, they saw it silvery under the pale moon, its houses in deep slumber. Milagros began to weep softly into her palms. Pablo hugged her awkwardly, whispering soothing words into her ear. Soon the last tiny lights of the village were left behind, and the train plunged into the vast darkness.

13

Buenos Aires

One Year Later, Grand Bourg, Provincia de Buenos Aires

It was dark in the room, except for a soft yellow circle of light on the table where Milagros was sitting at work. She was knitting a fluffy pink baby garment. She was fast and exact, counting stitches with a concentration that made the line between her eyebrows deepen further. Her dark handsome face – sharp cheekbones with aquiline nose – looked as if it was carved in sandstone. It softened when, often, she lifted her eyes from her work to look at the basket on the darker and warmer side of the room, where a small coal stove was burning. The basket was decorated with white tulle and pink satin bows and ribbons. There was a sleeping baby inside, wrapped in a cocoon of woolly covers, only its tiny face and fists visible.

Milagros looked at a large tin alarm clock on a shelf on the other side of the bed, across from where she was sitting. It was past ten o'clock. She strained her ears for sounds over the soft patting of rain on the corrugated roof. A dog howled, a rusty gate door creaked – then nothing. The furrow between her eyebrows deepened as the clock hands moved slowly and steadily on.

The baby stirred, then began to whimper. Milagros moved quickly round the double iron bedstead that took up most of the space, and picked the baby up. She felt the baby's hands: they were cold. She warmed them inside her own hands. She placed her face near the baby's and whispered softly.

"Come, my little Lucía, don't you cry now. don't cry my dove, my little sugar girl. Look! Mami is here. Mami is here, yes. You're smiling now, yes? You're smiling. That's Mami's girl! Look how pretty my baby girl is when she's smiling. Peekaboo! Look! Little moon is coming out of the clouds. When she's in the middle of the sky, she'll be watching over you. Peekaboo! You see? Ye-es! Everything's better now. Mami will keep you warm. Mami and her little Lucía, just the two of us."

Milagros lay down on the bed, still holding the baby in her arms. She closed her eyes. Listening to the baby's soft breathing made her drowsy. She was very tired. She was somewhere between sleeping and waking, and irritating thoughts buzzed around her head like mosquitoes.

How fast babies went to sleep! Look at her, she was just gone! Why did other women complain about their babies? Was she lucky? Wasn't Lucía just the most well-behaved and sweet baby in the world? Ever since she was born, she hardly ever cried. God, this girl of hers, what would she be when she grew up? This was Mabel asking, Milagros' neighbor. Would she be a teacher at the school? A nun? A saint? So young and so serious already! Imagine! Señorita Lucía Eva Suárez de Riquelme – school teacher! Perhaps even Doctora Lucía. You never know...Poor Mabel, she had those four devils for children. Milagros saw her Damián yesterday, he was collecting the sharpest rocks to throw at the dogs. "Stop it, you disgraceful child you," Milagros yelled at him. "Don't ever let me catch you doing that again!" And poor Mabel just shrugged. "What can I do," she said, "I don't even have the time or the energy to shout at them anymore." All this washing and ironing out in the neighborhood to make a *centavo* now her husband was out of work. So far they'd been lucky, considering. But Pablito was late again and she didn't like that at all. Was he up to something? Maybe those unions...God forbid! They could put you in jail for less. Could it be some other woman? She was afraid for the worst. Only she wasn't sure what the worst was in these troubled times.

She thought she heard steps approaching and rose, laying the baby carefully in the middle of the matrimonial bed, surrounding her with bolsters so she wouldn't roll over and fall off. Milagros went to the door and stood there listening for a few minutes, holding her breath. The footsteps had stopped, their owner probably turned round the corner towards another house. She went back to the table and sat down to do some more work. Under the bed there was a big basket with her knitting materials and another where a number of little woolly garments were laid out carefully, waiting to be washed and starched. These she would cover with a clean towel before Pablo came in. She didn't want him to know she took in knitting work. Some of it was pre-ordered, but most of it she gave to a woman who sold it at the square on Saturdays. The little pink garment she was knitting now was a present.

She went to the small kitchen next to the front door: a small sink with a water pump, a few shelves with pots and pans and crockery, a small cupboard with iron mesh walls where they kept the food, and a gas ring with a big green gas bottle underneath. She put the kettle on. She quickly brewed a *mate*. Pablo might still be a while, and she had to speak to him tonight. There would be no time tomorrow morning, when he set out for work before six o'clock.

As she was slowly drinking her *mate* from the wooden and silver gourd – a wedding present from her father – she took a letter from her housedress pocket and read it. The letter was soft and worn. She had been reading it for a week now, mulling over its contents.

Alta Gracia, Pca de las Pampas
June 28, 1957

My beloved daughter Milagros,

I hope the present finds you all in good health. We are still alive, thank God and the Holy Virgin. Papá has been feeling a little low lately. He's never managed to come around after the President's exile. It is not even permitted to mention his name now. Men are so stupid when it comes to politics! He stays in bed most of the time and only gets up a few hours a day to sit at his bench and finish only the absolutely necessary jobs. He is very weak.

Daughter, now that you are a married woman, you know what's best for you and yours but you must consider that we are your family too. Let bygones be bygones. We have forgiven you, and to tell the truth I am not sure why you and Pablo, my son-in-law in the eyes of God and the state, decided to do things that way. No one was going to stand in your way. Now that my only grandchild has been born in holy matrimony, may all the blessings of the Virgin of Luján be upon her, please come back to us. Old Man Suárez is heartbroken and we your old parents get more frail by the day. So it pleased God to take away from me all my other children, may they rest in peace, my own poor dear Mother being with them now to take care of them in their eternal sleep. But my one remaining daughter, you, and my little granddaughter whom I've never seen, I miss very much and hope to God you see what's best for you and for all of us and come back here. You will live in comfort, the Señora said you will stay in the gardener's house and Felix can go and live in the small house of old Martínez who died last month, may he rest in peace.

The Family are in good health. It was a shame about poor Don Faustino. Who would have imagined that old man Rafael would have it in him to do such a thing? To take a knife to another man's face, the man who is essentially your employer...Madness, no other explanation. The poor Señora took it very badly. She misses her old gaucho, and to tell the truth we miss him too sitting by the fireplace, being grumpy. But what can't be cured must be endured. At least now the Señora is better and with her new baby she is busy and has no time to mope. It's a good thing it's a girl, as she has already got her boy. Little Fito has grown a lot lately, and what a fine boy he is, but he misses you, and he is still asking, Where is Mili? and Why did she go? and When is she coming back? That boy loves you so much, more than his own mother. God forgive me for saying that, but the Señora admitted herself that it is so. She had a difficult birth and the new baby cries all the time and keeps me and Visi, the new girl, up all night. That Visi is an idiot. The other day she almost scalded Fito in the bath. The poor little soul, how he cried!

The poor Señora has put on too much weight after the last birth. She is as big as a mountain. She rarely leaves her room now. She, who was on her horse all the time! But time changes us all, rich and poor alike. Your Papá, how strong he used to be! And now he is only a little old man, sitting in a chair all day not saying a word to anybody. She said to ask you when you are coming back. She told me yesterday to tell you enough of this nonsense with Pablo's factory job and come back here where you belong. She asked me about your baby, too. I told her it's a strong and healthy baby, Lucía by name. She said, "Ah, so it's a little girl. Then all the more reason for Milagros to come back here and raise her girl and my Silvina together, and she can give the baby her milk because I don't trust that negra Visi." Please come back, daughter.

Till we meet again, receive many kisses and blessings from your mother,

María Celedonia Fernández de Riquelme

Not a word from him, Milagros thought. What would he be thinking now his wife was so fat? And would he try anything funny again if she returned? Had he turned his attentions to that poor Visi now? If she was a pretty girl, he sure had. That was who he was, wasn't it? I can't tell anybody, she thought. But what if somebody noticed how Lucía looked like him? She could see the family resemblance clearly. How white she was, and the color of her eyes just like his. And poor Pablo thinking that Lucía took after his own family! "My mother was Italian, from Venice," he said, "that's where my Lucía got her lovely golden eyes from." Men were blind, they only saw what they wanted to see. Thank God for that.

Raindrops began to drum on the roof, and outside the house there were men singing and shouting. Milagros put the letter quickly back into her pocket and went to the door. She opened it just a sliver. Pablo was waving noisy goodbyes to some *compañeros* who waved back and made their drunken way down the road, oblivious to the now torrential rain.

"There you are, light of my life, happiness of my house," said Pablito cheerfully, but he sounded slurry. He stumbled as he tried to embrace Milagros.

She hissed at him, "Shut up, don't you have any sense? You'll wake the baby."

"The baby, the baby. You think of nothing else ever since she was born."

The bed creaked loudly as Pablo sat heavily on its edge and began to take his shoes off. Milagros rushed to pick the baby up. She placed her back in the basket and tucked her in snugly. She wished they had a larger house, with a separate room for her.

"There is some *mate*," she said in a low voice. "I'm going to heat the water up again."

Pablo was whistling as lay down on the bed in his clothes. He followed Milagros with his eyes, and as she passed near him he grabbed her by the dress. She slapped his hand off and went about the business of preparing the *mate*.

"I don't want any," Pablo grunted and scowled.

"You can't go to bed like this, you'll still be drunk when you wake up to go to work."

"So maybe I won't go to work."

Milagros turned sharply to face him.

"What? Why? Did something happen?"

Pablo went on whistling, but not as cheerfully anymore.

"Speak to me. What happened? Did they fire you?"

"Maybe they did, and maybe they didn't. And maybe they will."

At moments like this, Milagros perfectly sympathised with those women who killed their husbands.

She took a deep breath and began.

"I wish you would tell me what is happening at work. And why are you hanging out with that crowd? They have no wives or children, they don't care. But you are not like this anymore. You're married now, you have a daughter."

"Oh, Mili, please stop nagging! I've got a pounding headache."

"Serves you right too! What will become of us if you go on like this? Getting drunk every night! And can you afford to buy all those drinks?"

"The *compañeros* buy me my drinks."

"And you buy them theirs! Watch out, Pablito, I may be a woman but I'm not stupid. I know you're up to something. You're not fooling me, do you hear? Do you want to spend your money with all those...those lost women, and those idiots who only think of today, so tomorrow they end up starving? Do you want our Lucía to starve, too?"

"My daughter will never starve!"

"Oh yeah? And how are you going to prevent it, by going out and getting drunk every night?"

Pablo was silent. He sat up cross-legged on the bed and took the *mate* gourd Milagros was offering him. His eyes were bleary and his shoulders hunched. Milagros was standing over him, hands akimbo, staring down at him, but inside she wasn't angry anymore. This is the man I married, she thought. A silly, irresponsible boy. How on earth were they going to manage?

"You promised me so much, Pablo," she said with a voice that she tried, failing, to keep both steady and low. "And I believed you! A house where I'd be the mistress! That I wouldn't have to go back to Alta Gracia, ever! That you'd provide for me and our children! Where are all those promises?"

"You are living in the capital and you are mistress of your own house," he said huffily.

"Not for much longer, if you carry on like this."

"Aw, come on, Mili," he said. "Give me a break. I work so hard, I deserve a break once in a blue moon."

"Once in a blue moon! This has been every day for a long time now. And what about me? don't I deserve a break too?"

"Why don't you come along once, to meet the boys and their... their fiancées?"

"Fiancées! Ha! Do you really want your own wife to mix with such women?"

"We could go dancing from time to time. Come on, Mili, we're still young, and you act as if we were a hundred years old already. Only because we've got a baby."

"And what do you propose to do with her? Leave her in here alone to cry and starve while her parents are dancing away? Or should we bring her along, leave her in a corner?"

"La Mabel could take care of her for you one night."

"I don't want my baby to be in that house. It's very dirty. Her boys are savages. If you have no ambitions about your daughter, I do. I don't want her catching something and dying. I want her to be well-fed and warm and happy. I want her to make something of her life. Not like us, just another *cabecita negra*. I'll see to it, do you hear? Nothing bad will ever happen to her. Her life will be so much better than ours, and if you can't offer this to her, I will!"

For a few moments, they remained silent as the rain tapped steadily on the roof. Pablo's face was streaked with tears. Milagros was still glowering. He extended his arms towards her.

"Baby, come here," he said. "Come to bed. I love you, Mili. What a woman you are! I don't deserve you, Mili, forgive me. Forgive me, and come to my arms, baby. Give your old man a little love, baby."

She said nothing, just stared ahead in the darkness, hating his maudlin mood and easy tears. She'd seen it all before. She felt less sorry for him every time.

"So, did they fire you?" she asked again, still looking straight ahead, away from him.

"No. Not yet. But they're laying off dozens by the day. They say the factory will close. They say there is no money for wages anymore."

"You must start looking somewhere else then, and the sooner the better."

"Ye-es," he said, without much conviction. "It's not easy. Hard times are ahead, don't you understand anything, woman?"

"Keep your voice down! You'll wake her up."

"It's my own house and I'll shout if I want to."

"You are a disgrace, Pablito."

"I'll shout louder if you don't come to bed right now. I'm still your husband and you must do as I tell you, do you hear?"

You are my husband for my sins. But you'll see what's what, thought Milagros, as she reluctantly switched off the light and began to take her housedress off, careful not to drop the letter from her pocket.

14

The Golden Age

Alta Gracia, 1964

In the rose garden the three children were playing hide and seek among the trimmed bushes. Trilling voices and shrill giggles mixed with birdsong. Felix the gardener ran after them, grumbling. Teasing him was as much fun as the game of hide and seek itself. They screamed with joy every time he was near enough to catch them, before squirming out of reach. Finally he got hold of the youngest child, a timid little girl of six. He shook her hard, and she, thinking this was part of the game, laughed and screamed happily. But soon the edges of her mouth turned downwards, as he spat at her:

"Shame on you. What are you doing running wild destroying the Señora's roses? It's okay for them two, but you should know better. I'm gonna tell your mama and then see what a beating you'll get."

The little girl started to weep. Then out of the bushes came the other two children.

"Leave her alone, you stupid man," yelled a dark-haired girl of about the same age but taller, with a fierce expression on her face.

She ran up to the old man and kicked him on the shin. He stopped shaking the little girl, but did not let her go. A blond slender boy of about eight followed behind.

Calmly, he said, "Felix, please don't shout at Lucía. It's not her fault. This game was our idea."

The gardener let the little girl go. She ran to the boy and took his hand, looking up into his face with a trusting expression. The boy dried her tears off with his free hand. The other girl was still scowling at Felix. The old man, still glowering, turned to go, muttering to himself. As the children watched him walk away, the taller girl said loudly enough for him to hear:

"What an asshole!"

The little girl gasped, shocked, then giggled.

"Silvina! You know you're not supposed to use such words," the boy said. "What kind of example are you setting for Lucía?"

"Well, he is," said Silvina. "I'm only telling it as it is."

The three children stood there among the rose bushes for a few seconds. Then Silvina said, "I know! Let's go to the pond!"

"I don't think so," the boy said. "Mama doesn't like it for us to play there. How about going to play in the folly?"

"Pond!"

"Folly!"

"I said pond!"

"And I said folly! I'm a boy and older than you and so you must do as I say!"

"No, I must not!"

"Yes!"

"No!"

Little Lucía was watching them with big fascinated eyes, reverting to putting her finger in her mouth, forgetting that her mother had absolutely forbidden it.

"Lucía, tell him," Silvina said. "You want to come to the pond with me, good girl, don't you? We girls must stick together."

"Leave the little one out of this," the boy said. "You're always getting her into trouble."

"No, I'm not," Silvina said, but with some hesitation.

"She's not," Lucía said loyally.

"Okay, I give up," the boy said. "Go to the pond, but don't blame me if you drown."

"Come on, Lucía, let's go," shouted Silvina running ahead. "We'll take our clothes off and go for a swim. I'm so hot with all this running."

The boy stood there watching them go towards the woods where the pond was hidden, torn between his wish to follow and his pride.

As she was about to walk into the woods, Lucía turned towards him and called, "Fito, come on!"

He stood undecided just a little longer, and then he ran to catch up with them, his long curls glowing in the afternoon sun.

Milagros turned away from the window. As soon as she made the Señora's tea, she would send somebody to the pond to make sure the children were safe. As for Felix, she would deal with him later. If he dared lay hands on her little girl again, the old bastard, she would go to Don Faustino himself, come what may.

Ramona was sitting in her large rattan armchair, fanning herself listlessly. Her eyes were half-closed, but Milagros knew that she was watching everything in the room. Ramona only didn't see what she didn't want to see. For example, that new girl, Betina, was sneaking into Tino's room every night. Ramona could not have cared less, it appeared. She and Tino had slept in different bedrooms ever since Silvina was born, and that seemed to be how she wanted things to stay.

I wish I could sleep alone in my own bedroom, thought Milagros, sighing, her heart completely cold and empty.

She made the tea and poured it into the lovely white tea set with the blue patterns. She preferred this tea set to the one they used back in town, the heavy silver one which was such a hassle to clean. On the other hand, this was more fragile. She had to be extra careful with it. She prepared the Señora's cup just as she liked it, strong with three cubes of sugar and a small slice of lemon, then she left it on the little table by her side. She put three small pastries on a little plate next to the cup of tea and made for the door.

"Don't go yet, Milagros," said Ramona, her eyes still half-closed. "Stay to keep me company."

Milagros went back to the window. She couldn't see the pond from there, but she could hear squeals and laughter. She should really send somebody to check on them, but she had to do it without Ramona noticing: she had forbidden them to go to the pond, and they would be punished. But what she didn't know wouldn't hurt her.

"Where are the children? I can hear them, but can you see them?"

"In the rose garden, I think, Señora. I can't see them from here either, but their voices come from that way."

"Come, sit by me," said Ramona, suddenly opening her eyes. They had the color of the weather, as people said: they would change from green to gray to light brown, according to the light and the season. They were darker now; they had been dark for a long time. Stormy weather.

They sat in silence as Ramona had a few sips of her tea. There was an overwhelming smell of white talcum powder, jasmine and warm sweat in the room. A fly was buzzing somewhere outside the window net. Ramona fanned herself and Milagros prayed silently that nothing would happen to the children at the pond. She trusted Fito's good sense and caring nature, but Silvina was a different story.

"So, is everything all right downstairs?" asked Ramona after a while.

"Yes, Señora, why shouldn't it be?"

"I hear old Felix is still not happy about you taking his house."

"It was your wish, madam."

"Tino's idea. But of course I think it's fair, you are a family of three and Felix is just an old man by himself."

"True, Señora."

"Don't you think about having more children, Milagros?"

"If it please God, Señora."

"I'm sure Young Suárez would like one of each. Yes, a little boy would be good. My Fito would have somebody to play with. He only has the girls to play with now." She was one of the few people left who still called Pablo the Young Suárez, even though he was the only one left, his father now buried in the little cemetery, keeping Abuela and Milagros' siblings company, and now also her beloved parents too, overcome with weariness and age.

"He's a good influence on them, madam."

"I know," sighed Ramona. "Especially for Silvina. She's a wild one. Who she takes after, I wonder."

Milagros said nothing.

"Is Young Suárez well? I hear he's been having some problems," Ramona said suddenly.

"What problems? Who said this? What did they tell you?"

"Come, girl, don't be offended now. It's not a secret your man likes his drink. He almost drove Tino's car into a tree the other day. Not that I would hold it against him, mind. Especially if..."

She paused and let it go, but Milagros knew what she would have said if it had been decent of a wife to speak ill of her husband in front of a servant. She agreed with the sentiment wholeheartedly.

She was a little surprised that Señora was speaking so candidly. The woman rarely allowed her true feelings to be known, except her displeasure, of course. Now Milagros was overwhelmed by displeasure too. And despair. Damn you, Pablo Suárez, she thought fiercely. You're doing it again. I'll kill you if we lose our places here too.

"You, on the other hand, you are a treasure, Milagros," Ramona said. "The children love you, and you are the only person Silvina listens to. I wouldn't let you go for anything."

Milagros breathed again.

"Thank you, Señora," she said.

"It's not your fault. What one's husband will turn out to be – it's pure chance. One can never know beforehand."

With a pang, Milagros thought of the thin long legs of Betina, of her childish mousy face. She remembered her first meeting with poor China, the rumors about the servant girls leaving from time to time to have an abortion. It was all true. Except in her own case. She thought of her angelic Lucía and her secret, that still no one seemed to have guessed – except *him* of course, the old bastard, whom she had often caught scrutinising the face of the little girl in secret, no doubt tracing the similarities, sensing the pull of the blood.

They remained silent a little longer. No voices could be heard, no buzzing; everything was perfectly still and quiet.

"You can take the tea things away now," Ramona said, closing her eyes again. "I'm done."

"You hardly touched anything."

"It's too hot to eat. Besides, I must lose some weight. I miss riding my horses."

Milagros got up and started to collect the tea things on the tray. She went briefly to the window and saw the three children walk back towards the house, their hair plastered on their heads, their clothes hanging limp and dirty. Lucía was running by Fito's side trying to keep up with him. Silvina was hacking at the bushes with a stick. Thank you, Virgin of Luján, thought Milagros, they are safe.

"You and I, Mili, we'll grow old together," said Ramona from the depths of her chair. She looked like an oracle, as she sat there, immense, majestic in her white dress and many necklaces, speaking with eyes closed.

"If it's God's will, madam," Milagros said, and left the room, closing the door softly behind her.

PART THREE

1975-1982

15

Liberation Theology

Buenos Aires, 1975

"So this is the young man at last. Welcome, son, welcome."

The man who greeted him and his father at the Jockey Club was overweight and sweating. It was a sweltering day. The room, large and comfortable, was hideously luxurious and seemed to have difficulty breathing. As his friend led young Fito into the room, introducing him to other rotund men, Don Faustino beamed with pride.

Fito assessed his surroundings with distaste. This place was very much like his own home, only more vulgar, if that was possible. There were men in crisp linen suits who smoked big fat cigars. He hated the smell and the choking smoke of cigars and had never, for the life of him, been able to tell a cheap from an expensive one: to him both varieties reeked. Only it was evident there wouldn't be any cheap cigars in here. The men lounged about, drinking out of tall glasses with chinking ice cubes, the sparkling drinks brought to them on silver trays by noiseless servants in white jackets and black trousers. Poor penguins, Fito thought to himself. Suffocating in this hot weather, climbing up and down stairs, so much energy wasted on attending to the stupid needs of men who are bent on slowly destroying their livers and their stomachs, only because they have nothing better to do.

Faustino felt slightly uncomfortable under the boy's critical gaze. He's too earnest for his own good, this son of mine, he thought, trying to look at the matter impartially, as an outsider would. Too serious. He takes that from his mother. The same disapproving silences, the scrutinising eyes that will only find fault. His blood pressure rose at the thought of Ramona, sitting on her throne, emitting judgement. Like the Holy Fucking Seat. But the boy was so good looking. A young Sun King. He needed nothing: no excuses, no explanations, no justification, just standing there, radiating beauty. He was innocent, too, and absolute in his judgements, like all the young. I was already corrupt when I was his age, Don Faustino thought. But it was different for us. We grew up more quickly. My father wanted me to get married before I was Fito's age. University was never a serious option, not that I had the aptitude. The old man was such a tyrant. At least I'm not tyrannical. Unlike the boy's mother. I wonder if he loves her. I wonder if he loves me. Don Faustino grinned at his son, and the boy smiled back.

Honor thy father and thy mother, thought Fito. It is a direct order from God, and there aren't many of those. I guess the ten commandments are reserved for the hardest things to do, the ones that don't come easy or natural. He remembered Father Agnelli's words:

"Even if you don't love them, act as if you do. This is the real and true meaning of love. Love is not to be fond of people, to profess good will for mankind and feel satisfied with yourself that you love everyone, that you are a good loving person, ultimately doing nothing for anyone. Love is action only, always action."

"Yes, but isn't this hypocritical, if I don't have feelings for them?" he had replied.

"No, it isn't. Feelings not accompanied by actions usually mean nothing at all. And hypocrites want to take credit for things they don't feel or do. In your case, you do the opposite. You recognize the lack of feeling and you make efforts to overcome this lack. Eventually the feelings will come, too. So don't worry about it."

Fito was not worried about his feelings for his parents very much. There was another kind of love he was more concerned about, but he hadn't dared speak to Father Agnelli about it. What would he say if he knew? He was a priest, after all, even if he was quite unlike any other priest Fito had ever met – not many, really. Would he change his mind about Fito, if he knew; would he think he was a bad sort? He would be disappointed, because the existence of such love in his life meant that Fito would never be able to become a priest like him. Fito would not follow in his footsteps or become his disciple. St. Peter was married, though. He had a mother-in-law. The face of Milagros came to his mind, dearer than a mother. What would she think? Wouldn't she be happy for him, for *them*, if they were as happy as he was certain they would be? He smiled to himself once more.

"It's nice to see you smile, son," Don Faustino said. "I knew you'd like it here. Now, how about a drink?"

Was it something I said? What *did* I say? thought Faustino, his heart clenching. He had seemed so happy, radiant, beaming like a young prince, and then all of a sudden he frowned. That was his mother all over: moody, unfathomable, volatile. That was why he could never be faithful to her. It was doomed from the beginning. She was never the sort that would attract him. He liked girls to be pliable, pleasantly predictable. Such a comfort. He loved it when they just let themselves go in his arms, they smiled when he smiled, they looked worried when he frowned. But that woman, there was no pleasing her. And unfortunately, the other one, her maid – same thing. Trained well by such a mistress. He sometimes wondered if they were in each other's confidence. He knew Ramona had never shown a deeper interest in another human being, not even her own children, but that maid Milagros was a rare exception. It seemed his wife had a lot of time for her, and of course for the mad old gaucho. He stroked the scar that had been disfiguring his face for nearly twenty years now. Just went to show the vulgarity of the woman.

Why did his faultless life get so tarnished so quickly, and why did he have to live like that, with the constant reminder of how much his wife hated him, and how much he hated her? There were the children too: his beautiful boy throwing his youth away being a do-gooder. And Silvina, headstrong, bullish, her mother all over again. The only light in that house was that angelic girl, Lucía. But her mother kept her well away from him, as if he was going to eat her. As if he would do such a thing to his own...he dared not even think the word. But he knew. He had eyes and he could see. He wondered why nobody else could. But there was nothing he could do about that or about anything else, Faustino thought, angry and miserable and sorry for himself.

He always looked so unhappy, even when he was trying to appear jovial, Fito thought. He could almost love him for this. Maybe if he was a ragged old man in the shantytowns, having only one meal every three days, abandoned by wife and children, surrounded by rats and roaches, maybe then he could love him, he could feel his heart ache for him. But how could anyone feel love for Don Faustino, with his immaculate clothes and the diamond pin in his tie, with his chauffeur-driven cars and his houses and the country estate and the servants at his beck and call? No, even if his father sometimes had the eyes of a kicked dog, and his scar always looked painful, a terrible memory made visible for the whole world to see, Fito could not love him. Sometimes felt sorry for him, yes, for a very short moment, until this feeling was replaced by maddening irritation, even shame on his behalf.

The drinks were served, the ceiling fan was turning languidly, the old boys were talking about the same old: politics and money, money and politics. It amounted to the same thing really, as Father Agnelli often said. They could both destroy one's soul. One of the things Father Agnelli would certainly agree with Silvina on, if he'd ever have a chance to speak to her. But Silvina would never give a priest the time of day.

Fito's first meeting with Father Agnelli was at an event at the Faculty of Medicine, organized by the Christian Students for the Poor. Father Agnelli was the main speaker at the event. Fito had expected an old man, stern and gaunt, wielding the Bible like an axe and accusing the young students of frivolous pursuits. Why he had gone to the meeting, he still couldn't explain. What he found was a boyish, jolly young man, with a wide forehead and unruly locks of hair, bright eyes and boundless energy.

Much of what he said at first went over Fito's head, although he was sure Silvina would love it: the man had studied in Paris and he was going on and on and on about anthropology and semiotics and the apparatus, the jargon nigh-incomprehensible to everyone else that Silvina used so adeptly with her pals at university. But then Father Agnelli began to speak of the poor, the shantytowns, the appalling conditions, the diseases that had been wiped from the face of the earth for most people except the inhabitants of those horrific places. He said, "Come and look for yourselves." He said, "We are here to offer practical love to our brothers, not good advice or ideologies or promises about the afterlife." He said, "I cannot talk to the poor about God and heaven and still be complicit in perpetuating their misery on earth. My duty is to show that God has not forgotten them, that He will send his angels to succor, and you and I are those angels."

So Fito *had* gone to see for himself. They headed northwest, driving past the leafy suburbs of Barrio Norte and its environs. They were on the road to Alta Gracia, and Fito had thought how long it had been since he and Silvina and Lucía were playing in the gardens and the large park surrounding the stately home. Lost in a sweet reverie as villas and roads and traffic lights gave way to shantytowns and factories and junkyards and then the vast, open country, he suddenly came to as he noticed that they were now outside the gated community of Las Tortorellas, its Italianate steeples and cypress trees peeking over high stone walls.

"Is that it? Are we there?" he asked, wondering if Father Agnelli had come here to collect another one like him. But the priest, looking quite amused, kept driving past the guarded gate, and turned east into a country road, full of lumps and ruts and potholes. The car swerved and bumped, bouncing almost off the road more than once.

"A bumpy ride," said Fito smiling, trying to show good sportsmanship. But it was quite annoying to be driving on such a rotten road.

The man at the wheel looked at him sideways and smiled, too.

"Does it annoy you? We're on the luxury stretch now, be warned. The really rough part comes later."

Fito groaned. Father Agnelli laughed.

They met few other vehicles on the way. Fito wondered if they were conspicuous in the plain, battered DC car, two young men, one of them with a priest's dog collar. Or did they just merge into the empty vastness and disappear? Who would care to be watching anyway? So many better things to do. He thought of the books on his desk, the invitation to the cinema, of dinner at La Perla. He thought of football practice, of his mother asking in her fake indifferent manner, "So where have you been today, son?" He thought of his father and the way he raised his left eyebrow and smirked and called him Señor Doctor. "What does Señor Doctor think?" "What is his excellency the Doctor's opinion?"

Fito laughed with him, but felt the disappointment and the disapproval. "These young men nowadays, they're just too serious for me, too eager," he had heard Don Faustino say in a languid manner to his friends. "Why can't they just enjoy life? You only live once, life is so short and youth is even shorter." People would think that deep down inside Don Faustino was proud of his son, that all this was just an effort to hide his immense pride at Fito. But Fito knew better. He knew that his father felt that Fito's choices were a criticism and a judgment on his own life.

"Do your parents know?" Father Agnelli asked him.

Fito shrugged. A little while later, he added, "I grew up practically down the road and I've never been here before, didn't even know this road existed."

"I know," said Father Agnelli.

"It is quite a distance. Do you think we'll be back in the capital in time?"

"In time for what?"

"I've told you, haven't I? I'm meeting my father at his club. I can't put him off again, he's been trying to get me there these six months."

"Oh yes, the club. No, you mustn't let your father down." The priest chuckled to himself. "Fancy visiting Villa 22 and the old club on the same day. That will be...edifying."

Fito said nothing. He was slightly irritated by Agnelli's chuckle, by the bumpy ride on the dirty road, by the miserably wet day.

"Are we there yet?" he asked. There was no reply. "Maybe this was a bad idea," he said after a few minutes. He felt contrary and obstinate. My God, I'm turning into my sister, he thought. Aloud he said, "I don't think I'm cut out for this kind of thing, you know. I'm not sure I can really help anybody. I mean, what if I make a mistake and kill someone? I'm not properly qualified yet, you know that, I've still got a long way to go to qualify..."

Father Agnelli turned and looked at him thoughtfully for a few seconds, then turned his eyes back on the road, looking fixedly ahead. His lips were twitching at the ends. Fito had the impression that he was trying hard not to smile.

"Don't worry, you won't kill anybody," he said. "And yes, I know you've still got a long way to go to qualify as a doctor. But there are others there who already have. You will help them. You can do simple things, taking blood pressure and the like, no? Actually we've got someone who knows you. A properly qualified one. Rogelio Otamendi de Grant. You do know him?"

"Oh?" Fito was surprised. "I didn't know he was into this kind of thing."

"It's hardly something he would talk about in social gatherings of your kind, is it?"

It's *your* kind, too, thought Fito. Or at least it had been. He remembered how his parents talked about Father Agnelli, how unbelieving and indignant they were every time he was on the radio or TV or in the papers. They could understand the Church as a career. It was proper for a man of their class, a second or third son: he could become a bishop, a Monsignor, he would live in a palace, he would keep his high social standing. The sex thing might be a problem, but Don Faustino was certain the chastity vows were for the common priests only; they did not extend to the upper ranks of the Church, especially those highly born. But someone like Father Agnelli, an only son of such pedigree. He was *criollo* on his mother's side; European aristocracy on his father's; intelligent and well-educated; a university professor before he was thirty; and a handsome man, too. For this man to throw everything to the dogs and become a priest in the slums! No, this was unacceptable, this was black magic. "It's that poisonous sect, that horrible woman's doing, Eva Perón," Don Faustino pronounced the name as if he was spitting, "she's still haunting us from the grave." "They are poisoning young minds," Doña Ramona had offered in rare agreement. Silvina had been at the dinner table, too, another unusual occurrence. "You can hardly call a movement with so many followers a sect," she said coldly, "and I can't imagine what makes you believe their ideas are poison and yours aren't." And then the usual fight had ensued.

The bumpy macadam road stopped abruptly. It almost reached the barriers of a large, complex, multi-levelled building site with pits and flat areas and high constructions. A large sign read:

La Primavera. Luxury condominium.

Duplex apartments and houses.

Sports centre, swimming pool, manicured gardens.

24-hour vigilance.

There were workers all over the place, moving slowly under the constant drizzle, their yellow helmets strokes of color against a gray landscape.

"Another one of those," Father Agnelli winked, alluding to the gated community they had passed a little earlier.

Beyond the building site, a dirt path began, with some sparse trees and a few signs of life and activity. Two or three skinny cows were standing in a thin, brownish pasture, and beyond that stood a settlement of precarious little buildings with tin roofs and muddy yards. A pack of mongrel dogs lay about on the side of the road; as soon as they saw the car they raised their heads and barked, with a few standing up and running towards the car wagging their tails. The car slowed down. A band of children then came darting from behind the trees, shouting and waving their hands.

"It's the *padrecito*, it's the *padrecito*," they were shouting. "He's come, he's here!"

"They seem to like you," said Fito. He wasn't feeling very confident. He wasn't used to young children, not children like that anyway. None of them wore any shoes. Sulky teenagers, younger children, toddlers clutching at their siblings' legs. Babies were carried by older siblings, looking severely undernourished. The whites of their eyes had a yellowish tint. Fito tried not to stare at any of their stick-insect arms and legs.

As they surrounded the car, Father Agnelli called out, "Get out of the way, little devils, I don't want to kill any of you today!" They squealed and ran in all directions, falling back and then coming onto the car again. It was clearly a game they had played often. As Father Agnelli eased himself out of the driver's seat, they surrounded him, holding up their hands for him to inspect, stretching their fingers, showing off their scrubbed nails. "Look, father, they're clean like you said!" "Not quite," he said, laughing, "but they will do." The kids beamed at him, and he turned to Fito and smiled. "As a doctor – sorry, as a future doctor, you'll sure appreciate this."

A few sulky, dangerous-looking young men came towards them. Fito remembered asking Father Agnelli, when he had first invited him to Villa 22, if it was dangerous. "Not for me or for those who accompany me," had been the reply. Now, as he saw the menacing youths approach, he couldn't help but wonder if they were there to cause trouble, and he then immediately felt ashamed for even thinking this. When they were near enough, Father Agnelli stopped in his tracks and a hush fell over all the children. Uh oh, Fito thought, noting how Father Agnelli stood upright at their sight, assuming a respectful stance.

"Oscar, Mario, José Luís, Pancho, this is Fito Goyena," said Father Agnelli, quite formally. "He's a doctor," he threw a warning look at Fito, "and he's with me. It's the first time he comes here."

The young men came one by one and shook hands with Fito. Their demeanor was so proper it was almost austere. It made him think of his grandfather, the Great Goyena, the father of the Nation.

"Welcome to our town," they said. "Doctor Rogelio is here," they informed the priest, as they shook his hand, too. Father Agnelli opened the car boot, got out bags and boxes, and gave them to the young men to carry with instructions. Some of them took the provisions and disappeared inside the maze of the shantytown. The rest took positions around the priest's car, standing guard. A quite unnecessary precaution, thought Fito, for who would steal anything from that battered car?

"You'd be surprised," said Father Agnelli laughing. Fito blushed, realising he'd been asking himself this aloud. But finally, he allowed himself to relax.

"And now to work," said Father Agnelli. "We'll visit a few people today and then we can go and see the school."

As they walked along the dirt roads of the villa, Fito looked around him in astonished, sombre silence. Of course he had heard about poverty and he knew there were poor people; he saw many of them in the capital every day, begging, peddling cheap trinkets, standing quietly at the edge of roads and train stations and bus stops, always in the periphery of his vision. So this is where they lived. Tin and cardboard rooms, thick plastic sacks of grain and animal feed turned into windows and doors. Pails and buckets of dirty water: Father Agnelli had told him there was no running water in the slum. No sewage either, judging by the evil-smelling pools of sludge and guck in the middle of the rutted roads. He carefully stepped around them thinking he should buy a pair of army boots if he was to come back here again.

There was hardly any privacy in the dwellings of the slum: thin walls, no doors but more torn sacks and bead curtains made of bottle caps and corks. All salvaged from the rubbish bins.

"Hello, Father. So you brought him here, have you?"

Fito recognized Rogelio Otamendi de Grant, in the company of another man, a doctor from Bolivia, and two women. One of them wore a nun's headscarf over a plain dark blue dress, very much like the one Lucía wore at school. Fito knew Rogelio socially and from medical school. Their mothers had also been at school together. Fito's mother disliked Alicia de Grant quite a lot, but Fito could never figure out why. The woman was a bit eccentric maybe, too educated for her class (too much education is generally wasted on a woman, was his father's motto), too liberal in her views, but she was quite correct and proper. Rogelio was his mother's spitting image. Fito had never met the father: he had been a distinguished professor of medicine but had died when Rogelio was still a child. Now he was greeting Fito warmly, as a friend and an equal. The two young men shook hands.

"Glad to see you here," he said. "We need all hands on deck. It's not easy work, you'll find."

Fito felt things were advancing too rapidly for him. Was he ever asked if he wanted to join? I'm here only as an observer, he wanted to say. I can't commit, I don't know if I want to. I haven't promised anybody anything. But he said none of these things.

They visited a few patients. One was an old woman with hardly any teeth left, her wrinkled face like a wise serpent's.

"How old do you think this woman is?" Father Agnelli asked Fito.

"In her late seventies?" Fito said politely, thinking that there was no way, she must be a hundred.

"She'll be forty next month," said Father Agnelli.

The same guessing game was played when they visited a little boy, barely able to walk. He was half-sitting, half-lying on something that looked liked a converted basket, more suitable for a pet than a child. This time I'll get it right, Fito thought. He can't be more than five. "Seven? Eight?"

"He's thirteen."

Most of the people they visited suffered from malnutrition. The children were often ravaged by parasites. The vinchuca bug was a big problem. There were cases of TB, of osteoporosis due to lack of calcium, even pellagra. While the doctors examined the patients – Fito helping to take blood pressure, open mouths and look down ulcerous throats, examine diseased skin and limbs – and the nurses administered medication, Father Agnelli sat next to the sick people and their families, held their hands, spoke to them softly. Fito was sure he was telling them all about God and the Holy Mother Church, until he heard this snippet of conversation:

"No way, *che*, Estudiantes will never stand for it. Two games in a row!"

He realized the priest was mostly talking about football, or telling jokes, or giving out recipes for broth.

There was a continuous movement in and out of the shacks: people who'd heard of the medical team's presence were coming to see them, to ask for their help.

"We visit as many as we can, but obviously one day a week is not enough," said Rogelio to Fito as they were walking out of a shanty. The drizzle was most welcome after stuffy rooms smelling of wet rags and paraffin oil. Father Agnelli joined them.

"If I could get a bottle of gas for each of the households," he said. "Just one bottle of gas, what difference it would make!"

"We treat quite a lot of burns here,'" Rogelio explained. "The people are trying to warm themselves and cook with whatever they can find. Fires are so frequent it's a disgrace. High infant mortality due to burn trauma." The Bolivian doctor was nodding, obviously familiar with the situation.

"Father, Father!"

A little boy came to them, breathless with running, glistening wet under the rain that was quickly becoming heavier.

"Yes, Chucho, we're coming just now," said Father Agnelli, tousling the boy's wet head. "Have you heard about our win? Racing FC for ever!" The boy made a derisory sound. He was wearing an old Independiente shirt. The priest looked at his watch. "Run along to the mess now, it's about time lunch was served. Tell the Señorita we'll be there sooner or later." The little boy ran ahead.

Father Agnelli turned to Fito. "Now this case is slightly different from the ones you've seen so far today. I only want you to remember that there is someone responsible for all this, and it's neither God nor bad luck."

Fito and Father Agnelli walked into a shack as grim and miserable as every other they'd been in, unique only in its combination of haphazard materials: plinth and tin and carton and cloth.

It was just the one room, appearing to contain few necessities, overcrowded with people. The hole in the wall that served as a window was covered with a very thick hemp sack which kept the light out but not the rain. There were about five or six children of all ages sitting on the floor or standing against the window.

"Why are you all still here?" the priest asked in a mock-angry tone. "Lunch is being served as we speak."

The children made an effort to smile and file out, the older ones carrying or dragging along the younger. There were some women from the neighborhood; they too left. A middle-aged woman was sitting on a low chair against the wall. She held a very puny baby in her arms. The baby was mewling weakly. She was trying to feed it a bottle with something greenish yellow in it. Fito stared. Was that *yerba mate*? And was the baby a new-born? The woman's skin was clinging tightly to her haggard features. There was another person in the room. A woman, lying on the only bed, with her face turned towards the wall. Fito couldn't see her very well, she was all covered up with a dirty sheet, but he could see her long black tangled hair. He knew somehow that she was very young and that she was the mother of the baby.

"She won't even look at him, Father," said the woman holding the baby. "She won't even lay eyes on him."

"Don't worry, Imelda my dear, don't worry," said Father Agnelli, stepping outside and making a sign to one of the nurses. She came in with a box of formula milk in powder, a new baby bottle, and a brand new small tin pan.

"Sister Clara will boil the water and will show you how to prepare the milk," said Father Agnelli. "Don't you cry now. All shall be well, all manners of things shall be well."

He approached the bed and sat on the edge of it. "Gladys," he said softly. "Gladys, daughter, wake up." There was no movement from the bed. The woman's body was as immobile as a corpse, yet it must have been soft and pliable not long ago. Fito was looking on. He could comprehend the girl was seriously ill, maybe dying.

The baby must have been hers. She didn't even have the strength to look at it.

"Gladys, daughter, wake up. Come back to your mother who loves you," Father Agnelli was saying, again with little success. His hands were wrapped tight around a rosary, counting beads, almost imperceptibly. He never moved nearer the girl lying on the bed, never touched her, only spoke to her in a soft voice, calling her back from wherever she was, and counting his beads, and waiting patiently. Rogelio made a sign to Fito and they both walked out.

"Gladys is thirteen," he said, lighting a cigarette and offering Fito one, who declined. "She went to work as a servant with a family in Barrio Norte. I don't know them, they are not...I didn't know them personally. A couple with two teenage sons. They took turns raping her, both the sons and the father. When they realized she was pregnant, they accused her of being a whore and kicked her out. She nearly died having that poor baby."

Fito looked at his colleague, feeling that the muscles of his face had long been rendered incapable of registering any reaction. Numb.

"The woman of the house, the wife – she knew all along but did nothing. 'Well, men will be men,' she told me when I went to speak to her about it. 'The little minx had it coming to her. She was always wiggling her ass at all the men. She had more than one boyfriend. But it's my fault, giving work to a no-account from the slums. I tell you, she deserved it.' I'm quoting her verbatim."

Fito said nothing but regretted having refused that cigarette. It would have given his mouth and hand something to do.

"She had bruises and all indications of sexual violence," Rogelio went on. "All black and blue. I took her to my hospital to give birth. She suffers from depression, a very serious case. I don't think she'll pull through. All those children you saw here are her younger brothers and sisters. Only the baby is hers, and she doesn't even want to look at him. You heard what her mother said. He may yet die, poor soul. They all depended on her for a living, too. Imelda cleans a few houses now and then, but if she goes out to work now, it's certain death for the baby."

"And the...the perpetrators of this?"

"We thought of taking legal action against them, but apparently there is not much we can do. How can you prove rape to a court who doesn't want to look at evidence? It will be her word against theirs: a poor little girl from the slums against respectable citizens. They'll claim her injuries were caused by a boyfriend, some delinquent youth here in the slums, and she wants to make money out of them. You know what it's like."

Fito looked around him, avoiding Rogelio's eye, feeling guilty though he didn't know what for. He thought of all the servants who ever lived in the same house as he, under the same roof, yet they had no more say in what was going on there than rats living behind the skirting boards. They had a life, too, and families, and things they needed done for them, yet they had to serve him and his own family all day long, every day, with very little time left for themselves. At least we treat them well, he thought, there is nothing of that sort going on in our house.

But of course, he'd heard the rumors about his father; he'd sensed his mother's stony face on certain occasions. And was it not true that Milagros avoided his father and kept Lucía well out of his way? Perhaps Milagros had heard similar stories to the one Fito had just been told, and was fearful for her daughter.

Fito brought to mind the sullen look his presence could sometimes conjure on Pablo's face: Pablo, the Young Suárez, who was normally so cheery and good-natured. Pablo, father of his beloved, who was constantly at the Goyenas' beck and call, living to serve them. Was he afraid of what Fito might do to his daughter? Had circumstances been different, had Pablo Suárez been a man of equal social standing, it would be Fito who would be afraid of him, eager for his good opinion; he would call him "sir" and tremble at his sight. And now it was just, "Pablo, get me the car," or "Pablo, take me to university." The father of Lucía.

He tried to chase away the idea of Lucía living in a house like
that poor girl inside had once lived in. The beautiful, sweet Lucía.
So trusting, so smiling. She was safe with them. And yet, and yet.
Was he much better than those other men? They only did to her
what he often imagined he'd love to do to her, but of course, never
without her consent. But would she be able to refuse him in the
first place, given his position?

On the way home, he confessed to Father Agnelli. He told him
everything about his love for Lucía, and his fear that this was an
impure love, not much better than the criminal lust of those men
in the Barrio Norte.

"Ah, but there's a great difference," Father Agnelli said.
"Thoughts and deeds are quite different things, remember. For a
young man to resist temptation in the flesh is almost superhuman,
and you are fighting a good fight there. The thoughts that come to
you, you can't help. Just don't give them space and time in your
mind. But of course there is a solution to every problem. St. Paul
has it for you. Celibacy is not for everyone. You can always marry
her, you know."

"Me, married! To Lucía! We grew up together. We're like brother
and sister."

"But you are not brother and sister, are you?"

"No, of course we are not."

"Well then."

But she's the daughter of our servant, was the first thought that
came to Fito's mind, and my mother and father would disinherit
me if I married a servant's girl. And then he thought: so what?

16

Lucía's Diary

The house was quiet. Señora Ramona had settled upstairs in her room for her afternoon nap, and Milagros had made sure she had everything she might need within easy reach: her cup of camomile tea with half a calming pill in it for good measure, her rosary, and her books of sentimental chivalric stories. Pablo was downstairs at the porter's, already being treated to his first drink of the day. The young people were all away to university and school, not expected for another hour at least.

Milagros went into the utility room, placed a heavy tin bucket behind the door with a jar of water on top, opened the dark cupboard in the furthest recess of the wall and got inside. She strained her ears to listen for any unusual sounds, but there weren't any. Then she put her hand inside the front of her dress and pulled out a notebook. On its blue cover there was a white label with garlands of flowers drawn on its borders. In the middle was written *The Diary of Lucía Eva Suárez Riquelme*. Milagros took another look at the door, again strained her ears for any sounds, and when she was satisfied all was quiet, she took a small torch out of her apron pocket, opened the notebook at a page towards the end and began to read.

14 September, 1975

Dear Diary,

I know I haven't written to you for such a long time, but I have been so busy at school you can't imagine! A history and geography test within the same week, and two essays to write about Sarmiento's Facundo. *Such a good book! What a great man and a great writer Sarmiento was! Profesora Bustos says my essay is probably going to get first prize in the school's annual competition! Mami and Papi are so proud of me.*

Something rather unusual happened yesterday. I met Don Faustino (not the hero of the book!) in front of the lift as I was coming in from school. He touched my chin with his hand (not in a nasty way at all, contrary to what malicious tongues would say!). He asked me how I was getting along with my studies. He said I had grown up very much lately. He said he heard I was a very good student and whenever I wanted I could go take any book from his library upstairs. Any book! Don Faustino! And he looked at me in such a strange way (NOT IN THAT WAY, OKAY). I think he looks at me in this strange way whenever he sees me, and it makes me feel so...so different. As if anything was possible for me in life. I don't know if you understand. I don't think anybody can understand. Then he said, "Don't tell your mother. It will be our little secret." I wonder if he knows how much Mami dislikes him. She has never said that in so many words but I know. I see how her face changes when he is around: it becomes closed like a wall without windows.

I wonder what SHE would think of that if she knew. The other day she scolded me because the mending of the little embroidered tea towels was not up to her high standards. "A girl of that age and not to be able to mend towels properly!" she boomed in that bullying voice of hers. No wonder Silvina hates her. I have better things in mind for my future, thank you, I should have said to her. I held my tongue, of course. Mami was sending daggers across the room with her eyes. Mami always tells me (in secret, when SHE is out of sight or hearing) that becoming a school teacher beats being a lady's maid any day and I shouldn't pay attention to HER nagging but be well-behaved and do my work as unobtrusively as possible. Mami is a bit of a scolder though. Papi, on the other hand, supports me in everything. That's why I adore him!

I have to go now, I must help Silvina get ready for that party. Oh, if only I was going to the party too! But Fito said, "They're just a bunch of idiots, Lucía, you don't want to be mixing with that crowd." If he is saying it, it must be worth something. A lot, in fact.

Yours,
Lucía

October 16, 1975

Dear Diary,

Look at the calendar! In less than six weeks' time we'll all be at Alta Gracia. Thank God for that! How I miss our little house there, and the beautiful Big House, and the gardens, and the woods with the pond! How I miss Abuelita, may she rest in peace, and all the good people I've known all my life! Silvina and I and Fito will go swimming in the pond, and we'll fish in the river too (I don't much like it, to be honest, but they both love it and could spend hours doing it – VERY boring, but there you go, that's life). Fito said he will teach me to ride this summer, and Silvina promised to lend me her horse sometimes. I told Mami and she scowled. don't you ever forget your place, her looks said, though she would never utter these words out loud. I'm sure she's thinking more about HER reaction: SHE won't approve of such a thing. I know in my heart that Don Faustino wouldn't mind. Somehow I believe he'd take my side. He's always on our side. I've heard the stories they tell about him. If they're true...Even if they are, who could blame him, with such a shrew for a wife? (If SHE ever finds this diary and reads it, I'm dead!) At any rate he's never tried to do anything funny with me. Fito says his dad is not a bad guy, just lives in the wrong place and time. He should be a nobleman in Florence in the times of the Medicis, he says. But Silvina says her father is a fossil and her mother a witch. She seems to love Mami more than her own mother. How many times she's told me, "Lucía, you're so lucky to have Milagros for a mother." Of course she doesn't have to put up with her all the time as I do!

Fito gave me La Razón de mi Vida *to read. What a wonderful book! It's really opened my eyes. Evita was a great woman, a saint. I've hidden it well at the bottom of the old linen chest that nobody ever uses.*

Yours,
Lucía

28 October, 1975

It is very late at night now so I'm writing with the help of a torch. The whole house is quiet. I think they had guests tonight, but Mami doesn't allow me out of our room after hours. I wish I could see if there is any light under Fito's door. I like to imagine him in his room, always well-ordered and quiet like a church, sitting at his desk studying hard. He will be a doctor. Imagine that! Maybe I should study to be a nurse rather than a teacher, after all.

I hardly saw him today. He left for uni early in the morning and only had time for a short greeting and smile as I was taking their breakfast into the dining room. But I looked out for him by the front door as he was leaving, and we quickly arranged to meet after school tomorrow; I'll take the Subte down to the medical school and we'll have a quick coffee at the café. The hours seem long, endless, until then.

I still have some work for school to finish. I should have done it earlier, but Silvina wanted to go shopping and she asked me to go with her to help carry the bags. In truth, she wanted to meet with those new friends of hers in the bookshop of Avenida Corrientes. If SHE knew where her daughter was, her hair would stand on end. It was kind of exciting, to be honest; the meeting took place in a room hidden behind a bookcase. Like in those films with spies! There were posters of President Perón and Evita and Ernesto Che Guevara de la Serna on the walls. I told Silvina I didn't think it was a good idea to be there, and what would her mother say? But she laughed and said, "Come on Lucía, since when do we care what my mother says? Besides, this is just a meeting about traditional recipes. We want to publish a book," she laughed. I didn't really buy it but I said nothing. Silvina is capable of anything, after all, even being interested in publishing traditional cookery books!

There were five of them. A young man with long hair and a beard was Silvina's friend – and perhaps something more? I think he was trying to look like Che, most students do these days! He eyed me up and down and asked Silvina if I had any idea of traditional cooking. She said that I was okay and had "the right ideas." I'm not aware that I have any ideas at all, especially about cooking. They should have asked my mother, not me! But truth is I generally do agree with Silvina's ideas. Who would dare disagree with her? Sometimes I think she's much more like HER than she'd like to admit, though of course she's good and kind, and SHE is anything but. The looks SHE casts me when Fito and I are in the room at the same time! Anyway, I stayed there with them for an excruciatingly boring hour. They were talking about the best way to prepare empanadas criollas, the way they make them in Salta. How many ingredients for twenty-two empanadas, if they should use tomato sauce, how to cut the meat and the cheese – that sort of thing. The only thing I said was they should ask my mother: she was the best cook and a specialist in empanadas. *They thought this was very funny! I noticed that the guy with the beard, the one who tried to look like a subversive, was devouring my legs with his eyes, the insolent man! Silvina noticed too, but didn't say anything. I hope not all of her friends are such creeps! His name was Cacho, though Silvina called him Gustavo once, which made him very angry!* "Compañera, *this is inexcusable carelessness,*" *he growled. They called each other* compañero *and* compañera *all the time, so I don't really know what the others were called.*

Afterwards we had to run down to Florida to buy some stuff at Harrods at the last moment, to avert HER suspicions. SHE would want to inspect the shopping later. As we walked down the street on the way back, many men were whistling and saying silly things. One called out at Silvina, "Hey, you're not bad yourself, but your little sister is a tasty morsel!" How embarrassing! I hope Silvina didn't get mad. Whenever we met policemen or soldiers on the street, she muttered "Pigs" under her breath. That scared me a bit. Anyway, we returned home without any trouble and nobody suspected anything. I decided I don't want anything to do with Silvina's friends. I didn't enjoy the looks of that man, and if Silvina likes him and he likes me she might be angry...I must stop, Mami is stirring and I don't want to wake her up.

Yours,
Lucía

2 November, 1975

The spring is finally here and the jacarandas have started to cover the whole city with fragrant lilac flowers. The sky is blue and full of fluffy white clouds. But my heart is heavy and all seems bleak and desolate. Because Fito is not going with the rest of us to Alta Gracia this summer. I overheard HER telling Mami this morning to start preparing everybody else's things for the summer, but not Fito's, because he was going to Europe.

To Europe. A million miles from here. A whole summer without seeing him, without hearing his soft voice, without his affectionate smiles and wise advice.

Cursed Europe.

All my happiness for the summer is gone. I have nothing more to write today, or ever.

Lucía

November 5, 1975

Oh, wonderful, wonderful happiness! The spring is smiling again, the world is a beautiful place full of harmony and music. Love is everywhere. In the trees in the park, singing in the branches. In the flame-red flowers of the palo borracho. In the song of the birds early in the morning when I walk to school.

There is nothing more wonderful in the world than love. There is nothing more precious than love. I only want to sing and dance all day. I want to embrace everybody in the street. I want to kiss all the children; I want to hug all the old ladies who go to the market dragging their shopping trolleys. I want to be forever kind, and good, and smiling. Because he loves me. He loves me. HE LOVES ME!!!

Last night, as I was sitting at the fire escape stairs doing my homework, or rather, looking at the buildings around me and thinking how ugly they look when you see them from the back, all gray walls with black humidity marks and dusty cobwebbed windows, surrounded by a sea of TV aerials and rusty chimneys, he came and sat by me. My heart was beating so fast. I didn't dare look him in the face because I was sure my feelings were plainly written all over, and I couldn't bear it if he knew. We sat there in silence for a while, and then he took my hand and said, "Lucía, I will tell you something I don't want anybody else to know. Promise me you won't tell anyone." I mumbled something or other. Then he said, "Promise." I promised. And he said, "I'm not coming to Alta

Gracia this summer with you all." "I know, your mother told my mother," I said, my voice barely a whisper. He went on: "I told my folks I was going away to Europe. But I want you to know that I'm not really going to Europe." "You're not?' "No, I'm not, and you are the only one who knows, except Silvina, of course." Of course. "Well, do you want to know where I will be?"

I didn't know what to answer to that, so I said nothing. Did I want to know? What if he said he would be somewhere with one of those girls SHE wanted him to be with? In a fancy place like Punta del Este, or on a cruise aboard the luxurious yacht of one of their friends? But something in my heart told me that this was not what I was going to hear. I remained silent. He squeezed my hand. "I will stay here, in the city. Father Agnelli and I are organising a relief group to work in the shantytowns." I said nothing, but my hopes rose a little. "The poor need us, Lucía," he went on. "They have nobody else to think of them. People like me can do a lot for them. We should do everything in our power for them. We have an obligation to our fellow men and women in need. But families like mine don't understand. Papá is lost in his own world, and Mama — well, you know her. I'm not saying she's bad or heartless. She just thinks that's the order of things, that's how God wanted things to be. But He doesn't, Lucía. Our first duty to our fellow man is charity. And it is also our first duty to our country. How are we going to move ahead, to become the powerful nation in the world we were meant to be with all this terrible injustice against the weak and the needy?"

I didn't speak. I just listened to him, and noticed how the sun turned his light brown curls into pure gold. He looked like an angel to me. That's what he is, an angel.

"They wouldn't understand if I told them," he went on. "They would be concerned. They would think I'm like my sister. I may not agree with Silvina on the principles, but I do agree with her on the actions. After all, Father Camilo Torres Restrepo was a Marxist, too, and he was a saint. Do you understand?" I nodded

yes. It doesn't matter that I didn't really. All I wanted was to hear the fervor in his voice, and to see his beautiful eyes the color of caramel shine with the fire of his conviction.

And then this is what happened:

He opened my hand and kissed my palm. I felt like I would melt. The touch of his lips on my hand sent shivers down my spine. And he said, "Lucía, will you help me? Will you come with me to share my work and bring relief to those who most need it?" There was no breath left in my body. "I...I don't know if I can," I said softly, looking into his eyes as if magnetised. "Yes, you can," he said. "You are such a wonderful girl, so intelligent, so beautiful, so caring. I have seen how you think of others first, how you put yourself last always. I have seen how you submit to my crazy sister's whims with such sweetness. I have seen how patient you are with the demands of my mother. How you seem to love those who least deserve it, my father among them."

Was he saying all these things for me? I could scarcely believe my ears.

"I have known you all my life," he said. "I know there are people who will think it's not right for someone from a family like mine to promise himself to a girl of your position in society. But they don't know you, Lucía. All they see is that your mother is a maid, and your father...well, you know what your father is. And how could he be any better, if he's faced exploitation and injustice all his life?"

Poor Papi! I felt a pang in my heart for him. But of course Fito was right. Still, it hurt a little — only a little thorn among the roses, that's all. The important thing is he was asking me to be with him. He and I together! What more could I need?

"Father Agnelli said a young man like me should either marry young or become a priest. I know I can't become a priest, Lucía. But as for the first option..."

I held my breath. I felt my face burn hot. I didn't dare lift my eyes to him.

"Will you marry me, Lucía?"

I could barely whisper "yes" because the breath had nearly left my body.

And then he kissed me.

Oh! I can't describe this. His lips on mine. His face so near. I could see little hazel spots dance in the pupils of his eyes. Oh, God, how I love him! I'll do anything for him. Anything he asks me to. I'll go to the ends of the world for him. I'll face HER wrath, my mother's sadness (though how can she be sad if she knows I'm so happy?), anything for him, all for him.

So it's all arranged now. I'm staying in the city, too, and Silvina is in it as well; she will say she needs me on that cruise she's supposedly going on. Fito and I will devote ourselves to the poor, and to each other, and be happy for ever.

I must go now, because I hear Mami coming and maybe she'll start asking awkward questions about me being locked in the room for so long.

With love,
Lucía, the happiest girl in the world

Milagros felt the sweat running down her back, between her breasts, pricking her scalp through the hair. The chill of the dark utility room had turned into a fiery furnace. Her knees gave way and she found herself sitting on the bare stone floor, unable to move. Her thoughts were racing madly inside her head that felt hollow and sore. She'd had her worries, yes, but not like this, nothing like...

Lucía. My Lucía. My little girl. How can this be happening? Did she...have they...? And to think that Fito looks so good, so innocent, such a loving boy, devoted to his mother, to me, his old nanny, and so kind to the poor, so sweet-natured.

But he is a man, after all. A man, his father's son. Damned men! Curse them all. Why did he have to do this to my little girl? Promise marriage to her too! He could have had anybody. If only he knew! If *they* knew! What can I do? How can I tell them? My little girl, my little boy, my favorite…Oh, damned, damned man. Look how the innocent are paying for your sins now. And if she falls pregnant? And if she has a baby? What sort of baby will that be? A monster, no doubt. Terrible creatures come from the union of blood relatives. There was this poor thing in the village once, Milagros remembered, half-human and half-fish: a peon had raped his own daughter and that's what came of it, an abomination. Everybody had been speechless with horror. Thankfully the poor thing didn't survive…

And all this other stuff. The dangerous stuff. Him playing Jesus Christ with the poor in the shantytowns. Look what Jesus Christ got for His pains. A cross and a tomb, that's what He got! There will be no resurrection for them though! And he has to drag my little girl into that, too! Damn him! Damn him! And what is that Silvina up to again? She's playing games, too, her mother all over again, riding inside the house on horseback, but what has she got to fear? She's a Goyena, and an Iribarren. The police, the army, they make subversives vanish from the face of the earth. But they will not dare touch the rich and powerful. They will just slap her wrist, there, bad girl, don't you ever do it again, now go in peace. But my Lucía, my Lucía…Good Mother of God, what is going on? Where was she now, out shopping with Silvina? She has no idea what she's getting into. How can I protect my little girl? I've only got her, I've got nobody else in the world, oh God, this husband you gave me was a useless son of a–

Forgive me, Lord. But please, help me now, you owe it to me, Holy Virgin of Luján, please help me to save my little girl from the lions, please help me, oh Lord, please.

But first she had to destroy the evidence. She tore the cover off the notebook and ripped the pages into shreds, then into small pieces, till they were a heap of confetti. She trampled on the hard cover; she soaked it in a bucket till it became pulp, then she trampled on it a little more till it was an unrecognisable mass of material. She wrapped a disgusting old rag around it and dumped it down the incinerator hole. She made as if to throw the shreds of paper after it, but changed her mind. Instead, she took an old pan from the cupboard, put the shredded diary pages in there, poured clear alcohol and a few pieces of cotton-wool over it, then threw a match on them. The material caught fire. She repeated the process till every little piece of paper was reduced to crumbly black ash. Then she emptied the ash into the marble washing basin, turned all the taps on and watched grimly as the ash went down the drain, until the last particle was gone.

17

Police Report

Capital Federal

URGENT. One copy. To be destroyed immediately after reading. We submit for your consideration.

Subversive activity detected in bookshop La Palabra Poderosa on Avenida Corrientes 3748, Capital Federal, registered to the name of Infanta López de Benedetti, wife of Donato Pascuale Benedetti, a subversive well-known to our authority, and son of Emilio Donato Benedetti, anarchist, organizer of unions and agitator, main instigator of strike at Urquiza factory in 1939. Donato Benedetti has escaped arrest and is now an exile in Italy. His nephew Gustavo Francisco López-Ortega is suspected leader of faction. López-Ortega is high up in the Montonero hierarchy. Known also as Cacho, el Negro, Che, and Rogero. Secret meetings monitored since November 1975. Faction members meet under cover of traditional cookery club. Subversive material circulates via bookshop disguised as recipes. Highly dangerous faction. Possibly implicated in bloody incident in the province of Salta on April 15, 1976, attack against police precinct 22. Imminent action advised. Utter care and caution suggested: member of faction known as Judit or Faustina or Reina may be special case. Real name unknown as yet but strong possibility person is of very high social standing. I repeat, utmost care and caution in the handling is advised. The Chief will deal with this particular member himself. All other members of the faction, confirmed or suspected, shall be disposed of in the usual manner.

(Private and confidential report by Chief of Police Daniel Hipólito Balseri to Comisario Mariano Cándido Arias, Security Services, Ministry of Interior Affairs)

18

The Black Pit

One, two, three, four, five, six, seven, eight, nine, ten, eleven, twelve. Turn right. One, two, three, four, five, six, seven, eight. Turn right again. One, two, three, four, five. Stop, lift foot or you stumble. One, two, three, you're there. The smell told her that already. But why was she there? Did she ask to be taken? It was usually just the bucket in the room. No, this was not the toilet. It was the other place. It was smelly, too. She didn't remember asking to go. But maybe she did and she couldn't remember. She was so forgetful lately. It's not easy to remember when it's always dark. She'd been in the dark for...how long? Had to be three days at least. She'd eaten how many times? Three? Once it was that sandwich, if it was a sandwich indeed and not a pizza – was it a pizza? No, the pizza was on the second day. It was cold but all the better, she always liked her pizza cold. Mami would make the pizza and she'd say, "I'm going to enjoy mine more tomorrow morning." "What a strange kid," Papi would say, "who's she taking after, not me, that's for sure." Then she had something else. It was hours and hours later and she'd slept twice since then. How long she slept was a mystery, she just couldn't remember. All she knew was she was getting the lift to go to Fito's room which was magically transported into that tall building opposite the shopping centre. She'd never been inside that building before but she thought that's what it looked like on the inside: it looked so sinister from the outside but look, this was just an apartment block like all the others. Then the lift stopped and she knew it was the upstairs floor and she made to push the door to get out but she couldn't reach the door because it was quite far from the cubicle and she had to lean very far to do it but couldn't because there was this gap between herself and the lift door and even if she did manage to push the door how was she going to reach it, she'd have to jump over that gap and under her feet she could see floors and floors of the apartment building all going down to the abyss and she could see the door openings on the other floors and they were so well-stacked one under the other, neat and regular like the cells in a honeycomb, an abandoned honeycomb waxy and yellowish brown, and then she realized the truth, this *was* a honeycomb, a giant one, and she was trapped in there and she was exasperated, thinking: this shouldn't be allowed, they should have placed a sign or something to warn people about this, and then she was awake because somebody had been shaking her shoulders and they were saying something to her but she couldn't understand what because the sounds came all muffled and she didn't want to hear anyway, she wanted to shrink back into her little corner of darkness and go away, please let me go I've done nothing I know nothing, I don't even know what you're saying to me, but they kept yelling at her. It was better in the darkness. When they pulled the hood off her head the naked bulb was a monster eating her eyeballs, and she cried out, and they laughed and said, Ah the little bird has started to sing see how much louder she'll be singing soon, and she was scared really truly scared although she thought there was nothing worse that could happen after what happened that day and they were laughing and it was bright and she was so scared and everything hurt, every bit and piece of her was hurting, and there was nowhere to turn and there was a permanent scream in her head and sometimes it bawled for Mami, and sometimes it bellowed in a voice she didn't recognise, Sons of bitches leave me alone, and sometimes it shrieked, Fito Fito Fito I'm here look I'm standing right here can't you see me, and then it was only the howling of the wind or of wild animals, wolves or jackals.

Where are we? whispered the girl into her ear or was it her who whispered in hers, Do you know where we are? and then another voice said, Nobody knows we are here, this is not on any maps, they came in the night, I've heard this has happened to others before and now it's our turn. But she had nothing to say, all she did was count in her head, one two three four how many steps to the toilet and how many steps into that other room and how many steps from the wall to the bed and then how many steps into the darkness and how many into the pain was all she could think of, not of what happened, and she must not worry about anything, your Mami will take care of everything, she's somebody your Mami, she won't let them take you too, you know she won't, and if Silvina hadn't yelled at them but where was she now, and Fito, Fito, that girl whispered into her ear and she said the men were held here but in another wing, she saw them, they brought them in the middle of the night and they were legion, and then she laughed into her ear but no she didn't, nobody was laughing here, she had dreamed that too, she had dreamed the girl was opening her mouth to laugh and her mouth was transformed into a cavern and there were no teeth only darkness and she wanted to sink in there and lose herself for ever.

One, two, three, four, fi – she couldn't count anymore. She'd pray she were dead if she believed in God, you puta daughter of a *puta*, but in here he was the only God, he was your God and master and see how you like that you godless subversive bitch, he yells no he whispers, and then she extended her arm to push the door of the lift and her arm was caught in the gap and mangled and wrenched away and she heard the scream in her head, Is this your voice? And then she heard a whisper and it was that girl and she said don't worry here's a little water and it was dark, and the water was spilled all over her clothes and she couldn't drink anyway because her throat screamed and her stomach screamed and then again it was one two three four into the darkness, don't be afraid of the dark Mami said, don't be afraid my baby I'm here with you, look, little moon is coming out the clouds and when she's in the middle of the sky she'll be watching over you. And then she was awake again but she had been spinning, where was she spinning round and round and round, my baby, Mami said, and Don Faustino said, Milagros, give the girl a fresh hot cake she must be hungry, studying for hours and hours, she deserves it, and there were cakes fresh and hot from the oven and she reached with her arm to grab one but it was darkness again and she was lifted up feet barely touching the ground and someone shouted, Prisoner L35 you are to be questioned now and you can't count steps because your feet are not touching the ground.

19

Looking for Her

Grand Bourg, Provincia de Buenos Aires

Milagros woke up with a start. It was time to go to work. But no, it was the middle of the night. The large tin alarm clock ticked and tocked. That's what woke her up. Or maybe it was the creaking and the groaning and the heaving of the decrepit little house. Sighing in its sleep, like a very old, very unhappy person. She stared at the ceiling. Nothing had changed since last night, when she had stared at it once again. She lay in her bed, she stared, she listened to the wind swishing over the flat roof of the house. The light was on over the outside door; she could see its pale orange glow out of the window over the wooden porch. It would be there till the sky outside her window became less solid, till the darkness began to dissolve like ink in water. She waited, stared, listened. Nobody would be coming again tonight. The light was on in vain. Yesterday, Pablo was angry with her about it. Again.

"Don't you see you are driving yourself and everybody else crazy?" he yelled. "What good does it do? Why do you want the fucking light on? It's no use, can't you see? It's no use. She doesn't know where we are. She's never been to this place before. How can she find us? How can she come back home?"

And then he started to cry, to bawl out loud like a beaten child. She just stood and looked at him and felt her insides harden to stone. She didn't have time for tears and helpless shouting. She could only wait. The light would be on – screw the electricity bills – for as long as it took.

She decided to get up and dress herself and have breakfast. The blue ring of fire in the dark was a comforting sight. She always used to get up earlier than everybody, to prepare the fire and heat the water, back when they lived in the Señora's house. They had their breakfast long before the Family had theirs. *Mate* for Pablo and herself, milk and cocoa for Lucía. But now there was no need. They didn't live at the Señora's anymore. And after the fight yesterday, Pablo had left. God knows where he was now. Crashing out on someone's floor, maybe, or in an abandoned shed somewhere. Everybody had been avoiding them recently. They knew or guessed what happened and they didn't want to be tarred with the same brush. Subversives. A word that equals prison, or worse.

A creak outside, a metallic sound as if a latch had been lifted from the yard door, and her heart leapt and began to beat frantically. Not for long. It was just the neighbor bringing out his cart, getting ready for his rounds of collecting cardboard and paper for the factories. She knew that. It happened every day at this time. When would she get used to it? Would she ever get used to it? Nobody was coming. Nobody.

She stared at a spot on the floor, congealed liquid of some sort, milky coffee, or cocoa milk, or blood, and she knelt down and scrubbed and scrubbed and scrubbed, till the water boiled over and put out the gas flame with a hiss, filling the room with an acrid stench that made her eyes water.

The man at the desk was having lunch. He had spread a chequered green and white towel in front of him, and he had placed a large plastic square box right in the centre, out of which he was picking huge dripping *empanadas*. They don't look very good, Milagros thought, underdone, yellow and pasty, not the deep golden brown they should be. He swallowed them in two bites, and as he sank his teeth into them the filling squelched out and oily sauce ran down his chin and onto his hands. He kept at it without looking at Milagros once. She knew there was nothing she could do but try to ignore him as he ignored her. It was impossible, though: all that squelching and munching filled the room and left no air for her to breathe. She swallowed hard. She gritted her teeth trying her best not to scream. She imagined jumping on the man's throat, slapping him, trampling on his food and spitting on it; she imagined suffocating him with his stupid towel and banging the stupid plastic box on his head like a hat. This offered some comfort.

"Come again tomorrow, we know nothing. No, there's nobody of that name here." "Sorry, madam. I wish I could help you. Leave me your address and telephone number. You have no telephone? Anywhere we could contact you? I'll do my best, don't worry." "Get a move on, my good woman, don't you see we're busy here? How are we supposed to know where your daughter is? If you ask me, she and her friends have probably robbed a bank and are living it up abroad now. You should know, you're the mother. The nerve of you people, you bring them up to be subversives and then come down here and pester us with your whining." "Go to office number 12 upstairs. Go to office 23 on the second floor. You've just been? It's not my responsibility, sorry. Wait till the Lieutenant Colonel can see you. Maybe tomorrow, maybe on Monday." "Don't you know who your daughter's friends were? Can you not give us any of their names? It would help her, you know." "I think you're delusional, personally. Watch too many American films. Disappeared persons? Nobody's disappeared." "If they took her away, she must have done something to deserve it."

Whenever Milagros passed outside that building, she turned her head away. The dark red color of the brick walls hurt her eyes.

On the large marble staircase, once a brilliant white and now gray with soot and dust, armed soldiers patrolled with guns always at the ready. There was always a long line of people waiting for their IDs to be checked before they got in. The long tail of a wounded beast. From up high, hundreds of square windows eyed the waiting crowd suspiciously.

Sometimes Milagros went up those stairs again in her dreams. She could feel them – in the dream – soft under her feet. She looked back and she saw her footsteps clearly marked on their surface. She climbed and climbed and the stairs seemed to have no end. As she got nearer the top, she could see the seasons change, children turning into adults, shops shutting down and opening again selling different merchandise, houses giving over their place, like humble guests at a wedding, to apartment towers. By the time she was at the top of the stairs, in front of the cast iron doors, years had passed and she was exhausted. The door was always shut and she had to knock. She heard the echo of the knocking travel through the immense doors down endless corridors, rebounding off walls sweating with humidity and floors smelling of disinfectant. She found herself walking down the corridor, following the echo. The corridor was branching out to other winding corridors. Some came to a grinding halt in front of blind brick walls. Others led her to gray iron doors which she pushed timidly, only to find out that they led to further corridors, or to the bottom of stairwells, and sometimes to small inner courtyards with stagnant pools of rainwater.

There were always people in the corridors. They stood and waited for hours leaning against walls. They walked up and down the stairs and wore them down with their footsteps. They peeked in and out of rooms. Their faces she could never see clearly in the dream, blurred and unfocused. But she didn't need to see them. She knew exactly what they look like. They looked like her.

There was also an old ponderous contraption made of glass and wrought iron, moaning and groaning as it went slowly up and down. The passengers placed their open palms on its transparent walls: captives wanting out. Milagros never took the lift, even if she felt her soles burning with exhaustion. She climbed up the labyrinthine stairs. Then she found herself upstairs, in a linoleum-floored antechamber that smelled, paradoxically, of hospital. This was where the Lieutenant Colonel office was. She felt like a fly about to be swallowed by a spider. She could feel its poisonous breath in the cold darkness beginning to conquer her, turning her insides into stone. Just before she walked into the spider's deadly embrace, she woke up.

20

Naval Hospital

There was a girl in the room, and she was about to give birth. The Lieutenant Colonel had forbidden all mention of it to anybody. Only Isabel and Dr. Figueroa knew about it. They were going to deal with it by themselves.

"What if there are complications?"

"I trust you and the doctor. You'll make sure there won't be any complications," he said. He smiled pleasantly, his colorless eyes glinting like steel. Isabel couldn't help shivering. It was a cold day, and it was even colder in there all of a sudden.

She wasn't allowed to speak to the girl, who was guarded round the clock. The cadets looked ahead in stony silence but Isabel could see their eyes following her everywhere. She couldn't even whisper. Every move, every word would be reported, she was well aware of that.

They said the girl was one of the subversives. It was for everyone's good, they assured her. "For your children, Isabel. They must grow in a peaceful, law-abiding country. You owe it to them. For the poor child's own good, too. Offspring of subversive parents. What could she have to offer to a baby, I ask you."

These people, these subversives, where did they all come from, what holes did they used to live in? Isabel wondered.

Though to tell the truth the girl didn't look like those desperate souls from the northwest, where the land was so poor they chewed leaves like goats. No, she looked different. Perhaps she was beautiful once. She was certainly very young. It was her first. She was all puffy now, dark bags under her eyes. Her skin was gray. Isabel didn't think she had long to live. But many pregnant women – to tell the truth, most of them, even under the best of circumstances – looked awful when they were near birth. Judging from what Isabel herself looked like, a real fright. All the sleeplessness and strange discomforts and extra weight, though this one hadn't put much on. Who knew if the baby would make it? This would definitely be a tiny one. Isabel's ankles had looked like huge balls, so swollen. She couldn't even put any shoes on. But the girl was slender like a twig, apart from the bump. Her ankles were still tiny. Her hair was stringy and dull. Most of the time she looked at the ceiling. She had wide eyes, a startling color: the color of pure honey, the sort you got straight out of the honeycomb. Isabel remembered her aunt's *quinta*, where her uncle was a beekeeper, God rest his soul. They used to eat the fresh honey with a stick, or with their fingers. Most people didn't know honey was bad for babies, for very young children. A boy in the village had died of it. So many things they didn't know in the old times. Thank the Virgin, they were more enlightened now.

Sometimes the girl placed her hands on her belly. She hummed softly. Isabel knew what she was doing: singing to the baby. The cadets just stood to attention, looking at nothing. She smiled when she did that. She didn't seem to know anyone was there.

Of course at first she had tried to talk to Isabel. They all did. But Isabel had her orders. There wasn't much she could have done. She just looked ahead when the girl spoke to her. Then she didn't try any more. It took most of the girls a long time to give up. But she had given up after few attempts. Perhaps she had been raised in a good home, where they had taught her to be polite. Her hands were slender, too. Her nails would've been a nice shape once, the oblong sort, like a Madonna. Now some of them were broken. One or two were missing.

She would hum a tune so faintly you could barely hear it. It sounded like a nursery rhyme, but Isabel couldn't be sure. Perhaps it was one of their revolutionary songs, how would she know? No talking and no singing, those were the rules, but the girl wasn't singing, only humming. She would stop when the Lieutenant Colonel came in. Isabel was glad she did; she wouldn't have liked to have to report that.

Isabel didn't know what he said to her and she didn't know what he might be doing to her in there. They all left the room when he was visiting. Even the cadets. She usually did the washing up and the sterilising during this time. She tried to make as much clatter as she could. She hated to have to listen to any sounds coming out of that room. It was none of her business – none of it.

She wondered if the girl's mother – did she even have one? did subversives have mothers? – would have told her daughter about it all, the birthing business? Did she have any idea of what to expect? Dr. Figueroa said it was going to be all right. "Women were made for this," he said, "their bodies would just do what they were programmed to do." He would be there during the birth, he assured Isabel, if anything went wrong he would take over. But of course he never had to give birth himself. Isabel could have shown her a few things. Women prefer to know, to prepare. For her part, she thought this was only fair to the mother-to-be, but Dr. Figueroa was what they call old school. "The patient," he said, "the patient must entrust herself to the doctor and obey his orders." He spoke through the nose in that rather annoying, old-fashioned style Isabel didn't care for very much. But it wasn't her place to judge doctors. Or anybody else, for that matter.

Isabel was well aware that she had already crossed the line. She had smuggled in a book the other day. She slipped it under the girl's bedcover. She wasn't allowed books, of course, but this one could not do any harm; it had nothing to do with subversives and politics. Isabel hated politics anyway, of all sorts and persuasions. When her husband and her brother began to talk about politics – and mostly such talks resulted in fights – her eyes just rolled and glazed over. What could anybody possibly object to in a scientific book? Even the Lieutenant Colonel, with all his obsession about subversives and how they were everywhere. Reds under the bed, ha ha. All right, it wasn't funny. But still, the poor girl. Obviously this was exactly the kind of thing that was strictly forbidden. It would cost her more than her job. But she had seen the marks on the girl's body. Had she been able to choose, Isabel would not have been there, an unwilling witness to...to whatever was happening. Still, a book about birthing couldn't possibly cause any harm. The girl would look at it, her large bright eyes filled with wonder, sometimes with tears. When Isabel heard a noise outside the door, she would snatch it from the girl's hands and shove it beneath the mattress.

Isabel had managed to convince one of the cadets to stay outside the room and give the girl some privacy. She would brew *mate* for him in the kitchenette. He was a nice lad, very young. He kept his counsel. They avoided looking into each other's eyes.

The girl slept like the dead. Once Isabel found her so still that she almost raised the alarm: her gray face looked so serene as she lay on her back, the blanket ballooning over her belly, her arms and legs spread heavily on the sheet, wax-like. She's gone, Isabel thought, and went to her, touched her: she was cold but not rigid. She looked so young and so ancient at the same time, a sight to break anyone's heart. Then she sighed in her sleep and Isabel could finally breathe. She wasn't dead. Better for her if she were though. Her arms and legs – especially the inside of her thighs – were covered in purplish and yellow shadows. What stories they told Isabel hoped never to hear. She had seen Dr. Figueroa appraise them with no expression on his face. He avoided looking at Isabel afterwards; he knew that she too had seen them.

As the pregnancy progressed, the girl would be too weak to look at the book, or to even sit up long enough to have a sip of water or a bite of food. Every day Isabel wondered if she would find the strength to bring that baby into the world. Dr. Figueroa did not allow medication, especially painkillers. "They might harm the baby," he said. "If she can bear childbirth pains, she can bear a few headaches, they can hardly kill her now." And he cleared his throat, seeming slightly embarrassed by his own callousness – if anything could embarrass an old army doctor.

21

Inside the Room

"You never smile," he said to her. "Come on, give me a little smile."

He traced a finger over her soft round cheek. Not so round as it used to be. Transparent. You could almost see the delicate bone structure behind.

She kept her eyelids closed. They had a dark blue tint. Her eyelashes were long and curved. There was a crust of salt on them: yesterday's tears. Their shadow fell upon her cheeks.

His finger followed a line down towards her jaw, deviated behind the ears, small and close to the skull, moved down the bruised berries of the mouth. She kept her lips tightly closed. He forced them open with his hard finger; she resisted, but not much. She knew better now, though he missed the early days, when she would resist longer and harder. She'd even bitten his finger once, and he gave her a good hard fuck, one of the best in his life. He was well aroused now.

"I'm your god and master," he panted. "Your life depends on me."

Her head fell on her chest, a flower snapped off the stalk.

22

Mothers

There were women waiting in queues outside police stations, ministries and government agencies. Always the same faces, grim and determined, hopeful or dejected. During the first weeks after Lucía vanished without a trace, Milagros would cling to them. The few minutes they spoke to each other, furtively, with low voices, sharing their common story, where only names changed, and sexes – Lucía, Alejandro, Irma, Rogelio – what difference did it make? They were all their children; these few minutes were the only ones in the day that mattered to her.

Otherwise it was all a bad dream, the endless rides on the bus, and the demands of the Señora, and the silence of Don Faustino, and Pablo's demeanor like a beaten-up dog. She had gone back to work for Ramona Goyena in her Buenos Aires residence, for she could find no other work – who would hire the mother of a subversive? But she had refused to move back into the house, even after Don Faustino's death from a heart attack, even though there was now so much space with the young people gone. It was that empty space that haunted her the most, the made-up beds in their rooms, school books and university notes tidied up on desks where no one would ever sit again.

Speaking to other people like herself, mostly women – the few men looked defeated from day one – made it seem certain, almost imminent, that the children would be found. The more they talked about it, the more certain and imminent it seemed.

"Any news, eñora?" they would ask each other as soon as they met. Then they would share their tiny crumbs of information, faint glimmers of promise. How one of them had been to yet another police precinct where the lady at the desk had seemed so kind and understanding as she had children herself. How a parish priest had prayed for the quick release of captives openly in front of military parishioners. How a lawyer had agreed to prepare a writ of habeas corpus free of charge. They aired their grievances as well.

"I can't find a lawyer who will make me one," a woman said.

"My own charged me five thousand pesos," said another.

The other women promised to get her in touch with the nice one who didn't charge the poor anything.

"What is this *habeas corpus*?" Milagros asked.

A prematurely white-haired, dignified lady wearing glasses with a round silver frame explained it to her. She had a soft, young-sounding voice. Her name was Alicia de Grant de Otamendi. It made Lucía's imprisonment illegal, that law of habeas corpus. The state would have to explain why she was kept in prison and clearly give them a date for a trial.

"But how can we prove she is in prison, if nobody will even tell us that?" Milagros wondered.

The woman nodded, her face sad but determined. "We will prove it," she said confidently.

After the meeting, they got on the subway together: Milagros had to go back to work and Alicia lived in Avenida Alvear, quite near the Señora's house.

They told each other their stories on the train. Alicia's husband had been a famous heart surgeon, but he had died five years before the troubles started. Her son Rogelio, also a medical doctor, her daughter-in-law Luisa, and three-year-old granddaughter Anita were taken away in the middle of the night, only two days after Lucía vanished on her way back from school. This gave the two women a kind of affinity, as if celebrating their children's birthday together.

"They take away children as well?" asked Milagros dumbstruck, when she heard about the little girl. She blinked as she tried to comprehend, feeling a numbing sense of dread in her stomach. Alicia nodded and turned her head away to look at the darkness outside the train window.

The mothers began to meet at a church, but one day soldiers were waiting for them outside and one of the women was arrested. They never saw her again. The priest got scared and shut the door in their faces. They believed he was the one who gave them away. Afterwards, the mothers decided to meet in the plaza. It would be more difficult for the military or the police to attack them in the open air in front of so many people. Attacking old women who could have been their own mothers – what would people say!

"Come and bring a photograph of your daughter," Alicia told Milagros. "We'll be there on Thursday after three o'clock. If anything happens in the meantime, here is my telephone number. don't hesitate to call me."

On that Thursday, the Señora had a late lunch. She always had a late lunch ever since Don Faustino's death. Milagros served her the soup and meat and a peach flan for dessert, casting oblique glances at the big clock on the wall. It was almost half past two. She had to see the Señora safely to bed for her siesta before she could go anywhere. She had prepared the things she wanted to take with her since the night before. A color portrait of Lucía, taken on the day she celebrated her eighteenth birthday, and blown up at the photograph shop. An old diaper of Lucía's, her very first one, made of gauze and cotton. Milagros had sewn it herself. How many times had she washed it? She couldn't bear to throw it away, her baby's very first nappy. She would wear it on her head, like a scarf. All the women would do the same, so people could see they were all together, like a uniform, a veil nuns or nurses wore. This would be their mother's veil.

The Señora was taking her time, today of all days. Typical. The one day Milagros had to go somewhere. She went on and on about the tea for the Philanthropic Ladies Society she was planning to give next week. Since when are you interested in Philanthropic Societies, Milagros yelled inside her own head. The clock hand was moving slowly and steadily towards three. If she is safely in bed before half-past three, thought Milagros, I can just skip out and take the bus and then the subway. It will cost a little more but it's just this once. With a little luck I'll be there before four o'clock. They will still be there.

"You must speak to the catering service tomorrow without delay," the Señora was saying. "Order fifty cucumber sandwiches, fifty cheese and ham, and make sure they use the good Spanish ham. I didn't like the local one they used last time. And foie gras, of course, the General's wife can't live without it, and the good puddings, the English ones. And the chocolate cakes. Make sure you tell them I won't buy from them again if they don't use Belgian chocolate, last time I think they used something else, but I won't be paying for Belgian chocolate if I'm lumped with something inferior instead. Are you listening, Milagros? You're looking at the clock too much. What is it, have you got a date?"

The Señora laughed at her own joke and went on about her catering requirements. I won't do the dishes now, Milagros was thinking, I'll just put them in the sink to soak and will do them as soon as I come back in, hopefully it will be before she wakes up from the siesta and if she's already up, I'll tell her I've been out doing the shopping.

The clock was showing three-twenty as the Señora put down her napkin and made to get up. Milagros ran to help her.

"No, it's all right, leave me alone, I'll just sit here at the sofa. I won't have a nap today."

"Not have a nap? But Señora, your health, the doctor said…"

"I know what the doctor said. Not having a nap for once won't kill me. You do the dishes and then serve the coffee in the small parlor. I'm expecting a visitor, and I want you to meet him, too."

"A visitor, Señora?"

"Yes. It's Chief Balseri, the chief of police in the capital, and he may have some news about Lucía."

What about Silvina and Fito, Milagros wanted to scream at her. But Señora was adamant: her children were abroad. Silvina was in Paris. Fito was in London. They were safe and in communication. Milagros knew this was a lie; she would have known about any communications. There was nothing: no telegrams, no letters, no phone calls. She sometimes wondered of late if Señora hated her own children and wouldn't mind if they were dead. But no, Milagros thought. Though the Señora's behaviour recently had been inexplicable, perhaps she wouldn't have arranged for Chief Balseri to visit, if at least a part of her maternal heart was not worried for her own children.

23

Where Are They?

The man Balseri had bright azure eyes and a genial smile. "I am so sorry about your daughter," he said. "Your mistress here assures me that she was a good girl. Unfortunately, we see many cases like that. Beautiful innocent girls led astray by some rogue, vanished without a trace, no word to her family or friends."

"No, sir, my daughter was not that kind of girl."

"Everyone believes that of their own children," Señora sighed. Milagros would have liked to kick her viciously on the shin. Instead, she said:

"There were rumors that a Ford Falcon took her, just outside her school. That she was taken as a subversive and put in prison."

He narrowed his eyes at her. "Rumours? Do not believe the rumors. If that was the case, I would have known. But it can't be. You have my word of honor as an officer that your daughter is not held by police or military."

Your word of honor! She wanted to laugh bitterly in his face, to use words that would cut him like broken glass, like razorblades. But she couldn't think of any such words. And if she could, she would have never been able to use them. A black cloud was hanging on the inside of her head; a migraine was certainly coming. She winced and realized this was a waste of time. She should still try and make it to the plaza.

Before he was to leave, he asked for permission to use the lavatory. Milagros was washing up the tea service in the utility room when she was shocked to feel his presence behind her. His insolent hand on her arm, almost touching her breast. "I can find out more about your daughter," he said. "But it costs a lot of money, making inquiries."

She thought of her savings, collected over the long years, like an ant patiently collects and saves its stash, grain by grain. She nodded. What else could she do?

A few weeks later, Balseri returned. He and Ramona were together in the smaller office, she on her wide pink velvet winged chair, he sitting on a stool near her. Milagros had been listening to their conversation, her ear glued to the keyhole, holding her breath like a diver in the deep dark sea. After what Balseri had proposed to her, any time he visited she tried her best to glean more information.

"Your daughter is better off in Paris," Balseri was saying. "Yes, we know she is there. We know you are sending her money, but you should think about what you are doing. Our liaison there says she is in contact with a known group of subversives."

"I have a right to send money to my own daughter, and I won't accept any advice from you," Ramona said. "You have no reason to complain yourself. Swiss account and all. But I need my son, I need to know where he is. What is going on in this country – it's unheard of!"

"I agree with you there. Such levels of subversion."

Ramona was thinking: and what's wrong with subversion? If only I was young. If only I could leave this goddamn chair and walk down those goddamn stairs on my own. She had a vision of herself riding down Avenida Santa Fe on a big black stallion, running down anyone she met on her way, taking revenge. Avenida Santa Fe was a valley and she was riding through it to freedom and victory.

She pinched her nose with her hands.

"If madam is not feeling very well–" he began.

"No, stay!"

She took a deep breath.

"Please, don't go yet," she said in a softer voice. "There's another person I am interested in. Lucía Suárez. My maid's daughter. I want you to find out if she is…if she was taken at the same time as my son. And where she is now. I'm not buying that nonsense about a seductive villain you sold her poor mother. Just find out and tell me where they are."

His eyes glinted. "Cash for that bit of information."

"Cash," she agreed. "Just tell me where she is, where they are, and I'll give you more cash than you've ever seen in your miserable life, you rat."

He got up and bowed to her and made for the door.

Milagros scurried back into the kitchen, her heart beating fast. Her little stash was almost depleted by now, no doubt in the Swiss account Señora had just mentioned. So he's taking advantage of us both, she thought. Double advantage of her. She thought of the disgusting hands, how he sneaked into the kitchen whenever he called and pressed his body onto hers and rubbed himself against her backside. She wanted to throw up, to claw his face until blood ran down. She comforted herself with violent fantasies of him on the floor, her kicking him hard all over the place, turning him into a rag that she would wring and toss in a bucket of dirty water.

Ramona was sitting alone in her bedroom. She had locked the door. The heavy drapes on the windows and the incarnadine velvet furniture made the room stifling hot. She liked that. It reminded her of the northern lands where she grew up, the jungle reaching to the threshold of her father's house, creepers obscuring the day and creating a warm humid womb of a world where she found herself forever young and all-powerful.

She opened a sandalwood box inlaid with mother-of-pearl. The key to its dainty yet secure lock was always hanging around her neck, hidden among the folds of flesh and the silk layers of clothes. There were all sorts of things in the box: locks of babies' hair, amulets, silver teething rings and christening souvenirs, prints of babies' feet and hands, children's first drawings.

She inserted her hand in a narrow slit formed in the heavy satin lining of the box. She took out a thin folded piece of paper. It was a letter she had read such a number of times that she knew it by heart. She stared at it, her eye falling on phrases here and there:

...she loves me and I love her...my intentions were always honorable and now she is mine and I am hers in the eyes of God and the law. Father Agnelli has blessed our marriage. Lucía is the woman I want to share my life with, and you must accept it... when this nightmare is over...I don't know what happened to her. I don't know where she is. I hear things too terrible to believe... It's all my fault. But it is she who is paying the price now...I know you have the power to save her, and me, because, dear Mother, if anything happens to her and our baby – your own grandchild, Mother, your first grandchild, do you realize it? – if anything befalls them, forget you ever had a son...you will prove yourself a true Mother and a true Christian...

Doña Ramona looked at the letter for a long time. She was as rigid as a carved idol. Her eyelids never flickered. But she would have liked to scrunch the letter into a small wrinkly ball. To throw it on the floor and stomp on it. To tear it into a thousand little pieces with her teeth. Instead, she folded the letter and put it back in its place in the satin lining. She locked the box and passed the key through the solid gold chain around her neck. Then she sat erect and glared at the wall, till the room was filled with long thick shadows.

24

Letters from Paris

Well, here I am, Gustavo, a nobody among nobodies, a dark spot in the City of Lights. A blur. All fuzzy and bleary at the edges. I don't have edges anymore. Even you with your strict ethics of revolutionary poverty would find nothing to reproach me with. Think about it for a minute, if you please. Consider my position. I know you always looked with distaste at the unequivocal marks of my family's affluence. You examined the quality of my clothes and calculated the price to the last centavo. You were furious with my carelessness in spending; you said you found the lack of any mental or material obstacles in attaining my own way obscene, but we all knew what you meant: "You're just a rich bitch and it's not fair that it's you and not I."

I live on very little now. My family won't send me very much and I don't want their help anyway. My room is spartan enough even for your standards. There is no hot water. I walk up and down six flight of stairs several times a day – no lift. I've lost quite a bit of weight, which is also something you'd approve of. Revolutionary ethics or not, you wanted your women to look like models. I live on bread and cheese. Being poor is not as terrible as people make it out to be. Okay, I know what you'll say: "It's terrible when it's thrust on you, when it's not your choice and you can see no way out." In that case you'd be arguing for poverty being a state of mind rather than material lack, all about what one might feel one has a right to and yet is denied to them. In the final analysis, it's about position and being accepted. I'm not talking about being destitute, mind, that state of overwhelming and appalling lack of necessaries which so outraged Fito and made Lucía tearful. I can't say I've experienced that.

Who am I without my privilege?

Still, I'm alive. I suppose I ought to be grateful.

It's so pathetic to be an exile, Gustavo. It's so much more difficult to make friends when you are in need. Making friends was always a problem for me, as you well know; much more so now that others can feel my desperation. I just don't know how to hide it. It's as though they can smell my need and it puts them off. It only attracts ghouls: those who enjoy other people's misfortune and misery, who will use it for their own ends. Journalists and the politically ambitious. Faux do-gooders. And of course others like me, from home or from other places where misfortune has hit. Those are the worst; I can't even bear to look at them. Sometimes people think they'll please me, or maybe it pleases them to think they are doing a good deed by a homesick exile, when they tell me: "You must definitely come tonight, there will be so and so from your own country, have you met them?" Those I especially avoid. It's not that I don't want to hear the news from home – and besides, bad news always finds a way to be known whether one wants it or not – but I don't want to see the look on their faces when they learn who I once was.

And what good news could possibly reach me now? I know she is dead, and I don't want to think about it. And Fito…He's safely out of reach now, I think, in some Patagonian desert. And you, Gustavo, you are not one of those who die. You and I are so much alike. *Maybe this is why it was so hard for us to be together. Maybe this is why I find it so much easier to love you and to talk to you when there is a whole ocean and all those border crossings and military police guards between us.*

To cut a long story short, lately I have been spending my days avoiding people. I haunt the city instead. I love the bridges, the gray sculptures, the pigeons, the overcast skies. The sky here is nearer the earth, I think. So like, yet so unlike home. I enjoy losing myself in crowded streets, bustling department stores, as sullen-looking in my raincoat as any of the passers-by, pushing and shoving in my hurry to go – where?

Truth is, I have nowhere particular to go. I stopped going to lectures long ago. I find them boring and they just go over my head now. I've lost all appetite for critical theory and highbrow words. What do these people know, I would ask myself as I sat among the eager faces of students younger than me, lapping up like grateful kittens the nonsense a smug professor uttered about the Revolution with a capital R. What does he know of the revolution? He once stood among a crowd who shouted and chanted in a demonstration? Or he may have written one or two clever quips on a wall ten years ago. Standing opposite the police and shouting at them. How revolutionary! I wonder what they would do if they knew about me and you, Gustavo, about actually killing cops, not just standing there and shouting abuse at them. Ha! How about making the bomb and setting it all up and then seeing it detonate, debris and human body parts raining down upon the black crater in the earth, the noise, the blood, the smell. Well, you and I, we know what it was like, the real thing. The unsuspecting poor sod, the copper, whistling and eating a hotdog, then the look of unbelieving terror only a second before, the incomprehension, the panic. You wanna play revolution, kiddies? Come, I'll show you revolution and how to play it.

But I never say anything. I've just decided to stop going to university instead.

How sick and tired I am of your July 1789s, May 1968s, of your Octobers and your Junes. But you like that kind of thing, Gustavo. In this you and Fito are similar, in this devotion to calendars, to red-letter days, to symbolic dedications, to icons and myths, the Holy Church or the Holy Subversion, St. Mary or St. Evita. All this I find stifling, all this I wanted to escape from, and I thought what we did was a way to do it, to put an end to it forever, to deal with it once and for all. But maybe you will say, like M.me Jouvet – my analyst, and spare me your sneers about how bourgeois psychoanalysis is! – that violence was my own mythology, and terror the most powerful myth of all.

But I digress. This is supposed to be a letter with my news.

There is no news really. I just spend my days studying and reading. I plan to set up a psychoanalytical practice someday. It's as good a job as any other, and I need a job, since I decided I will owe nothing to anyone anymore. I'll stop accepting money from my mother. But what would be the point in forcing myself to take any odd job that would come my way, for wages that would barely keep me in cigarettes? What would be the point in me living in rat-dens and wearing rags? No, I need money, after all, and I'm about to begin earning it.

So I read and write letters to you – letters you'll never receive – and immerse myself in the city and spend hours in the cafés in the Marais. I walk down the Champs-Élysées, watching the long black chauffeur-driven cars going by with their sullen passengers, usually women behind enormous sunglasses, in fur coats, surrounded by shopping bags with ornate logos, the de rigueur *poodle on their lap. Sometimes they get out of the car and walk rapidly past me to meet a man in a café. I can distinguish whether they are meeting a husband or a lover by the scowling or smiling expression on their faces. I look at them and think, This could have been me. Me in Calle Florida, me in La Biela, me in the expensive boutiques on Avenida Santa Fe.*

I can see the sneer on your face, Gustavo, the ever-emerging suspicion, the forthright accusation. I know what you are thinking:

"There, I told you so, you're nothing but a bourgeoise deep down inside, that's what you are, that's why you're enjoying watching those airheads, those rich bitches, with such pleasure, and what else – longing?" No, Gustavo, I am not one of them and never will be. My pleasure in watching them consists only in knowing that here I am safe from that fate. Here I am an immigrant, Gustavo, an exile. I cannot belong and this is exactly what makes me happy. I can watch everybody from a safe distance. Nobody wants to cross it, Gustavo, nobody cares to cross this distance and meet me in my own territory. For the first time in my life, nobody looks at me, and I am really free.

True, I am sometimes caught unawares, it may hit me when I walk down a road and then turn and suddenly find myself in small plaza with a broken fountain, or a quiet, tree-lined road with a bakery, a sudden breeze wafting the warm fragrance of freshly-baked bread and petit-fours. Or when there is a street lantern in the fog, casting its muted orange light with economy and sadness. At these times, I seek refuge at the river. I know I'm safe there, because the Seine is so different from the River Plate, and its bridges look nothing like the bridges over in that place, which is no longer home. At night especially I'm happy; watching the city lights from the bridges I feel that I'm at last in a real big city, a metropolis, where any and every wonderful thing may happen. Buenos Aires always gave me the impression during the nighttime that it was reverting back to its original character, to the poor, timorous and temporary fort it was born as, and was meant to be.

Silvina X

September, 1981

Dear Gustavo,

I have been thinking of my father. I wasn't there when he died, and regardless of what M.me Jouvet says, I haven't got the slightest remorse about that. What good would it have done him? He disliked me, I think; he positively hated my mother, and I don't know if he ever forgave Fito for being a good Catholic and an upstanding young man and not a rake like himself.

No, I don't care about funerals. I was only thinking that my father would have been a happier man had I been a beautiful girl. Everybody knew about his passion – or vice, according to the way you looked at it – for women, and of course they were all pretty, but sex is not what I'm talking about. He had the passion of a thwarted artist for beauty, and he had learned to look for it mostly in women. I have often wondered how he came to marry my mother: a plain, brooding thing who had never been good looking in her life, not even in extreme youth, judging by old photos. Most people do go through a phase when they look at least tolerably presentable, especially in their late teens, but I've seen pictures of her just before she was married. She wasn't as fat then, which for her bulk doesn't say much; she was only a little short of looking like a beached whale. It can't have been solely about the money, as he belonged to a rich family too. And I know for a fact that a lot of other, more attractive women of his class would have died to have had him.

It's a mystery, and what would life be without them? When I was a kid I used to think I'd much rather have Milagros for my mother than her, then Fito had explained that if my mother had been somebody else I would have been somebody else too, and I remember saying, "So much the better." I haven't mentioned this to M.me Jouvet – but why should you care, you don't believe in psychoanalysis. It's just that I can see for myself what it means and I know exactly what her answer would be, so what's the point in spending good money to talk about the self-evident?

Back to my father now. I remember how he looked at Lucía at times; I caught him unawares. How can I describe that look? A yearning, a possessiveness, a pride…She was only the daughter of a servant, though a beloved one, almost a member of the family, but he treated her as if she were his own flesh and blood. Or maybe I *should say better than his own, because my father never had much time for me. It was because of her beauty, of course. No, it's not what you think, if you've heard the stories about him. Lucía was not just another* chinita, *one of those puny, sly-looking, sexy chits (they are sexy when very young, I must admit) he loved to sleep with. I have seen him gaze at paintings the way he gazed at her, following her with his eyes as if she was something very rare and precious. He was almost timid in her presence, awed.*

You of all people, Gustavo, should know what Lucía did to people when she walked into a room. And she did it without even suspecting she did it. That was what made her irresistible.

It was difficult — no, difficult doesn't begin to describe it — it would have been superhuman not to envy her. And I am not superhuman, Gustavo, though I sometimes believed I was. But I did love her. Looking back now I can see that I often bossed her around and maybe treated her more like a beloved pet than a person — but what was Lucía to me exactly? I often wonder. Was she a friend? But we were not equals, for she was a servant's daughter. We were raised together, by her mother too, but we were not sisters; as the servant's daughter, she was a kind of servant herself. Not exactly a sister, not exactly a friend, not exactly a servant. But whatever she was, I could never imagine a life in which Lucía didn't play a part, a presence as necessary and as taken for granted as my own self.

I speak of her in the past tense. In my gut I know Lucía is dead, as I know that Fito is not, and neither are you.

So yes, I envied her. You know that quite well. When you all spoke with trembling voices to her and shook at her presence; when you devoured her with your eyes. Oh, I could feel every look, every word, every sigh as a stab in my heart. Especially yours, Gustavo. You see, I loved you. Regardless of what we claimed: true love should be free, unrestrained, enjoyed without limits or petty notions of possessiveness and exclusivity. Yes, yes, I know, we talked about it, we accepted it. Or pretended to. I never really got any enjoyment or fun out of it. Maybe because this was another instance, like school and being picked up for teams, where my popularity was tested and found deficient. Maybe because I only wanted you. When you love someone...but no, I won't go down that road again. Let me just say that sometimes I wish I had been beautiful for your sake, too, as for my father's.

Silvina

November, 1981

Dear Gustavo,

I find it harder and harder to go on living in this city where I am nobody and nobody cares for me.

November is always such a difficult month. In Buenos Aires the jacaranda trees are painting the city in bluish purple strokes, lush carpets of the blooms being crushed beneath people's feet. November, the month of spring and hope, but here it is a month of deepening gloom and constant, freezing drizzle.

I keep thinking about the past. They say it's something that happens to you in midlife, this examination of your history and what went wrong; since, of course, most lives, at least the ones requiring examinations and revisions, must have gone wrong somehow. M.me Jouvet asked me the other day, "What would have been your best-case scenario? Would it be that the revolution happened for real in your country, as it did in Cuba?" I just stared at her. Was she really so ignorant or was that meant to be a joke? But it did start me thinking. What would have been my best-case scenario?

Honestly, I don't know. The obvious answer of course is that some things that happened actually wouldn't have, in an ideal world. We wouldn't have been arrested; I wouldn't have been forced to leave the country. I would have known that you and Lucía and Fito were all alive and well. You may all still be, but it would be nice to know for sure. And then I wonder: if I had the power to unmake things, what would I have changed, what would I have done differently? Would I participate in the events of that day? Would I bring those men back to life, the coppers? Would I give them their lives back by simply not participating in those events that led to their losing them? Would I leave Lucía out of all involvement? Would I go even further in the past, change who my parents were, their own past and their own ancestry too? Would I have made myself die before any of this happened? M.me Jouvet says that editing the past is a sure sign of survivor's guilt. I have often caught her asking me the same question, to see if she gets the same answer. She's not as clever as she thinks she is. I never change my story. I am very well aware of what happened, and why, and I would do it all over again. It's the outcome I would have changed. It's the rest of the world I would have changed. Not myself. Not what I did. Not what we did. Whatever is done, is done – and it was done for the best.

December, 1981

Dear Gustavo,

One of the strangest things about living here, one of the things I'll never get used to, is the turning upside down of the seasons. Christmas in the winter always felt weird to me. Even though I have been to Europe in the past, many times, it's one thing to be here for a few days or even for a few weeks, as a visitor, and quite another to live permanently, with no assurance of returning home. It's my third Christmas here and I still can't get used to the fact that we won't be planning a holiday in Mar del Plata at my Grandmama's, or Punta del Este, or doing the Christmas shopping and then eating enormous ice creams in the terraces of the cafés in Calle Florida. The gardens in Palermo will be lush green, the water fountains in Recoleta gushing and sparkling.

I remember Milagros taking us to the Zoo and the Botanical Garden back when we were all kids. The four of us — Fito and myself and Lucía in tow — boarded the Subte. It was a secret and we kept it faithfully. Mother didn't like her children to ride the Subte; she thought all sorts of unspeakable crimes were committed in there. I think she had a fear of all public places. Maybe she was agoraphobic. Or maybe she was just too embarrassed to be seen in public, being so fat. (Amazing how my mother can interfere with my fondest memories.)

Anyway, we rode on the Subte and this was an adventure in itself. How I shivered when the train left the brightly lit underground stations and faced black blind walls. I used to shut my eyes very tight till I saw orange explosions in my visual field. Then Fito laughed at me and I stopped doing it. No, it wasn't that — it was the monsters that lurked in the Subte. I imagined them coming out of the dark tunnels. There was a beggar we came across often: half his face was missing, or rather it was replaced by a hideous mask-like purple skin, eaten away by God knows what acids or flames. "Poor man, his face must have caught fire," Milagros said, but she turned us all away from the door to stare at the tunnel walls instead. But I could still catch glimpses of his hideous reflection on the windows. Later I found out it was quite common: shanties in the villas miserias *often caught fire as they were heated precariously with all sorts of dangerous contraptions. Fito treated many poor* villeros *for burns in medical school. But I was fascinated by the horrible sight, by the sharp drop under his nose and by the full teeth exposed as in a skull. Lucía started to cry, and she kept her eyes tightly shut. Now that I recall, I never shut mine after that. I opened them wide and peered in the darkness outside the train windows, but all I could see was shadows of our reflections, Milagros unsmiling and ramrod straight in her crisp gingham nanny's uniform, Fito explaining something to Lucía who looked up to him and listened in concentration, and myself, scowling, staring, the enormous bow on my head as annoying as a gigantic fly I'd like to squash.*

I often ride the metro here, and every time I start walking down the steps and the smell hits me, this particular smell of metallic rails touched by a million hands, of hot steam and dug-out earth (the smell of a grave), of sweat and tar and rats, I fear that I'm going to find myself back in Buenos Aires, and even come across our familiar faces, the four of us solemn and scowling, or rapt in conversation, on our way to the Zoo and the Botanic, and the hideous half-burned face of the beggar directing his skull's grin towards our backs.

Sometimes when I am dreaming, Gustavo, I sigh deeply in my sleep and wake up startled because I think there's someone else in the room, and only when I am awake do I realize it was me. And then it hits me, it hits me like a blow, a real blow, like in the boxing ring, it hits me that I don't live in Buenos Aires anymore, that I am so far away that even if I could go back, even if it was safe to go back, even if I wanted to go back, there is an enormous sea between me and there, an ocean in all its dark depths and its strange surfaces of islands and algae and sea monsters, hostile continents and strange cities and towns between me and Buenos Aires, and to my shame I tell you that at those moments I cry, and you know very well it should take more than a fucking city – what's more, a city where I've mostly been unhappy – to make me cry.

December, 1981

Dear Gustavo,

Often I walk the streets conducting conversations between you and I in my head. Sometimes I just continue discussions – arguments, I should say –we've had; at other moments I do a lot of editing, mostly of my words, at times even of yours. I was never good with words, unlike yourself. I was, and still am, one of those people who says any odd thing that comes into their head, and later stews for hours over what would have been a more suitable response. I relive arguments and get very angry, all red in the face and thundering down the road, so that people sometimes turn to stare at me in the street. Apparently I speak aloud to myself, and they stare; not very often though, they're used to lonely, ranting people here. I am good at anger. It's what I do best.

Maybe this is why I always thought my vocation in this world was rebellion. Revolution was my path and my duty. I wasn't beautiful and obedient like Lucía, so I would never be happy with the common lot of women: love and marriage and children, or clothes and lovers and shining at parties. I was not kind and compassionate like Fito, so it was out of the question to help others the proper, slow way: following a suitable career, doctor or teacher (it was assumed ever since my school days that I would go to university to study one thing or another). And of course I could never be like my mother. This choice to be as unlike her as possible was one I made myself; it was not imposed on me either by nature or by conventions. Revolution was my vocation, and I don't mean it in the same way as you, Gustavo, because for you revolution was, and apparently still is, a career. And you do very well at it, I have to say this for you. I'm sure you have far to go yet, once the dictators fall. And they are bound to fall any day now. They all do in the end.

Anyway, I've been thinking about revolution. Of course in my textbooks I find all sorts of bullshit about the parents and rebellion and what children decide to make of their lives, just to assert themselves against what they take to be their enemy. They say that in the hour of confusion and chaos, it is difficult to identify the enemy. Well, I never had any such problem; for me the enemy always had a face and a name and a figure, and what's more, it lived in the same house as I – and if you are going to come up with some three-penny Freudian psychobabble about it, remember that you are speaking to a trainee psychoanalyst. And for the record,

I want to clarify my position here: I never believed in the real capacity of psychoanalysis to solve anybody's problems. I see no problem in practising a profession – a lucrative one, too, and that's the important thing, otherwise why bother? – in which I don't believe. I am not the first or the last to do so. I bet you anything that a large number of priests are atheists in their heart of hearts, and I have personally known an even larger number of professional revolutionaries who didn't give two shits about a better future for humanity. Maybe I was one of them, too. And maybe so are you, my dearest Gustavo.

January, 1982

Last night I dreamed again. Of that day. You know what day I mean. I was walking down the road opposite the police station. I was looking for signs of you or the others, feeling that something dreadful had happened, that we were betrayed, and I had to warn you. I was running, I was out of breath. My heart was pounding so loudly, ticking like an alarm clock in a completely empty room, it was going to explode in due course. And I had to find you all and warn you before the explosion, and suddenly the street was full of cops; they were all running towards me and shouting and bellowing like deranged bulls, and I panicked and started to run blindly, madly, but I didn't know where to go, there was nowhere to go because all the side streets were blocked, chockful of pigs, and they were near enough for me to see their faces, they had no eyes at all, no eyes, only black holes, screaming, gaping holes in the face, nothing else, nothing else.

Sometimes when I walk down a crowded street I see a beautiful face in the crowd and my heart beats quickly because I've recognized Lucía. She's seen me and she's smiling a strange smile, lopsided, unusual – almost evil. I am petrified with fear. In my panic that in a second's time I'll have to speak to her and explain, I freeze. Then I look again, braced, but the face has disappeared. It couldn't have been her, of course – how could it? Lucía has been dead for years now. And it's my fault.

To go back to the dreams again. I wake up afterwards and this makes me so sad, Gustavo, so miserable, because it's slipping, it's fading away, the revolution is only fodder for nightmares, and one day it will be as if it never happened, as if we never stood up, as if we never did anything, as if all those beautiful times when I was really alive, when a true feeling pierced the thick fat around my heart for the first time in my life, and all those beautiful, real, flesh-and-blood people, brother, sister, comrades, those people so vibrant then, so untamed, so free, they have all become shadows, shadows visiting surreptitiously in dreams, just looking in, for a few seconds perhaps, once in a while, till they forget and are forgotten, till they stop visiting. And it will be as if they never were, as if our struggle, our revolution, our real life, Gustavo, never really happened at all.

I don't want therapy. I don't want closure. I only want justice.

Silvina

Spring, 1982

Dear Gustavo,

Here is a snippet from a recent session with M.me Jouvet:

"Describe a street."

"Long, winding, endless. Tarmac, asphalt, hot. Long. Dusty, hard on the soles of the feet. Endless."

"Endless."

"Yes. It feels as if...it's like no matter how long one walks on it, there's still more of a distance to go. How else do you want me to say it? Endless."

"Keep going."

"The shops are closed. Only the almacén in the corner is open. It must be the oldest building in town. I can see the ornate awning over the entrance, the wooden panels with the peeling green paint,

the ghosts of gilt letters on the glass panes. I know for sure that
the owner is snoring peacefully behind the counter. He has been
taking a nap in the shop for the last forty-five years. He never
closes at siesta times; he trusts in the tinkling bell over the door. It
has the same effect on him that a cannon shot would have on most
people. Sunlight bounces back and forth on blinded shop windows,
on inert brass handles and heavy window shutters. It is still too
hot for the season. As I walk down the empty street, I feel the sweat
gathering under my armpits, and I know that by the time I reach
the end of the street — my destination — there will be moist patches
under the sleeves of my already stained white shirt."

That's where I stopped with her. I didn't want to go any further.

"Now write any word that comes into your head below this
word," M.me Jouvet said, and pointed at a word on the blank page:
Noon.

I wrote: Noon. Moon. Soon. Loon. Loom. Doom.

She peered at the paper. "Doom. Interesting."

"Interesting? I would say boring. Banal as anything."

Spring, 1982

Carpintería. Mercadería modas de París. Panadería. Libería.
Facé. Almacén. Dorrego. García. Izaguen. López. Benedetti.
Goyena. Olmos.

I write words in my own language, constructing the place, the
time, the scene, the perpetrators. I am unable to stop myself. There
is a town hall, too. A clock tower. Too far to see the time, always,
in the recurring reconstruction, though I know exactly what time
it is. "The police station, please?"

"At the end of the street, Señorita. Straight ahead. Four more
blocks."

Soon after that I will see the young man. He could not have
been more than twenty years old. He had the kind of mouth you
want to bite, full red underlip, swollen, then a pouting upper lip.

The cigarette between them made it all the more enticing. He was neither tall nor short. He had broad shoulders, narrow hips. His black hair caught the sunlight and absorbed it. I wished I were he; I wished his spare elegant body was my body. Gun slung on his side. A sudden gust of wind and dust, whirlwinds, tumbleweeds on the empty street. His cigarette was out and he lit it again, cupping brown hands with shiny nails, black-edged, over the invisible flame.

Spring, 1982

"October."

"Funny you should mention October. The most beautiful month in the year. That is, it used to be, once upon a time. It is one of the many gloomy months here, isn't it? For me it was always the first real springtime month. The lilacs blossoming...Lilac is a color connected with death, isn't it?"

"Is it?"

"Is it?"

Summer, 1982

"Cigarettes. Oral stage."

"Is this what you were really thinking?"

"No. I was thinking of the light. Fire. Fuse."

I remember I was in a two-piece white piqué suit, a wide-brimmed hat, sunglasses. I was swinging a boxy leather handbag. Not a very large one. No keys or wallet inside, just lipstick and a compact, generic, bought at one of the less interesting pharmacies on Avenida Córdoba. The bag was not mine and not real leather: cheap but expensive looking, at least to the eyes of small-town boys. Not that he would pay specific attention to my handbag. The idea was the whole image should be striking, otherworldly, the rich bitch once again. That was my part and I played it well. From experience, you see. Nothing beats experience in this sort of thing.

The bag would be found later, examined. To no avail. I was also wearing a pair of short white gloves. Perfect for sweaty hands and the added bonus of no fingerprints. "You look like Jackie O." Gustavo, Gustavo, I should have known then, I should have seen, but I didn't, as I walked down that street, graceful and poised, almost languid in the hazy heat, and that young man – a boy almost – hair shorn so near his skull I could even see the nicks of the barber's razor. But no, that wasn't right. It was black, shiny, curling on the nape of the neck – no, no, wrong, it must have been shorn near the scalp, it must have been...

Summer, 1982

"Memory is a tricky mechanism," M.me Jouvet said.

Mechanism, tool, machine. M.me Jouvet likes to use such words to describe the inner workings of the brain. Brainworks. Roadworks. There would have been roadworks there that day. The truck would come to collect orange cones and road-repairing machinery; there should be at least two workmen. In worn overalls with badges on them, letters, as plausible as could be. Nobody pays any attention to workmen, they are part of the landscape, they can get away with anything.

"This wasn't Gustavo's idea. It was mine. It would have made everything so much simpler. But as it wasn't his idea, nothing came of it. I was sent out on my own. Why do I remember this? It's an insignificant detail."

"There is nothing insignificant," M.me Jouvet said. "If you remember it, it is there for a reason."

I smiled. How often people tell me this, present the world to me like an elaborate network of cause and effect where every little detail has its place. Much like a fancy hairdo. I shrugged under M.me Jouvet's hard, unhurried, non-committal eyes.

Summer, 1982

"What else do you see, in your recurring dream?"

A white lace collar. I remember Milagros perpetually knitting one of them with very small, very slender crooked needles, with hooks at the ends. Milagros's hands and needles worked so fast they formed swift butterflies; the frothy little white collar was what remained of this flight. A white lace collar. My heart explodes in my chest with agony. My heart wants to flee my chest, Gustavo, and never come back again. My throat is dry, everything inside me, all movement of fluids or gas, all the back and forth inside my body, it's all stopped. The whole world has turned into a terrified beating of a heart that wants to flee. Because this is the lace collar Lucía wore on the last day I saw her. And still it keeps turning up in my dreams, like flotsam and jetsam on the shore after a terrible shipwreck.

Does this mean anything to you?

25

A Telegram

SOUTH ATLANTIC

14 June, 1982

The soldier Adolfo Faustino Goyena Irribaren fell in the field of honor this morning at 06.47, defending the right of the motherland to sovereignty over las Islas Malvina, and upkeeping the noblest military traditions of our beloved country. Viva la Patria!

Lies. All lies, Ramona thought. Why do we have to fill our lives with lies? She was oddly proud of her dry eyes, the more so as she could hear Milagros's inconsolable sobs through the door.

I hope this breaks his black flinty heart, she thought. And then Ramona remembered that he too was dead, and that the worms would have feasted on his heart long ago. It was a minor consolation.

26

Death of a Hero

DEATH OF A HERO

One of our Best Families Loses a Son – Our Motherland Gains
Another Hero to Decorate with the Laurels of Glory

Adolfo (Fito) Faustino Goyena Irribaren (26), heir to the Goyena
Irribaren family's enormous wealth, a philanthropist, a medical
doctor with a future full of promise, and a most eligible bachelor,
epitomised what was best in the high society of the capital. Yet,
this young man who had everything, who only knew riches, comfort
and luxury in his life, for whom all doors were opened wherever he
went, who could have had any woman with his striking masculine
beauty, gave up everything as a sacrifice to our beloved motherland.
He chose the path of honor and glory. He fell defending our rightful
property, the pearl of the South Atlantic, from the grasping claws of
the rapacious English. His father, Don Faustino Goyena, who died in
1979, was spared the pain of losing a son. But this son from now on
will live forever in the memory of a grateful people, and his name will
be written in golden letters in the books of Time and Memory.

Adolfo Goyena Irribaren is an example for all our young people. He was always a serious young man, devoted to his family, especially his formidable mother, Doña María Ramona Irribaren de Goyena, and to his studies as a doctor. He had been abroad for many years, perfecting his medical talents in the university of Sorbonne and in Harvard Medical School, and in his spare time he participated in philanthropic expeditions in the poorest regions of Africa and Central America. He had been planning to return home and combine his scientific and charitable works by building a hospice for the poor, when the voice of the motherland calling all her children to defend her inalienable rights called him forth.

Sources close to the family reveal that Adolfo enlisted in the army contrary to the wishes of his mother, who did not want to lose her only means of support in her old age and infirmity. A family friend told us that disappointment in love may have played a part in his decision, too: there are rumors of a tragic love affair with an exquisitely beautiful French girl who died in an aeroplane crash. There are also hints of his unrequited love for an unnamed childhood friend pertaining to one of the oldest aristocratic families of Buenos Aires. But others say that Adolfo, a modern-age saint (and at one time linked with liberal priest Father Vittorio Agnelli, the "Angel of the Shantytowns," killed in a car crash in 1976), enlisted in the army out of a sense of strong patriotic duty, and to make up for the sins of his own sister, Silvina Goyena Irribaren (24), the black sheep of the family, who has been linked to subversive circles. Her whereabouts are unknown at present, but she is rumored to be either in France or in Mexico.

Adolfo's remains, covered by the time-honored flag, will be carried by military escort, in the presence of the President of the Republic, the Minister of Defense and top-ranking officials from the military and the civil service, to the cemetery of La Recoleta, where he will be interred in the imposing Goyena family mausoleum, built in 1886 and rumored to have cost the then astronomical sum of $20,000. The famous sculpture of the weeping angel standing on top of the golden dome of the edifice was made by Claude Leblanc, a disciple of the world-renowned French sculptor Auguste Rodin.

Rest in peace, Adolfito. Your ever grateful country will never forget you.

(Printed in society magazine, "FACES," issue 4757, July 1982)

PART FOUR

1983-1985

27

Witness

I was taken from the house of friends where I had been hiding for some time. It was in the middle of the night, April 14, 1977. I don't know what kind of place it was they took me to. It looked like some sort of abandoned factory or car repair shop. It was completely dark and I couldn't see well. The faces of the men who abducted me were covered in soot, and they wore no uniforms I could recognize. [...] I don't know why I wasn't hooded; most of the women they brought in after me were hooded for days on end. It was an awful sight [...] I had nothing to eat or drink for the first three days. They made us sleep on the concrete floor, no covers. It was freezing. Sometimes they made us take off our clothes and told us to keep each other warm and they made indecent jokes and gestures about our bodies.

On the second night I was there, they raped me and beat me. There were many more times. But for a long time I didn't know if it had all happened on one and the same night or different ones. I suffered from delusions and lost all sense of time. [...] I was taken for interrogation every day. I don't know who my interrogators were. I couldn't really see any faces as I was under very strong light and they kept themselves in the shadows. They all called each other by the same name. "Pedro" here and "Pedro" there. But I know who the chief torturer was. I recognized him from his voice; he had a slight lisp. I could tell this voice among millions of voices. I learned who he was later, of course. The Butcher himself: Julián Dos Santos. They wanted names of other members of the union, and when I pointed out they must know them already, the unions were not secret organisations, they beat me. With a thick rubber stick, a metal bar, a wrench – anything. They used the picana for electroshocks, too. It wasn't only me, every woman and girl in the camp suffered the same. [...] I had a letter and a number. I was prisoner D67. They shouted it at me all the time. It was forbidden to use our names. There were pregnant women there. They had no mercy for them, they tortured and raped them, too, like the rest of us. The Butcher himself did it, and others. They mostly had their faces covered or painted black when they did that. It was too painful to look at them. But I remember one of them had thick hairy hands, lots of hairs on the back of the hands, like a boar's hairs. [...]

When they brought Ester in, I pretended I didn't recognize her. Of course Ester wasn't her real name, we never used our real names. She was completely broken down. She screamed and whimpered most of the time at first. We helped her, we nursed her secretly when they were not looking. She was there for about three months, till her pregnancy started to show. She told me she and her husband were kidnapped on the same day. She told me her mother didn't know she was pregnant. She was afraid she would lose the baby. Then one night they came and took her away for good. I don't know how she knew that she was going for good, but as they were leading her outside she cried, "My name is Lucía Eva Suárez Riquelme, please let my parents know I was here." She was still shouting from the door and one of the soldiers hit her in the mouth with the back of his hand as they dragged her out.

(Excerpts from the testimony to the Special Committee for The Detained and Disappeared given on July 27, 1983, by Mirta Aléida

*Campos, ex-detainee of the secret detention camp known as El Pozo
Negro, the Black Pit.)*

28

The Baby

Carlos Durand Hospital, Capital Federal, July 2, 1985

The young nurse smiled at Milagros as she showed her into the doctor's office. She leaned over her with solicitude and said something to her.

Milagros made a negative gesture with her head. The nurse left the room, closing the door behind her carefully so as not to make any noise.

Milagros was standing in the middle of the room. She kept her purse tightly to her breast. She looked around her. The room was painted a cold green color; the ceiling was white. There was a metal desk, a bookcase and a filing cabinet, and two metal chairs. The usual smells of hospital – white spirit and gauze and something like a clean linen cupboard that had been closed for too long – made the office feel even smaller and more cluttered. Milagros sat at the edge of a chair facing the empty desk. There was a closed window with the shutters down over it; the noise of the traffic outside was muted, traveling all the way up the twelve floors. She sprang up from her chair as soon as the doctor – a tall, somewhat gaunt young woman with chestnut hair and surprising light blue eyes – walked in.

The doctor shook Milagros's hand, introduced herself as Analía Guzmán. Milagros sat on her chair again. The doctor hovered undecided for a few seconds, then, instead of going to sit behind the desk, she pulled another chair and sat next to her.

Milagros's eyes were firmly fixed on her handbag, which was old and a little scuffed at the edges. Her hands, gripping at the handbag tightly, were slightly trembling.

Guzmán began to speak to Milagros, looking straight into her face. Milagros listened attentively. At some point she nodded. The doctor stood up, went to the desk, opened a drawer and took out some documents. She sighed as she leafed through them, then she went and sat by Milagros again. She placed a neat hand with short, squarely cut fingernails on Milagros' hands, white from the exertions of gripping. She peered into her face, and slowly spoke to her.

The handbag fell to the ground.

The doctor took the older woman's hand and held it helplessly. Milagros's head was bowed and her shoulders were heaving. The doctor patted her on the back softly, then leaned over and hugged her tightly.

A few minutes passed.

Then Guzmán stood up, went to the desk and picked up a large envelope. She went back to the chair and sat down. Milagros slowly looked up. Her face was tear-stained, but calm.

The doctor slowly started to speak to her again, but soon her tone became more urgent.

Milagros sat up and listened. At first she seemed to be distracted, listening only out of obligation, but soon her expression changed. The doctor took some photographs out of the envelope and showed them to her. She looked at them, listened to the doctor's explanations, nodded, her mouth set into a thin line, its edges shaking a little.

The doctor pointed out a large photograph of a skull. Then another photograph: the skull from the left side. The doctor pointed with the tip of her finger at a dark spot – a round hole – above where the left ear would have been, when the skull was still a living person's head.

Milagros took the photograph with both hands. She brought it closer to her face, then moved it far from it. She fumbled inside the handbag for a pair of glasses with a thick black frame. She put them on, while the doctor was holding the photograph obligingly for her, and then took it back again.

Milagros peered at the photograph long and hard.

The doctor shuffled the other photographs she was holding. She stopped at another one. This one showed a skeleton's pelvis. The doctor turned and picked up a pencil from the desk and with its tip, pointed at various bits of bone. Milagros squinted in her effort to see. The doctor held the rest of the photographs on her lap, then she changed her mind and left them on the desk. Then she faced Milagros and very slowly and carefully spoke to her.

Milagros's lips moved, as if repeating the doctor's words. Her eyes were round and uncomprehending. She looked old and childish at the same time.

The young doctor spoke, becoming increasingly animated, but Milagros had ceased to listen. Her head was bent again; her whole body remained motionless.

As she walked out of the building, Milagros felt strangely light and unreal. She walked down the stairs of the hospital entrance, thinking she might just soar into the early evening sky, like a loose balloon, over Avenida Díaz Vélez, over skyscrapers and apartment towers and rusty chimneys and television aerials, all the way to the river.

She took a few steps down the avenue, hardly knowing where she was going. Passing cars with their lights on, motorcycles, pedestrians – they were all a jumbled mass of muted colors. She looked up and the sky seemed so empty. Abandoned by God. The earth had plummeted, gone down a hole. She felt the weight of every car, bus or truck thundering down the avenue passing over her back; her bones were laid down on the asphalt and all the vehicles were running over them and grinding them to dust. Every now and then she stopped and tried to breathe. It was difficult.

She stumbled along the road till she stopped at a *kiosco*. She bought a bottle of water and asked if they had a telephone she could use. The man showed her in the little shop: there was a telephone booth. It was taken, and she had to wait. She took out her handkerchief from her handbag – the Señora's old handbag – and wiped her face. How can it be so hot in the middle of the winter, she thought. When she went into the booth, she sat staring at the phonebook, hands trembling, sweating profusely. Then she dialed a number.

"Hello? Yes? Is that Families Investigating for Memory and Justice? I would like to speak to Señora Alicia Otamendi, please."

Some time later, she found herself still in the booth, staring at the handset, till she heard tapping on the glass. It was the owner.

"Señora, there are people waiting to make phone calls. If you are not going to use it, please let others. Are you feeling okay?"

No, she was not feeling okay. She never would, ever again.

"Now, come along." He unscrewed the cap from her bottle of water, gave it to her. She looked at him but saw nothing. There was nothing where the voice came from; it was just shapes and colors, ugly colors, dirty, dusty. Like a beige wall in a hospital. The gray surface of a mortuary slab.

She didn't know how or why, but next thing she knew she was walking in the street again.

One step. Two steps. How many steps till I get home? Maybe I should count them. Just to keep my mind busy. I must not think of anything else. I must not think of legs that will walk no more. She had the sweetest, roundest little legs in the world. She was born on a hot summer's day and I was thinking then, Oh holy Virgin, this is how the *asado* felt when stretched over the *parilla*. I was being fried alive, torn apart, and then I heard her cry and she was all blue from the strain, and she was beautiful. God, how beautiful she was! How did that little fairy come into my life; where did she come from? She would toddle into a room, little arms extended, laughing eyes, giggles. And light and heat came in with her. I could even put up with that disgrace, Pablo, because she loved him. She loved everyone. Everyone loved her. How could they do this to her? Didn't they see how lovely she was? Didn't they see how kind, how sweet she was? How could anybody do this to my little girl? How could they bear to see tears in those eyes?

And where did she go? Where? Why dear God, why, where, how did it all happen? Without your mother, my baby, without your mother. And your mother was somewhere else and she was sleeping and eating, the fat pig, the senseless, worthless pig! She could eat and drink and sleep while you were dying, sweetheart, while they were doing things to you, my love, and your disgusting pig of a mother was not there to help you, sweetheart, she could bear to breathe and walk and even smile maybe, and where were you all that time, daughter, where did you go, why did you go?

It was dark when Milagros inexplicably reached a street corner near her home. She had been dragging her steps all over the city, had walked streets and passed places she'd never seen before, had wandered in strange neighborhoods full of unknown faces. Children had run after her calling, "Crazy old woman, crazy old woman!" Dogs had barked at her. Old ladies had stopped her and kindly asked if she was all right, only to move away from her as quickly as possible when she looked at them with wild, inflamed eyes that couldn't see. And now she was back. And she had something to do.

29

Inés de Castro

Milagros laid the bones out of the box in rough approximation; she didn't know exactly how a human body was supposed to be, though when Fito was small he had been given a toy skeleton and the children had spent hours trying to put it together. She remembered watching them and shaking her head at the macabre game. But now she tried to remember exactly how that was done, because these were real bones of a real person and she had to put them together. With steady movements she placed them in the long luxurious box, all shiny and smelling of frothy tulle and silk. She placed the skull tenderly on the satin cushion, then the collar bone. She taped them in place using double-sided tape and she pinned broad satin ribbons on top of them for good measure. What a small skull, she thought, had it really been so small? She couldn't remember. There had been all that thick and glossy hair on top of it, and of course the eyes, the cheeks, the–

No. She wouldn't think of that now. She had work to do.

The dress gleamed softly in the semi-darkness. It smelled of sugared almond bonbons and of starch. It draped softly over the sharp angular yellowish bones. Milagros opened a small cardboard box smelling faintly of lavender and mothballs. She remembered how her breath was taken away when Señorita Delia had brought it out and put it on the table; had it really been she, Milagros, who had taken the pink glossy lid off with a fast-beating heart in that remote room? She unwrapped the layers of tissue paper, rustling under her fingers; she lifted the veil. It was yellow in places, and some of the seed pearls had fallen off the coif, but it was still her lovely lace First Communion veil. She remembered the day she had shown it to Lucía and told her she could have it for her wedding; Lucía had wanted to play with it ever since, though she was forbidden to. Yet one day Milagros had returned home to see Lucía preening in front of the mirror, wrapped in the veil which was much too long for her and swept over the floor. Milagros was furious and had a mind to give her daughter a good thrashing, but then the little girl turned round and her eyes were shining under the white tulle, and she was smiling, and just like that Milagros found herself smiling too amid her tears, as she remembered.

30

Homecoming

Capital Federal, 21 September, 1983

Silvina was walking, walking, walking. From Avenida Alvear she crossed Cerrito, then 9 de Julio, largest street in the world, widest avenue, whatever, everything too large there, everything over the top, large numbers of cars, vast numbers of people, walking fast on the overly broad pavements, going about their business. Nobody knew her; nobody paid attention. Shop windows; she didn't want to look at them but caught glimpses of her image on them passing quickly, at moments almost running. "What a rude woman," someone said, someone she pushed in her frantic effort to escape from her own reflection, trench-coated, hands hidden in the pockets. She didn't even say sorry, she was too panicked, M.me Jouvet had spoken of it, too, or was it the other one, the Swami, the fake Indian, telling her to breathe deeply and visualize a serene place. Silvina laughed bitterly and was aware that people were staring. She walked even faster.

On Avenida Corrientes the bookshop was not there anymore. She stopped on the pavement opposite and muttered, "So it was nothing, after all, no big deal." Here she was, looking at it, where it used to be, and inside she felt nothing. Nothing at all. Is this what you meant by *closure*, M.me Jouvet? Or was it the man in New York? He wore a trimmed beard. She should have suspected him merely for that. What kind of shrink wants to look like an iconic, stereotypical shrink? Exactly, only a phony. The bookshop was boarded up; they would be doing work there soon; it would be converted to something else, something that wouldn't hurt because it would not bear any memories. How long would it take for the eyes to adjust to the new images, for the new images to replace the old ones? Deep breath, serene place. With water. Yes. A lake. A holiday in Bariloche. No. A holiday in Mar del Plata. Children running on the beach. Three children, shrieking with laughter as they splashed about, throwing water on each other. She went underwater, feeling it filling her nostrils, pounding in her ears, she must come up for air, quick, some fresh air. But if she stayed under then she'd start feeling euphoric. It only took a few seconds; she'd read all about it. The only fear was the fear of the unknown.

So why worry, she thought.

She went down the steps into the Subte, a meaningless descent into an urban Hades. No consequences. Well, for some there were and for some there weren't. Had she noticed how consequences always meant the bad things that happened to someone, never the good? The air down there was warm and smelled of engines and oil and human presence. It was comforting. She got on the Line A to Plaza de Mayo. More people on the train, sitting, standing up; she tried to hide among them and then remembered there was no reason to hide anymore; nobody knew her and it was unlikely she would meet anybody from the old days. They were most of them gone, dead; they would not ride the Subte anymore. But now it was just ordinary people: mothers with young children, students, old men and women. I look ordinary to them too, she thought, but who knew what horrors they might be carrying with them, locked safely in their own heads, same as me. There are no ordinary people; there are only survivors. Survivors like myself. We are all survivors. I'm certainly not the only one.

A little boy was dressed in rags and holding another, even younger boy by the hand. They were swaying to the rhythm of the carriage. The older one was singing old tangos, slightly out of tune, pathetic, the melodramatic lyrics with their world-weariness sounding eerie from such a young voice and face.

> *My beloved Buenos Aires*
> *when I see you again*
> *there will be no more pain*
> *no more forgetting...*

His little brother was holding a torch which he placed beneath his chin, lighting his face in a grotesque way; he made faces and lit them up and laughed to himself. His laughter was clear and high: the sound of a musical instrument that hadn't been invented yet, a celestial instrument.

Most passengers looked ahead with glazed eyes, pretending the two little beggars did not exist. Some young people laughed at the song; they thought it was too old-fashioned, a relic from times long forgotten and irrelevant. But a few old ones looked at the boy solemnly, with moist eyes, shaking their heads slowly, remembering heaven knows what episodes from a past nobody cared about, involving people long gone. They searched in their pocket for coppers to give the boys. The older boy collected them in a cap; he bowed gallantly as he went on with his singing. Every time a coin fell into the cap, the younger brother flashed his torch and let off a tinkling silver bell of a giggle.

She left the train at the station Plaza de Mayo, standing at the bottom of the stairs, many people going down past her, men in suits old and worn, with shabby leather shoes and briefcases, just people struggling to make a living. Some of them might have had blood on their hands; some of them might still be mourning lost ones, who knew? Who can ever know the human heart, who can ever decipher it, children begging, more beggars than in the old times, or maybe back then she didn't see them. Whatever I've done I've done for you all, all you spent and calm-looking people, the look of people after a long weary journey. But the best...the best were gone, dead or disappeared, and they'd taken her Buenos Aires with them.

And who was going to assume their place? The cowards. The silent ones. The privileged. What I'd like to know, she thought, is whether anything, anything at all, has changed for all this pain and suffering and death. And if it hadn't, then what was the point? What was the fucking point?

She was still standing at the bottom of the stairs, still not sure she wanted to go up to the surface again. It was warm and dark in the Subte. Almost like a womb. Maybe that was my problem from square one, she thought, my mother's womb was just not hospitable enough. Ha! Back to the psychoanalytical nonsense.

She climbed up the stairs slowly, until she was back on the surface of the earth again. There were people everywhere, but they looked different from the ones on the subterranean train. They were all standing, and they were white, and ghostly, and they didn't have faces or hair. There were pregnant women with huge bellies, and babies crawling.

What was this? She blinked and looked again. It was only silhouettes, cut out of pasteboard, drawn on walls, on the sidewalks, even on the road. There were words written on the walls, too. She read: *Where are they? We want them back alive!* There were people, real people, around the silhouettes, pointing, whispering to each other; some had tears in their eyes, some glared, but nobody spoke out loud. Slowly the avenue and the plaza ahead – the Casa Rosada rising behind the mist – were filled with people who glided among the silhouettes, looking more ghostly and unreal than the paper figures, set up by students from the College of Art to commemorate the Disappeared.

"Silvina!"

Her name hit her like an arrow. Gustavo had spotted her and was now walking fast towards her, smiling, and too late did she realize that there was nowhere for her to hide, not in this city where there were still people from the old days, survivors like herself, but alas, not the best: not those who should have been spared. Only the second rate, the opportunists, the unworthy.

31

The Stone Maidens

Recoleta Cemetery

Milagros would have liked to think of them as sleeping peacefully, but the image never quite worked for her. Put them to bed, arrange their covers neatly and snugly so they won't catch cold in the night. Yes. Sit next to them, watch their little breasts as they breathe, up and down softly, listen to their breath coming out of tiny nostrils. Okay. Switch off the lights, see the room bathed in the ethereal light of the moon and stars, stay in the soft sweet darkness and dream a little with them – fine. God knows in what grassy gardens they roamed in their dreams. God only knows.

But here, no, it wasn't working. They did not sleep. They were dead. They were in boxes. Fito in his large polished ebony one, with the silver carvings. Sealed with lead. They hadn't even been allowed to look at him, to say goodbye. "You don't want to remember him like that," the kind man had said. What did it matter; she had seen so many bones by now. She wondered if there really was anyone in that coffin. And then Lucía in her little chest. A small heap of slender bones. No, how can you say they are asleep? The children are not even there. They've left those horrible remains of themselves behind; they've upped and gone. Where did they go?

Milagros dusted and cleaned and polished. She washed the white lace doilies and polished the silver and bronze candelabra. She made sure there was not a speck of dust on the marble altar. The cross of our Lord and the statue of our Virgin of Sorrows were shining softly in the gloom.

Gold and velvet chairs, carpet, chandelier.

Marble floor, mosaics, tiles, crystal, silver, bronze, expensive wood.

She scrubbed the floor. She even used wire brushes. Steel wool. Soda powder. Beeswax polish for the caskets. Spray for the glass. Hot water, vinegar, and lemon for the crystal. The silver kept its sheen when rubbed with a soft woollen cloth, no liquid necessary at all. A small spatula scrubbed off the candle wax. Some people burned incense. She always planned to, then found she'd forgotten. Would they like its bittersweet, cloying fragrance?

She left the older coffins for Pancho, the caretaker. She didn't like climbing down the steep stairs. It was so cold down there; what little air there was stank, musty and old and rotting – if air could rot. She feared it. She might be breathing in God knows what, dust of decades, years of decomposing bodies. She had seen a decomposing dog once, a very long time ago, out in the pampas. She shuddered when she remembered the sight. She thought: if I could open all those boxes and peer inside, is this what I would see? She tried to chase away the images coming, leaping out, crowding her brain. Shoo. As if they were flies, all those flies on the carcass, the heaving white mass of maggots...No. Stop. Concentrate on the floor instead. It has to shine like a mirror. The Señora might slip and break her leg, she thought maliciously, as she had been doing for some time now.

She looked at Doña Ramona, sitting on the elegant sofa like a grotesque idol, uncomprehending, lost. It should have been you and me in those boxes, thought Milagros, overcome with weariness and sudden, unexpected pity. But not them. Not them, oh dear God. Outside the mausoleum, the maidens bent towards each other, tears of stone gliding down their immovable, pensive faces.

32

An Announcement

Doña Maria Ramona Silvina Irribaren de Goyena (54) – R.I.P. – Peacefully in her sleep, in her domicile in Recoleta, Capital Federal. Her beloved daughter D.ra Silvina Estela Goyena de Irribaren invites close family and friends to a burial service at the family mausoleum, cemetery of Recoleta, tomorrow 11.00 a.m. No flowers. Donations to be made to the non-government organisation Families Investigating for Memory and Justice.

(Printed in national evening newspaper, LA VERDAD, Funerary Announcements, 15 August, 1985)

PART FIVE

2003

33

Remains of a Family

Everything was ready for Silvina's party. The apartment was entirely clean and polished; mountains of sandwiches were arranged on the table; on the sideboard were enough drinks to fill a reservoir. Milagros finished laying out Silvina's new clothes on the bed for her. She was taking her bath when Milagros left.

"I'm off! Have a good time, see you tomorrow morning," Milagros shouted as she was going out the door, but she heard no reply over the running water.

Downstairs Milagros met Norberto, the *portero*, sitting at his large mahogany desk opposite the glass and cast-iron entrance door. He winked at her:

"Another party tonight, eh?"

"Keep an eye on her for me, Norberto, make sure she doesn't misbehave."

They laughed and said goodnight.

When Milagros got home, about two hours later, she was exhausted. As soon as she put the kettle on for the *mate*, Mabel's head appeared over the fence, turning this way and that like a periscope. She came round to pass the time every evening, but that night Milagros didn't have much appetite for conversation. Mabel was going on and on about the neighborhood assembly and their new plans to install street lighting in the *barrio*. They'd have to pay a hundred and forty pesos per house.

It was all right for Mabel: her Damián was in the building materials business, and he was making good money and took care of his old mother. He had just had a new roof installed on her house, and a brand-new security door. Her grandchildren had two mobile phones each, the thugs. They tormented animals too, just like their father used to. While Milagros had nobody to take care of her. Where was the justice in this world? And where was she going to find that kind of money?

While Mabel was chattering and Milagros was yawning as ostentatiously as she could, the doorbell rang. It was a polite young man from Salud Integral Insurance Services. Señora Riquelme owed them three months of instalments, seventy-five pesos and twenty *centavos*, to be precise. Would she be obliging enough to make a payment? She gave him twenty pesos under Mabel's prying eyes. He said he would come back next week.

And then the doorbell rang again. All misfortunes come in threes, thought Milagros.

She knew it was Pablo. He always came round towards the end of the week, when he knew she would have been paid. At least that drove Mabel away. But Milagros was sure she would be hovering in her backyard for a while, trying to overhear. The old crow. At least she was going deaf lately. Served her right.

"Ugh! You've been drinking again. You smell awful," Milagros said.

Pablo shrugged and looked sheepish as he walked into the room.

"Well, you're late this time. The insurance collector has already been. Sorry!"

His face fell, and Milagros felt like laughing out loud.

"It's nice to see you still care enough for me to visit though. Well, virtue is its own reward. I'm having a *mate*, want some?"

"Isn't there anything else? Beer?"

"No, and there will never be."

He sat in his chair – it shouldn't be called his chair anymore, as he hadn't been living in the house for years, but old habits die hard – and switched on the TV.

"I've got a headache," Milagros said. "What is it you wanted?"

Pablo looked smaller and thinner every time she saw him. It was one of the mysteries of life, how men became all shrivelled as they grew old, whereas most women expanded, taking up double and triple the space compared to when they were young.

"I'm going away," he said.

"Oh yes? Where to this time?"

"What do you mean, this time? Have I ever gone away before?"

"No, but you always promise you will, and like a fool I believe you. The fares I've paid up so far, you could have gone to the moon."

"You make fun of me again. Go on, make fun of me, if it pleases you so much."

"Why don't you go to hell once and for all, Pablito? What do I care where you go and what you do! I've stopped caring a long time ago. A very long time ago, do you hear?"

"Keep your hair on, old woman," he said.

They sipped some *mate*, watching TV. There was a riot somewhere downtown: a journalist was screaming himself hoarse into a microphone, while behind him people wearing kerchiefs round their noses and mouths were throwing stones and Molotov cocktails and police on horseback were hitting them with truncheons.

"Goddamn bastards, sons of bitches," Pablo muttered.

Milagros sat at the table and drafted her accounts on the back of an old electricity bill, mumbling to herself.

Two hundred and forty la Silvina owes me, fifty-five twenty I owe the insurance, twenty-three fifty-nine for the gas, the electricity I paid last week, won't have to pay for it for another two months, thank God. No need to buy food tomorrow, there'll be plenty of leftovers from Silvina's party, they don't eat much, they only drink and I have no use for drink, though better not tell Pablo anything about the party. I wouldn't put it past him to go and beg from Silvina, though God knows how he could show his face there anymore after the fiasco with rehab, what a shame, the woman tries to help, secures a free place for him at the clinic and he up and leaves before the first week is over! Disgraceful son of a...why I put up with him I don't know. Others in my position would have shut the door on his face long ago. The fact he's still alive is also somewhat mystifying, his liver must be like a rotten sponge by now, but he's still kicking around. For my sins.

"Look, they're in it as well," Pablo said, pointing at the TV set. "It must be something important, if they're in it."

There were many of them, white scarves on their heads, holding up banners, chanting among the havoc. The women from Families Investigating for Memory and Justice. They seemed to be in everything nowadays: protests, rallies, TV shows. Good for them. Milagros searched for the tall, dignified figure of Alicia Otamendi de Grant among them, but it was impossible to identify anybody in the chaos. Besides, she'd be too old now, too frail to go to demonstrations like she used to. Her son and daughter-in-law were still among the disappeared. Her granddaughter hadn't been found either. She had said so on a TV documentary the other day. Milagros regretted having watched it.

Pablo got up and changed the channel. There was a prize show on this one: every time the contestants got an answer right, blond girls dressed in tiny bright-colored dresses screamed and danced up and down like the idiots they were. Pablo was looking at them with his mouth hanging open.

"Shut it or a fly may get in," Milagros said.

He didn't even turn to look at her. He sipped his *mate*.

Two hundred and forty she owes me. The new dress she bought for the party cost twice that. What use is it buying all that stuff? She hasn't got a husband and won't ever get one. Too late now. She looks more like her mother as she grows older. "Time passes for everyone, daughter, rich and poor alike," my poor old mother used to say. Only for the dead it doesn't pass. They remain the same age for ever and ever. Forever young, forever beautiful. Ah, what will become of me?

Pablo looked at her in a strange way.

"What is it, you old good-for-nothing?" she asked. "What's the matter now?"

"I'll get out of your sight if that's what you want," he said. "Only...only..."

"Only you need some money again, right?"

"Well...if you can spare a bit for me–"

"How much?"

"Um...let's see...one hundred pesos?"

"One hundred pesos! For what reason? Are you really leaving town then?"

"Eh...no, not exactly. I need it to pay for the license."

"License? What license is that?"

"For a stand at the Sunday fair in Lezama Park."

"Oh, so you're going into business! What will you be selling, if I may ask?"

"It's just food. *Empanadas*, pasties, that sort of thing. Inés will be making them; I'll be selling them."

"Inés? Is that the Bolivian widow?"

"The very same."

"And she'll be baking and you'll be selling.'"

"Yes, what's wrong with that?"

"Well, there's no shortage of fools in the world is all I say. Though in this case I don't know who's the more fool of the two."

"Come on now, Mili, you can't be jealous!"

"Jealous? Me? I assure you, all I feel towards this woman is gratitude. That is I *would*, if she managed to keep you away from here permanently. Unfortunately, I don't see that happening anytime soon. You're always here begging from me. Does she know you're here now?"

He shrugged, went to the TV and changed the channel again.

The austere face of Alicia Otamendi in the advertisement for Families Investigating for Memory and Justice, said solemnly, "If you were born between 1976 and 1983 and have doubts about your identity, approach us…"

Pablo moaned softly and changed channel. Milagros looked through the window. It was pitch dark now. He changed channel again.

On Channel Noticias there was a press conference. The Minister of Public Transport in front of many microphones, large and small, was saying, "…the new plan to solve the capital's increasing traffic, which, on the other hand, is a sure indication of a healthy, growing economy…" The man looked tired; his face shone with the heat from the camera lights. Surely he should have been at the party right now?

"Ah, look!" Pablo said. "It's that guy. The Minister! Silvina's guy. Gustavo Whatshisname. The ex-Montonero!"

Milagros went to the TV and switched it off.

They sat in silence for a few minutes.

Pablo was stirring uneasily in his chair.

"Well, what about that money?" he said finally.

"What about it?"

"Aren't you gonna give it me? I'll pay you back this time. I promise. Every *centavo*."

"I haven't got a hundred pesos, Pablo."

"Come on, Mili. You always have some stashed away. I know you. Please!"

"I haven't got it."

"Then fifty. Forty. As much as you can spare."

"Oh, so forty would be enough for your license, eh?"

"No, but I'll find the rest somehow. Just help me this once."

"I've helped you a million times and what good ever came of it?"

"This time I promise – just thirty, twenty, please!"

"I haven't got any money. I haven't been paid for more than a week now. La Silvina has had a lot of entertaining to do. Partying with the Minister, no time to remember the old housekeeper's wages."

"Oh, come on Mili, You know you have something to give me. For the love of God. I was your husband once, I was her father–"

"What did you say?"

"If she was here you wouldn't be like this to me. Lucía loved her old Papi, and she would have–"

"Don't you ever dare put her name into your foul mouth again, you disgusting drunkard! How dare you! Get out now! Out of my house. Go on, get lost, never come back here again!"

"Don't be angry now, Mili, I only said–"

"I don't care what you said. Go! Here, take these ten pesos, it's my last money, go drink yourself to death."

She slammed the door with all her might. Oh, Lord, what were You thinking? Why is this wretch still around to torment me, and my beautiful girl is only a little bunch of bones in the ground? What were You thinking, Lord?

34

The Last One

Avenida Libertador & Montevideo, Recoleta

Milagros got off the bus at exactly 8.06. She was more than half an hour late. Thanks to the new roadworks of his excellency the Minister of Public Transport. He wasn't the one who had to ride on crowded buses. She stopped at the bakery to buy a kilo of mixed pastries, the ones Silvina always asked for after a party night, filled with *dulce de leche* and chocolate. There was a pregnant woman with two small children outside the bakery, begging. They looked as if they had slept there on the street. Milagros scowled but gave the mother her loose change and the children one pastry each.

She walked quickly, aware of the sweat coming strong and musky underneath her armpits. She wondered if she had time for a quick wash before she began the day's work. She wanted to have the mess of the previous night cleaned away, ashtrays emptied, dirty glasses washed, the large drawing room aired, before Silvina woke up. Then they could have a *mate* together, and she would ask her about the money. Then Silvina's patients would start to arrive. You've saved others but you cannot save yourself, Milagros thought, shaking her head with pity.

She stopped at the dry cleaner's to pick up the laundry: two dresses, a trouser suit, three shirts. One of them was a man's shirt. It was not the Minister's. He never left any clothes behind him; his wife was very jealous, though she was at least twenty years younger than him. Why was she so jealous? It was more than obvious that her husband was not going to leave her for Silvina. If he had loved her, he would have married her back then, when they were young, wouldn't he? And poor Silvina still living in hope... This didn't stop her from enjoying herself though. Whose shirt was this? It looked like something a young man would wear.

When Milagros reached the building, the deputy *portero* jumped up from behind the desk and rushed to open the door for her. She thanked him and he nodded. He was a silent one, that young man. His name was Juán Domingo. Like the President of old, whom her father used to revere so. Good thing he died long before things transpired the way they did. This Juán Domingo here was from down south. Unfriendly people, those southerners, reserved. She could not complain, though, he was always very polite and proper. She would just rather have seen Norberto at the *portería*, to ask him about last night; he always kept a discreet eye over things and gave her warning. But Norberto was never at his post before nine o'clock.

Juán Domingo opened the lift door for her. As it went up, she looked at herself in the gilded mirror. Her hair was already untidy and coarse with dust and sweat. She looked tired and haggard, and she had put on a bit of weight lately. She must not eat too many pastries today, only a couple of crackers with the *mate* and that should be it.

She reached the fourth floor and pushed the door open with her backside, trying to balance the pastry box and avoid dragging the freshly laundered clothes on the floor. When she was in front of the door, she realized that she would have to put the pastry box down on the floor and hoist the laundered clothes over her back in order to get her keys out of her handbag. She cursed herself for not thinking of it earlier; she could have asked the Patagonian porter to hold her stuff for her. With difficulty, she unlocked all three heavy locks and pushed the door. It only opened a sliver. The chain was on from the inside.

So a man had stayed the night. Good thing Silvina put the chain on. Milagros hated it when she walked into Silvina's bedroom with her dusters and there was a naked man in the bed. It was just not right.

Milagros rang the bell. Waited. Rang again. And again. No sound of steps or any movement came from inside the apartment. She kept on ringing, pressing the button longer and longer, and she felt the sweat drenching her, getting colder on her back. The ringing sounded hoarse and desperate, like a baby crying and crying in an empty house and nobody there to pick it up.

At 9.15 the door was broken open by the combined efforts of the building's private security and the two *porteros*. They had accidentally trampled on the box of pastries in the process, and Milagros had stepped on the hem of one of the freshly laundered dresses, leaving the dusty imprint of her *alpargatas* on the white crepe de chine. She threw the bundle on the Queen Anne chair next to the entrance door and made straight for Silvina's bedroom, barely registering the chaos in the rooms, the debris from last night's party, the stale smells of tobacco and alcohol and something more acrid which she knew to be marijuana (Mabel's Damián still indulged in the stuff from time to time, although these days he was more likely to sell it). The floors were sticky with spilt drinks. The security men and the *porteros* picked their way carefully in the semi-darkness. They were awed by the size and luxury of the rooms; they very rarely got the opportunity to enter any of the apartments it was their job to guard. They all registered the strange silence that made the grand apartment feel completely empty. They were wary of it. When they heard Milagros scream, they jumped, but they couldn't say they weren't expecting it: they rushed towards the continuous wails in the depths of the apartment.

35

Fancy Words

November 2, 2003

Dearest Gustavo,

At last this is goodbye. This time for good. I can't take it anymore. So I'm leaving. I don't think you'll miss me, or maybe you will, but it doesn't matter much now anyway. The thing is, I'm just too tired and I can't carry on. "Move on, put everything behind," say the ignorant, the common, those who have no idea, who can't even begin to imagine what it was like, what it's still like. And isn't it ironic I have to use this particular cliché myself in my professional life, day in, day out, though I know very well what a lie it is? There is nowhere to go. It is impossible to move on, there is nothing, only the conviction – no, the knowledge – that they have won this war, that they have won and we have lost, no matter if you are now His Excellency the Minister and the pigs surround you as honorary escort wherever you go and they guard your beautiful house and your young and beautiful wife and flick the dust away from your Italian suits and lick your handmade English shoes. And what am I doing here, alone at 5 a.m.? A middle-aged woman getting older by the day. And everything around me shrinks and vanishes, and whatever I touch turns to dust. We've lost this war, Gustavo, we've lost every war, and let me tell you, those who left early were the lucky ones. They were the lucky ones and I wasn't. I don't believe in an afterlife so I don't expect to meet them there, Lucía and Fito, they won't be waiting for me with reproaches and hurt looks, no, there is no ninth ring of hell. I won't be punished because nobody will be, traitor or assassin or torturer, no one is ever punished, and that's our misfortune. We just have to move on, Gustavo, but I have nowhere to move on to in this world, and so I'm getting out, and this is goodbye. Remember me, but please no obituaries and no fancy words. You know how much I hate them.

  Silvina

(Private letter sent to Dr. Gustavo Francisco López-Ortega, Minister of Public Transport)

36

In the Garden

Even from a distance it was immediately obvious he was dead. There he lay in his old worn out suit the color of liver. His face was the same color as his tie: a putrid yellow. It was a hot day, and moths were already flying around his eyes and mouth, ready to take possession. His legs were rigidly extended in front of him, shoes scuffed at the toes but polished all the same.

Just a few hours earlier he had been standing in front of the elderly shoeshine, putting his foot on the box with the metal base. The shoeshine talked non-stop as he worked with a dexterity belying his frailty and age.

"We're going to the dogs," the old boy was saying. "Where oh where are the good old days? *Che*, you could walk out safely in the middle of the night then. You didn't ever have to lock your front door. I say bring on the military men, that's what the country needs nowadays with all those corrupt politicians and their palaces and their luxury holidays abroad."

Don Julián frowned as he listened to the ancient man garbling on and on. Why is he telling me this? he wondered. What does *he* know? Don Julián was not pleased. He'd heard all this talk before but he knew it didn't mean much. He knew how quickly words and ideas changed, congratulations turned into condemnation, the "Hosannah!" into "Crucify him!" as the wind blew.

The shining over, Don Julián paid the man, who accepted the torn banknote gratefully, murmuring thanks and blessings. Then the blessings turned to curses muttered between decrepit false teeth, as soon as Don Julián had turned his back. He ignored them.

Don Julián had nothing to do and nobody to see and nowhere to go. The old café where his friends used to meet, friends from the old days, his own people, had closed down recently. There was a building site there now, promising to be ready by the end of the year, with luxury apartments. His friends had scattered. Some of them dead. Others gone away, God knew where. Now his schedule was sparse and fixed. He would go back home at noon and have his lunch. It was waiting for him on the small folding table in the kitchen. A piece of the *torta pasqualina* from yesterday. Mashed potato. A small piece of cheese. A soda to wash it all down. Then he would go to that new café on the corner and have a cup of coffee. He would read the paper. Someone would have left one. Time would pass. He would go back home for supper. But what to do till then?

Go to the garden in the park. Sit on the bench. If his favorite bench was free. The one behind the statue of the naked nymph with ivy coming out of her mouth. Stone ivy. He would spend the day looking at the nymph's beautiful round stone ass. He had been dreaming about this ass. More than once. He could feel its round shape under his hands. He wanted to caress it. But people watched. People always watched. They had nothing better to do. Always spying on others. Ready to criticize. To judge. None of their business. None of anybody's business. He couldn't stand them. Secrecy was a great thing. A great virtue. What you did in secret – it didn't exist. There were so many people who believed this, even now. After all those TV shows. The newspaper stories. Good men taken out to market and made a spectacle of. They had confessed. They had been forced to sign something they didn't mean. They had had to. One had to go on living. Even in prison. It was still some kind of living.

Don Julián had seen the crowds, disfigured faces, mouths wide open, screeching, screaming. Masses flocking outside the court-room. Cameras and long microphones threatening, terrible. He didn't care about the judges with their self-satisfied smirks of righteousness. He didn't care about the families, pale and silent behind the line of the defendants. He didn't even care about the miserable dogs, the rank and file, the traitors, who pointed a finger at him and said, "That's him, he's the one who made me do it." Some people thought that was what hurt most, the low turning against the high, the treason. But he knew this was what happened in such situations. They would do that. They were sons of bitches, the lot of them, hounds faithful only so long as they were fed, then they turned and bit your leg. Let them all go to hell. No, the only thing he minded was those long microphones shoved into his face. The treacherous cameras following his every blink, his slightest change of expression, as he sat in the dock. He had been advised to look straight at the lens, straight at the eyes of the public. The lawyers had told him, "This means you have nothing to hide. Everything you did, you did in good faith. For the moth-erland. For honor. For the army. You have nothing to be afraid of and you have nothing to hide. Just refuse everything."

Easy for them to talk, ignorant bastards.

He had a family once. But this was a very long time ago. They upped and left. "If only I had known what you are," she had said. Yes, you did. You did, madam. Only it didn't suit you when every-body else knew too. You wanted this, you wanted that, and as long you had it, you were happy. "Señora de Lieutenant Colonel." You enjoyed the salutes, the car, the young conscripts collecting your laundry from the dry cleaners and doing the school run for you. And the brats. Papá, I need a new dress, all my friends have new dresses. Papá, I need a new motorbike, all my friends have a new motorbike. Then they upped and left. The old man was useless now. What to do with him now that everyone knew? Out with him.

Who needed them? He had a family. The army was his family. But yes, most of his companions were dead. Or gone away, what was the difference?

He needed to decide what to do today. He couldn't sit on a park bench all day. Maybe he would go downtown. He'd walk to the plaza. The breeze came straight from the port there. It was fresher. The plaza would be full of people. It was better among large crowds. He would not be seen there. But how could he be sure? That old shoeshine now. He surely knew something. He recognized him. Why else mention the military? Better not go that way anymore. He would find another shoeshine. Someone young who would not remember. But they all knew these days. They did. Cursed television. Hadn't they anything better to show? Only old stories. Stories better forgotten. He couldn't understand people sometimes. Why did they want to remember? As if there was anything good to remember.

Those crazy women especially.

No, he'd better not go to the square. That was their haunt. And they knew him. They knew, all of them. "You old devil, old torturer," they had shouted at him the other day. "Murderer! Assassin!" Some of the women were older than him. Some were his age. He could have been their husband, their brother. Didn't they feel sorry for an old man? "You are a disgrace," they had said. "You should not dare show your face here. Go find a hole to die in." Their mouths, horrible grimaces. Now *that* he could understand. Pain is the one thing he understood. He grinned at them. "You make my day. I like it. It still hurts, eh?" "Go to hell, you old pervert," they shouted at him. A young man wanted to hit him. "Your old man was not as brave when the *picana* was up his ass," he called out, a leer on his face. Oh, there was still some fun in it all right. "You old son of a bitch, shame on you," they screamed back at him. "Will you not repent? What forgive and forget nonsense are we talking about? These people would do it all again with pleasure." Then a policeman had come along. "Officer, this man is an assassin and a torturer. Surely he must not be on the loose." "Come on, now," said the policeman to them, "move along. You are disturbing the peace. Quick or I'll take you all down to the precinct." "Those days are over," a young girl said, her words dripping with impudence – she had a nice little pert ass in her tight jeans. "You can't do this to people anymore." He had been trying to catch the officer's eye, to ascertain their connection, two men on the side of law and order, even after all that had happened, but the officer wouldn't look at him. He was looking at the girl and he spoke to the old woman, who was obviously the ringleader, the young man her lieutenant. What is the world coming to, Don Julián wondered. All order destroyed. Exactly what those subversives wanted. They won that war, and that was the truth.

He liked it in the park garden early in the morning. Hardly anybody around. Thank God. No mothers and babies. They would come later. Their babies would scream until they were red in the face. He didn't like babies. He didn't like children. But he would not kill them. Who said kill them? We were not unnatural men. Raise them good and proper. It was the only solution. A charitable thing. A wise thing. That was how you beat the enemy. Beat them at their own game. Catch them before they indoctrinate them. Be there first. Take their children away, hand them over to good families where they would be raised properly, with the right ideas.

See? It was simple.

The park bench was empty. He sat there, carefully wiping the bench dry with his handkerchief. He didn't want his trousers wet. It was not good for his health. He might catch cold. He was always careful about that, his health. Would he catch something from them? Not if he was careful. He remembered the army doctor, his inferior. He liked that man. Always with his stethoscope at the ready.

"Stop! You don't want her to die on you." "Stop it. Give her a break." "Less voltage, if you please." "Careful there, Lieutenant Colonel. This is a line you don't want to cross. I'm not averse to this kind of treatment for subversives, but..."

"It's not a matter of personal opinion, doctor. It's what has to be done."

"But they are too young."

"So much the better. Subversion needs to be nipped in the bud."

Here, he remembered the doctor laughing. "Chicharrón, you are a gross pig, if you don't mind me saying so! Ready to fuck whatever moves on two legs. Even four maybe. But think of the danger. The diseases you could catch."

"But you just said they're too young. They can't carry any diseases."

"But we all know what these subversives are like, the rotten lives they lead. All promiscuity. No respect for family or morals."

It was a nice day. It would have been a nicer day if the air was a bit thicker. Why so thin today? It must be the heat. Coming up from the river. From the earth. Did you know, bodies send up heat? Yes, it must be all those bodies. Buried everywhere. In the foundations of downtown skyscrapers. In the underground tunnels. Beneath the tar and macadam on avenues and highways. There were bodies everywhere. They were blazing hot. Going to burn us all. Stealing the air we breathe. They decompose and cause combustion. They ignite. Strange how that round little bottom was really fuel for the flame. Or was it the flame itself. Try the *picana* on it. It's gonna shake and tremble. It drove him mad. The bastards, they enjoyed it. They enjoyed it, the bastards.

He moved to another part of the park. Another bench. Dirty beggar children were playing around. Two of them approached him: a girl dragging a boy by the hand. They were so dirty. Their noses running. Disgusting. He made as if to raise his stick and they ran away.

And then he heard them. Not the children. The bodies underneath his bench. He heard them screaming with horrible shrill voices.

"Where do you think you'll hide? There is nowhere for you to run, old bastard. We'll get you. We'll burn you alive. See how you like it." And they were laughing. They were laughing. He could hear their sickening laughter coming through long teeth. Unmasked by lips. They had been eaten away, the lips. Too many years under the ground. He hated them. He hated them!

But they were everywhere. He had managed to keep them at bay for a long time. Now they knew where he was. They shouted at him. They whispered. They sighed. They heaved. "Old son of a whore," they screamed. "We'll hunt you down. Hunt you down. We'll burn you alive." He felt them dragging him down, towards the graves. They flared up around him. The world was on fire.

The white van of the forensic team opened its doors. Various people came out, medical masks covering the lower part of their faces, hands covered by plastic gloves. A young man was putting yellow tape all around the park bench. People started to gather around the marked enclosure, staring avidly at the dead body. Mothers with babies in their buggies, teenagers bunking off school, a few old men with hands behind their backs.

"Poor old man," they whispered to each other. "Dying all alone like this. Poor old man..."

37

Death of a Torturer

DEATH OF A NOTORIOUS TORTUROR
Another Chapter of the Dirty War Closes

Bs. As. – Julián Dos Santos (81), alias Pedro, alias The Butcher, alias Chicharrón, died of natural causes yesterday in Buenos Aires. Dos Santos, a former Lieutenant Colonel in the Army Engineers Corps was implicated in the abduction, torture and disappearance of at least two hundred persons in the years of the Proceso and was condemned to twenty years in prison for crimes perpetrated against humanity during the Dirty War, in the famous trials of 1985-1986, only to be pardoned a few years later due to the general amnesty granted by the then President Menem. Efforts to prosecute him in the early 90s for human rights violations, after allegations were made against him for participation in the kidnapping and illegal adoption of children of the disappeared, failed for lack of sufficient proof. Alicia Otamendi de Grant (76), representative of Families Investigating for Memory and Justice, said, "Dos Santos was yet another unpunished criminal implicated in one of the most horrendous crimes our country, and indeed the world, has ever known. He may be under the jurisdiction of another Judge now, but this must not mean that our own human judges should not do their job properly. We demand that all perpetrators of such abominable human rights violations like Dos Santos be brought to justice and tried in a court of law, which is much more than they allowed their victims."

There was no statement from the Retired Army Engineers Association concerning Dos Santos's death.

See also: The Legacy of the Dirty War, by Fernando Rojas-Walsh, p. 8.

(Story published in national evening newspaper, LA VERDAD,
November 3, 2003)

38

The Day of the Dead

November 2, Grand Bourg and Capital Federal

The young man got out of his car and looked around him. What he saw were low houses, dirt streets with patches of cement here and there, children playing, dogs barking. There were very few cars, and those there were old. In the corner a kiosco was advertising its super large hotdogs with a rather rude illustration; some men were hanging out there, standing or squatting against the wall. One or two of the houses down the street looked like junkyards. This is where *cartoneros* live, the young man thought. He had never been to a place like this before; he had only seen barrios like this from inside his car, on the way to his own home ensconced in a private neighborhood, surrounded by high walls, protected by gates. Yet this place did not look dangerous or threatening. Rather like a place in a retro movie dealing with the lives of the working class in the 1970s. This would have been a much more cheerful place twenty or thirty years ago, he thought.

The house at the address he was looking for was small, built slightly higher from the ground, with a tiny dust yard around it and a porch in front. The whitewash on the walls had fallen in places to reveal the bricks underneath. The shutters on the windows were closed. He climbed up the four steps to the small porch, where there was only a single white plastic chair sitting empty, a clothesline with two or three pegs, a couple of flowerpots. He sighed with relief. It did not look abandoned. People still lived here. He rang the bell.

A small fat woman peeked outside her front door from the next house.

"She's not in," the woman shouted, a bit more loudly than necessary. "She's at work all day, over in the capital."

"Oh, good afternoon, madam," said the young man pleasantly. "Would you know when she'll be back?"

His voice had the polished tones of an educated man. Encouraged, the woman went on:

"She usually returns at six, seven o'clock, depending on traffic. She comes down there at the bus stop, but sometimes she takes the train and walks from the station. It's a long journey from the capital, you know. Two hours, just about. Do you come from the capital yourself?"

The young man did not reply, just smiled and looked at his watch. Still two, three hours to go, if what the nosy neighbor said was true.

"I guess I'll have to wait," he said.

He walked back down the steps to his car and leaned on the door. He rolled himself a cigarette and lit it. The woman was still there, looking at him with unconcealed curiosity.

"Might you be from the Salud Integral Insurance Services?" she asked.

"No, ma'am," he said, still smiling.

"If it's anything urgent you might be wanting her for, I can give you the number at her work."

"Oh, no, it's all right. I'd rather see her in person. I can wait."

He did not want to say that he already had the number but he preferred not to use it. Some things could not be said over the phone.

The woman hesitated, then said, "Would you care to come in and wait in my house? Maybe have a nice cup of coffee?"

"No, thank you, ma'am. I'm fine."

He smoked his cigarette and looked nowhere in particular.

"Are you from up north? I know Milagros has family up north, though she hasn't been to see them for a very long time. It's so expensive to travel nowadays, you know."

He smiled, said nothing, smoked his cigarette.

"You're not a journalist?" asked the woman abruptly, as if inspired.

"A journalist? Oh no, I'm not a journalist."

"I'm only saying this because there were a lot of journalists here once. They were doing a program, you know, for the families of the...you know, those who disappeared. It was such a shame about poor little Lucía, such a gorgeous girl she was! They asked questions all over the place, and I said no, we had nothing to do with these horrible things, it's such a shame people do that sort of horrible thing. But my son Damián, you know, my youngest, he says, Ma, you have no business talking to people you don't know who poke their nose everywhere and ask questions. He was always a bit, how should I say, my son..."

The young man took his car keys out of his pocket.

"I think I'll leave and maybe come back tomorrow," he said.

"No, no, wait, Milagros will be here soon, I'm sure she'll want to know who you are, I mean, she'll be sorry to miss you. I know, why don't you go to wait inside her house?"

"Really? Could I do that?"

"Yes, yes, of course, you look like a nice young man, you're not a thief, surely, not that you'd need to be with such a nice big car. I can tell you're an educated young man, and if you don't want to say who you are…I mean, if you can go in and wait, Mili will soon be here and find out. Look here, I've got it, her key, take it. Go in, please, do go in. I would come to keep you company, only I have to wait for the children, they'll be home soon and very hungry, too, my grandchildren, you know."

Milagros left Silvina's building at around two in the afternoon. She had had two cups of tea at the *portero*'s rooms first, prepared extra strong and sweet by his wife. The police and the forensic team had stayed for over five hours. The paramedics had left first, taking the body with them. The chief policeman had said Milagros would be required down at the precinct for an official statement, probably the following morning.

"You are lucky there were so many witnesses that the door was locked on the inside, it simplifies things for both of us," he had told her.

As they were all leaving, she had overheard one of the younger policemen say to another, "Those high society broads, what on earth is their problem that they go and kill themselves?"

"Maybe her boyfriend left her."

"There must be something in the air today, they're dropping like flies," said a third. "Day of the Dead and all."

"Who else?"

"An old man in the park a few blocks up."

"Really?"

They were sniggering as the lift doors closed behind them, their voices being cut off abruptly.

Milagros had remained silent all the while, her face stony, cold sweat running down her back.

She boarded the bus which mercifully was not as crowded as usual. She hadn't been on a bus at that early hour for a very long time. She found a seat at the back and sank into it. The city passed in front of her eyes as the bus rushed down the avenue, but she didn't see it. Her eyes were closed; her head was resting against the high-backed chair.

The young man let himself in with the key that the obliging neighbor – Mabel, he thought she'd said – gave him. He closed the door softly behind him, looked for the switch and pressed it. A feeble light came on.

He found himself in a front room, rather cramped with furniture that obviously had once belonged to a much larger and wealthier house. There were two doors, one leading into a small kitchen, the other into the bedroom. There was a tiny washing room and bathroom off the kitchen, added as an afterthought. And that was the whole house. There were photographs all over the front room: on the old TV set, on the table, on the bulky sideboard. Some were in cheap metal frames, some in cardboard, and some were unframed, stuck into the side of the mirror or the pictures on the wall. He gently picked them up to scrutinise.

A framed black and white picture of a baby girl with dark hair and large light-coloured eyes in a white frothy dress.

Another framed picture of a little girl with her hair in pigtails, sitting on a school desk in front of a large map of Argentina. She looked directly into the camera, her sweet face serious and eager. He smiled: there existed a picture of him in the same pose exactly, only he was wearing his expensive private school uniform instead of the white duster coat of a state school.

Another picture of three children: a tall blond boy of ten – he believed he looked exactly the same at that age – a sulky dark girl with unruly hair, and then the pretty light-eyed girl, all three of them standing at the feet of a statue of a goddess in a beautiful garden.

The beautiful girl as a teenager, dressed in a long white dress, her hair done up, in a sparkling tiara, smiling with a dazzling smile: she really was a vision. She was probably celebrating her fifteenth birthday. That was a colour picture.

Now, the golden-eyed girl and another, bigger, plain girl, the sulky child of the garden picture, both in mini-skirts, wedge shoes and long straight hairdos.

The beauty again between a small wrinkled old man, smiling, and a solemn woman with a middle parting and a perm. The man had his arm round the girl's waist; the woman was standing with her hands clasped in front of her.

A very fat, haughty woman loaded with jewellery, chains, bracelets, and earrings, sitting in a huge rattan armchair, staring straight into the camera, and the woman with the permed hair in a bun, wearing a maid's uniform, slightly smiling, standing next to her, a little to the back.

A passport picture of a young man with curly light brown hair – the blond boy from the picture in the garden? – in a white shirt and tie.

A very old, framed photo of a family taken in a studio: a grumpy-looking man; a dark haired, sturdy woman seated in the middle; another native woman, very old and frail and withered, with a rosary in her hand; four children of various ages sitting down in front of them.

Another faded photo, of a dapper young man with hair slicked back, in a bow tie, with a dreamy expression on his face. Long eyelashes, bright, liquid eyes.

More pictures of the stunning golden-eyed girl, now smiling, now solemn, now sitting in front of a table full of books, now standing outside a shanty house with a small dirty child in her lap and many older children surrounding her.

A picture inside a shanty house: the young handsome man – the one who looked like him – with a stethoscope, examining an old woman, and a priest standing next to them, looking at the camera, his mouth open as if saying something to the person who was taking the photo.

The young man looked at the pictures for a very long time.

The bus was thundering down the Autopista del Sol. Very few people were left on it.

So that was what a body looked like, Milagros thought, a body that had been shot, recently, the hole in the head, the mess. She couldn't clean up that kind of mess, they were bringing their own people to do it, specialists. There were a lot of shootings in the world, a lot of mess, the body so rigid, did it hurt? Did she have time to think about how much it hurt? Was she dead before the bullet came out the other side? Her body just a heap on the floor, a wax doll, an effigy, how strange that a body can end up like this, a lifeless heap of flesh and bone. The flesh didn't feel like flesh at all, it was waxy and cold, rigid, like stone? No, not like stone, like something horrible, something that doesn't belong in this world. It was warm and soft before.

How many times had you held her in your arms, helped her put on her socks and shoes, wiped her nose, fed her? Please, one more spoonful darling, one for Mami, one for Papi, one for the teddy bear, one for you. And all the times you bathed her – don't splash the water all over the place, you naughty girl, look, I'm soaked, what have you done? Sit still now, I'll tell you a story if you're a good girl, but there will be no stories for naughty girls, now sleep my treasure, quiet now, I'm not going to say it a second time.

And then she's a big girl all of a sudden, they transform overnight. Look Señora, straight As, clever girl, don't talk back. What do they teach you at that school I wonder, why don't you take a leaf out of Fito's book, Fito who was always so kind and respectful, Fito whose body we never saw? And there was nothing in that casket, I knew it, but what a day it was. Señora standing like a tree hit by lightning, never shedding a tear, just sitting on her armchair and whispering, "I'll never see him again, Mili, I'll never see him again," while the whole time I was thinking it's true what they say about God, his mills grind slowly but grind they do, and I never got to see the body. They took my little girl away, my little girl who would shine when her birthday came along, my, aren't you the prettiest girl in the world? God, what have I done to deserve such happiness, thank you good Virgin of Luján, and then, then... So many men in the world, so many women in the world, pretty rich women who would've died for him, and he goes and picks her, and she, she, she knows nothing. Mami will be happy for me when she knows I'm happy, she said. Dear God. I know I've sinned, God, but why her? Why not me? Why, why, why?

"Tickets, please! Are you okay, Señora? Are you sure? Here, let me open this window a little. It's too hot for the season, I know, imagine what it'll be like in December. No, don't worry, no trouble at all."

The young man put the last photograph back in its place, wedged between the looking glass and its frame. The mirror was old and slightly tarnished. He looked at himself. He saw what he had been seeing every day. The same oval face, wide forehead, eyes the color of the weather, changing from gray to green to light brown, regular nose, tiny brown mole on the left side of the lips. But who was he? Until a few weeks ago, he was Roberto José Malbrán, twenty-six, intern at the Hospital Británico, son of retired army officer Eduardo Malbrán and his wife Josefa, brother of Elena María. Of course he had seen the woman on TV, the advertisement – who hadn't seen it? "If you were born between 1976 and 1983 and have doubts about your identity, approach us, Families Investigating for Memory and Justice." But how could it concern him? He had never given it a thought.

But then Josefa – could he call her mother anymore, after what she had told him, tears streaming down her face – had confessed.

"I can't die with this on my conscience," she'd said. So she'd waited until the very end. And that man – his father up to that moment, now a stranger, no, an enemy – had cursed and stormed and threatened his wife, but what can you do to the dying? The dying never lie, for they have nothing to lose.

Then Alicia Otamendi de Grant told him his story, what she knew of it. They had gone to the Genetic Data Bank together, where they took his blood. They had looked at him solemnly. They had shown him the result of the tests. The files of his parents. Their photos on the files. A very beautiful, dark-haired, golden-eyed girl. A light-brown-haired, smiling young man. Goyena Irribaren Suárez de Riquelme. That was his real surname in full. His mother had been Lucía Eva Suárez de Riquelme. His father Adolfo Faustino Goyena de Irribaren. They were both very young when they died. Younger than he was now. How could you be older than your parents? He had heard about the young man, his father. How he was a saint and a hero, close friend of the martyred Father Agnelli, how he died a hero's death in the Malvinas. Then the rumors that he hadn't died in battle after all, but had been murdered, thrown off a plane in one of those death flights years before, all those stories from way back, from the Dirty War, terrible stories that the man he had been taught to call Father had told him not to believe. "The leftists and the subversives made up all those stories to undermine the army," he had shouted, hoarse from all the shouting. But Roberto could believe everything now. Every single story.

Milagros got off the bus and walked slowly home. She was very tired. Spent. All she wanted was to get into bed and sleep, a deep sleep without dreams, without waking, even. As she turned the corner, she saw a large shiny sports car parked outside her house. She felt her blood pressure rising. That disgrace of a boy, Mabel's Damián, must have got a new car. Why couldn't he park the blasted thing in front of his own house? She would give that Mabel a piece of her mind. She'd had enough!

As if on cue, Mabel ran out of her house, and before Milagros could open her mouth, said breathlessly, "There's a young man waiting for you inside your house. I let him in. He looks quite nice, though he wouldn't tell me who he was. Were you expecting someone?"

Epilogue

2008, Alta Gracia, Provincia de las Pampas

The summer wind comes from the north and brings with it the fine dust from the vast deserts thousands of miles away, deserts that shine like glass in the sun and are full of strange and wonderful rocks that sigh and sing and sometimes sweat. When the children come here for the Easter holidays, they enjoy the strong wind very much; they don't mind the dust, they run up and down, they squeal and laugh, and their hair and clothes get all tumbled and dirty. But they go to bed tired and happy. Little Lucía is the leader of the pack.

"You're more like your Auntie Silvina than your namesake," I tell her.

She shrugs and runs away. Children are not interested in old stories about dead people.

"Abuelita, look, look, I've got a lizard," says Pablito. The girls scream and run away, then come back to tease him with sticks and branches. He lifts the lizard up from the tail and brandishes it at them, like they do with crosses at vampires, and the girls wave their sticks and branches at him and scream.

"Children, please don't disturb Abuelita Milagros," says Elena María.

She's a nice woman, Roberto's sister. She and her children come and spend their holidays here, with Roberto's family. I'm not sure she gets along very well with Joanna. But the house is so large, there is plenty of space for everybody. The children enjoy it very much. They run the place down; the rose garden is a mess after they're done with it. Sometimes I think I'll see the ghost of poor old Felix running after them, yelling at them to lay off his roses. But he, too, is now sleeping in the little cemetery with the wooden crosses.

Yes, that Elena María is a good girl. Always asking me if I need anything, if I like this or that. Sometimes I have the feeling she does this – I don't know, maybe I'm not fair on her – because she wants to show she has no problem that her brother's grandmother was a servant. A lady on the one side, a servant on the other. I am not her real family, anyway, not her blood. I look at her sometimes and think: this girl's father might've killed my own girl. But it's not her fault. She was born after all this happened. We never talk about these things with her, it won't do.

Joanna sometimes asks me about those times, about Lucía, Fito. Their work with the poor in the shantytowns especially. She is a sociologist, has all those diplomas from the university, but she doesn't use them now with the children being so young.

"One day I will write a book about you all, Doña Milagros," she says, "and the world will know what happened, and it will not happen again."

"Ah, my girl. It will take much more than books for this to come true in this world," I tell her.

I'm not complaining about anything: life has been kind to me now at the end. Roberto is a sweet boy. He's got the good nature of his father, the obliging smile, the eagerness, the easy charm, and the beauty and sweetness of his mother, my poor darling Lucía. But I think Joanna is not very happy about this, the charm I mean. I can tell that women like him a lot, and he likes them back. Buzzing around him like bees around honey, every single one of them besotted. There was an incident with some phone calls last summer...Let it be. He's young and he'll grow up.

He is a good doctor. Sometimes when he bends over me to take my blood pressure, he reminds me so much of Fito. But he has my Lucía's eyes, not the color – the color is his other grandmother's – but the shape, and he squints when he laughs, just like she used to. Ah, Lucía, Lucía. They say Time heals. No, he doesn't heal, he just makes it more difficult to remember.

Roberto insisted that I should leave my old house in the *barrio*. He thought I should come here to the Big House and live out the rest of my days in peace. In the summer I like it, but it gets a little lonely in the winter. There is nobody left here anymore. China, whom we sometimes called Chancha – shame on us! Her real name was Marta – was the last one left from the old days. She died shortly after I moved back here. Another wooden cross in the cemetery. Her granddaughter Martita, the girl who keeps me company, is a kind little soul with large mild eyes and a very slow mind, God love her. If she wasn't, she wouldn't have been here with me; she would have been trying to make something of her life in the capital. But she is a good girl, eager to please. She rarely speaks, and that's a good thing. We sit and watch television together in the dark quiet winter afternoons. I was given the large corner room on the first floor that used to belong to Doña Ramona. I didn't want it, I said the couple should take it, but Joanna said she didn't like the view of the woods – it was creepy. She preferred the rose garden. They are in Faustino's room, now dead so long that even his ghost is gone from this house.

I don't spend much time looking at the view anyway. I watch television in my room. There are often stories about those days, documentaries, news. Sometimes another lost child is found, or another mass grave with bones, or another torturer brought to justice. Last year Alicia Otamendi de Grant died. They had a special program for her and the work she had done with Families Investigating for Memory and Justice. What a nice lady she was. Really kind. I have the greatest respect for her and everyone in my family feels the same.

When the wind is howling, in the night, be it summer or winter, I still hear the voices. I recognize them. Pablo's constant whinging – a good-for-nothing even in death, may he rest in peace. Faustino, haunted. "Never let them know, Milagros," he wails, "never tell Roberto the truth." "But everyone has a right to know who they are," whispers the serious voice of Alicia Otamendi. "Mami, protect my boy, it's not his fault," says my Lucía. "She's right, it's not his fault, Mili," says Fito. "We were young and we loved each other very much and we didn't know." I listen and listen, and beg them to speak to me more often, and promise I will never tell their secrets. They are such good company for me, especially in the winter, when everything is quiet and all I have is the silence of Martita, and the low steady murmur of the TV, and the howling wind over the long and endless pampas.

THE END

Author's Note

I moved to Argentina in the early years of this century. The country was reeling from a financial crisis that had crippled its economy and invited IMF intervention. The capital, Buenos Aires, stately yet dilapidated, was eerily quiet, its huge avenues empty of traffic, sidewalks filled with shabby men slowly pushing carts laden with junk. Outside meagerly stocked supermarkets, well-dressed beggars timidly asked for money to buy food. Families slept on the steps of the magnificent Teatro Colón. In the street where I lived, workmen with toolboxes gathered every morning near the bus-stop, waiting to be offered a job for the day; I could see them walk away a few hours later, having waited in vain. It was heartbreaking – and from the vantage point of twenty years later, eerily prescient of what kind of century we were heading into.

At the University of Buenos Aires, one of my fellow mature students told me: "The best of us were taken away, murdered or disappeared. That's why we've ended up in this state." He meant the Dirty War, waged by a brutal regime against its own people, between 1976-1983. He had survived prison and torture, but lucky not to be among the 30,000 who had died or vanished. As a Greek,

I could relate; we too had experienced a dictatorship that had left deep scars in 1967-1974. But nothing comparable to the mass disappearance of young students, workers, professionals, intellectuals, journalists; nothing like the kidnapping of their babies and small children, illegally given for adoption to the very people who had exterminated their parents. This was still a painful matter many decades later. When my son was born, an Argentine citizen, the paperwork I had to carry with me at all times, especially when travelling, to prove he was my own child, weighed as heavy as a tome of *War and Peace*: I understood perfectly the compelling reasons for this. I watched the news avidly for stories of lost children reuniting with their grandparents, of old torturers and kidnappers finally facing justice. It was not enough, but it was something.

Odd as it may sound, I spent a lot of time in cemeteries at that time, especially in the necropolis of Recoleta. I pushed my baby's buggy among marble and granite houses of the dead, day after day, while outside the walls Buenos Aires was slowly recovering from the crisis: grand, sprawling, vibrant, teeming with life. And yet sometimes there fell a hush, as if the sound of the world was muted, as if absences, not presences, haunted the living. The horror of that absence and my need to fill it resulted in this novel years later. Its characters and the plot are completely fictional, even though the events that inspired them are sadly not. Fiction is a way to make sense of true and attested events that the mind and the heart find hard to accept.

With every history book recording such events, with every fictional work inspired by them, we hope to stop them from happening again. *Nunca Más* (Never Again) was the motto of the great reckoning that took place after the fall of the dictators. So far, all over the world, such hopes are dashed time and again. And yet, we keep on writing.

Acknowledgements

I would like to thank the people who helped the writing of this novel in many different ways. This novel started its life as a project during my MSc in Creative Writing at the University of Edinburgh, and I am forever indebted to the people who read it and offered invaluable feedback: my tutor and supervisor Dilys Rose, and my fellow writers Amanda Block, Diane Chang, Nada Dajani, Gero Gutzheit, Kat Schaup, and Spencer Thompson. You are all amazing writers, and it was such a privilege to learn from you.

I am very grateful to Morag Pringle, Sasha Greene, and P.S. Livingstone for their wise and thoughtful advice and for taking the time.

To Blackwater Press I will be forever indebted for giving this novel a place in the sun, taking it out of the vault in which it was hiding: Elizabeth Ford, John Reid, Vivien Williams, thank you. Very special thanks and gratitude to John, patient and meticulous editor. He is a writer too; he understands.

Eilidh Muldoon for her beautiful, haunting art; every cover of yours is a treasure. Giuseppe for his illustrations, too; I did not know I needed them until I saw them.

Finally, Nena, who heard all the stories and wishes she could read them; and Richard, who planted a tree that will survive us all in a garden in Gran Buenos Aires; and Andrew, my own *porteño*, whose existence ties me forever to Argentina.